Praise for the writing of Cari Silverwood

Iron Dominance

"This book is a page turner that will sweep you into its story from the very first pages."

– *Dark Haven Reviews*

"With sex scenes that will make your palms sweat and your pulse race, this is a book that will make any BDSM fan happy."

– Nix, *Scorching Book Reviews*

A Recommended Read! "This is a delightful book…"

– Becky, *Guilty Pleasures Book Reviews*

Three Days of Dominance

"…creative, erotic, sexy and full of adventure."

– Clea R. Gellar, *Book Wenches*

"…full of heat, passion, and intrigue."

– *Whipped Cream Reviews Site*

"…a juicy tale that will keep the reader's attention til the end."

Penelope, *Kinky Book Reviews*

LooSeId®

ISBN 13: 978-1-62300-031-8
IRON DOMINANCE

Originally released in e-book format in August 2011

Cover Art by Valerie Tibbs
Cover Layout and Design by April Martinez

Printed in the U.S.A. by
Lightning Source, Inc.
1246 Heil Quaker Blvd
La Vergne TN 37086
www.lightningsource.com

Steamwork Chronicles:
IRON DOMINANCE

Cari Silverwood

Dedication

To all those at ERAuthors who offered critiques and to my intrepid beta readers, Nerine Dorman, Bianca Sommerland, and Kimberely for all their help wrestling Iron Dominance *into shape. Also a big thank-you to my editor, Crystal Esau.*

Chapter One

Beneath Claire's feet, the timber floor vibrated in harmony with the airship's engines. Opposite her, through the brass-lipped oblong porthole, at the end of a long pylon, the port engine shone with reflected light against the backdrop of night sky. She stayed at parade rest, both hands behind her back, pretending to be unconcerned with how little of her was covered by the skimpy evening dress.

The Common Room door was latched back. Whenever crew passed by, they tended to slow and give her an appraising look before continuing on. Even so, she'd rather the door be open—for apart from the four square tables and their chairs, she was alone with Lieutenant Inkline.

As if he exuded frost, whenever Claire was near the lieutenant, her fingers and lips grew cold. With his arm propped on the table, Inkline leaned over studying the papers fanned out before him. He'd not spoken for ages. His name badge falsely declared him an officer of the PME Diplomatic Corps.

Inkline—a diplomat. What a laughable cover identity. Except no one, especially she, would ever dare to laugh.

"Sir," she ventured, "permission to put on an overcoat before we land?"

Lieutenant Inkline looked up, one corner of his plump mouth twitching. He smoothed his palm down the leg of his immaculate uniform whites as if wiping off sweat, then across his bald scalp. Already, she regretted speaking. "You're a frankenstruct. You don't question me. You don't speak without permission. And you certainly don't feel." He casually swung his hand and smacked her face.

The force jolted her sideways.

"See?"

She tasted blood, felt the sting from his fingers, but didn't make a sound or do anything more than move her head until she once again stared over his shoulder. Tears wet her eyes. She blinked, ignoring them. *Don't feel.* What an illogical statement. She could feel. She could, but no one cared, so yet again she curled her mind up in that dark cold place where others couldn't see, and there she wept.

"Your instructions." Inkline read from the folder in a monotone. "After arrival at Helspin Airport, you will be conveyed to a residence where later this evening, there will be a state reception. Meet your target. Get him alone, seduce him, then kill him by whatever method you can, preferably using the poison spike in your shoe to make his death appear natural." He glanced up and asked drily, "You do know what seduction is?"

Confused as to whether she should reply, Claire stayed mute. From Inkline and the other trainers, she'd been taught enough to approach a target. The lessons, despite the subject matter, hadn't been pleasant.

"Let me remind you." He took a step forward and put his hand around the back of her head, pulling her to him. His lips bit down, crushing her lips onto her teeth, his tongue snaking into her mouth. She didn't struggle even though his foul breath almost made her gag. That would only earn her a reprimand.

"Pah!" He released her and wiped his mouth. "Let's hope you can do better than that tonight!" The glitter in his eyes told her the kiss had stirred him. The man had a cruel streak.

"Now, for the target's name. Theodore—"

With a loud *bang*, the airship shuddered and slewed sideways. Through the porthole to her left, Claire saw the pylons of the engine twist like taffy. The engine broke away, propellers shrieking. Sparks of flaming metal and timber streamed backward into the night. Another *bang*. In a staggered line, three holes pocked the wall, spitting debris and shrapnel into the room. The lieutenant fell screaming, arm flung out sideways, a cloud of blood spraying from his shoulder. Knocked off balance, Claire grabbed at the back of a chair and barely stopped herself skidding across the floor. People yelled and cried in pain. An acrid, burned odor overlaid the sweet smell of blood and the perfume she wore.

Still clutching the chair even though the damn thing's legs had little more hold on the carpet than her shoes, she prayed the ship had enough buoyancy to stay in the sky. Prayed whoever shot at them lost interest, real fast.

She kicked off her high heels and let her mind slide into a state of honed awareness, thanking God for her training. *Sharp time*, they'd called her ability, once they knew of it. Skin and muscle sizzled with tension. Time slowed. With a warbling whistle, three pieces of shrapnel tumbled toward her, scorching the air, leaving trails of gray smoke and a burning flutter of fragments. She threw herself sideways. A fist-sized chunk grazed her head.

Another, louder *bang*; then an exploding *crump* shook the whole airship. Her head filled with smoke and blackness...and silence.

* * * *

Theo rocked up and down on his toes, reassessing, wondering if there was anything more that could be done. Smoke rose from the crash site, marking a tattered line across the pale blue morning sky. To his right, a flock of crows cawed from their perch in an enormous fig tree.

Thick roots at the base of the tree spread across the rock at the edge of the cliff. Below, deep at the bottom of the narrow ravine, ran the torturous Yang River. The airship crew were lucky they'd not crashed a few yards farther west. Bouncing off the cliff walls would have made survival impossible.

What a mess. He coughed and spat to clear his throat of the sludge from the smoke. His hands were gray from moving pieces of the airship, and he was sure his face was no better. He eyed the wreckage. Though it had come down in one piece apart from the nose, fire had destroyed the section that lay a few yards away.

"Found another survivor?" he yelled.

Dankyo stalked toward him, the holster of his Gerwelt pistol slapping against his crisp gray trousers, his flattop of shaven black hair cutting across the sky like a steam ship across the ocean. Trust Dankyo to find time to dress formal on an emergency mission in the wee early hours. Though Dankyo was originally a refugee from the Greater Asian Monarchy, Theo had never regretted making him head of his personal security.

From the position of the sun, it was past nine. Theo put a hand to his stomach, sorely missing breakfast. He tugged out his gold pocket watch. Close. Forty-two minutes after eight.

“No, sir. Still only five survivors.” Dankyo saluted. No matter that Theo had been out of the air fleet for two years, the man insisted on military manners.

“Cause of the crash?”

“Well.” Dankyo rubbed his chin. “We’re smack on the border here. A Pancontinental Mexican Empire airship with multiple blast holes and the front section blown away by maybe an electro rocket? We didn’t do it, that’s for certain.”

“The Brito-Gallic League.” Theo sighed. “Once the PME find out, we’ll have another flare-up of the war, and just when things were calming down.” The PME was touchy to say the least.

Dankyo shrugged his immense shoulders then asked, “Can I hope, sir, that you might reactivate?” Despite their long years together, in the air corps as well as outside it, Theo still found himself startled at times by the *Englishness* of Dankyo. It was as if a butler had morphed into a Sumo wrestler.

“No. You may not. I’m headed for politics as you well know, man. The horrors of war can be another’s worry from now on.”

Horrors of war indeed. Too many men had lost their lives in the name of war. Lunacy. When he’d seen betrayal of fellow countrymen become the norm, he knew there were better ways to spend his life.

A uniformed arm waved from the smoking mound of black and twisted metal. One of his house guards had found something. Above the man’s head, emblazoned across a slope of undamaged metal, was a yard-high white and orange eagle—all that remained of the PME flag.

“Hoy! Sirs!” the guard yelled. “Another one! A woman!”

“Come, Dankyo.” Theo set off jogging across the disheveled landscape, hopping here and there to clear small piles of debris. A lone crow took off, flapping and cawing, as he approached the man who’d waved.

At his feet lay a slender woman, blonde hair still partly pinned into a chignon, the diamantes on her wine red evening gown dulled by smears of dirt. One strap had slipped from the shoulder, revealing the upper curve of her breast. Near the jagged hem of the dress, three deep yet neat cuts had bled and left red trails along the outer curve of her thigh.

The unexpected sight of womanly flesh among all this blatant destruction was as jarring as a rose floating in a swamp.

He slipped off his leather jacket and squatted to cover her. Her eyes snapped open—polished amber irises full of pain and confusion. From the rubble by her side, her arm swung weakly up; a broken metal strut tumbled from her hand.

"Uh-uh." He easily intercepted her wrist. Those big golden eyes slowly closed. *A spirited one.* Her arm flopped back above her head, jolting her breasts.

She's barely conscious. Having me looming over her must have frightened her. Casually his gaze traveled up to her shoulder, around the curves of muscle, up to her wrist...and he imagined her with both arms tied that way.

He shook his head. "Where's the doctor?"

"Coming." Dr. Eastway crunched across to them, his boots slipping on the loose earth. The last few strands of gray hair straggled across his forehead, and his black medical case swung from his hand.

Though the doctor was bleary-eyed, Theo knew him to be competent and backed away to let him through.

"Ah. Hmm. She's breathing easily, sir. Pulse strong. Color good. Upper leg lacerations plus looks like a blow to the head from the abrasions on her temple. I need to get her back to the house, sir. Ah." Dismay tinged the doctor's last word. He peered at and probed the skin of the woman's neck and shoulders, then rose slowly.

"What is it, Doctor?"

But the man merely flapped his hand at Theo while shaking his head. "A moment, please." The brusque tone was normal. An early career tending soldiers hadn't encouraged a good bedside manner.

Having given instructions for the loading of the woman onto a stretcher, Dr. Eastway took Theo by the arm and led him to one side. "Ahem. Colonel, there's something I should tell you about that young woman."

"Yes? Is she going to be all right?"

"Perhaps. Most likely. Though spending the night out here has not helped any of them. I expect she will regain consciousness soon. But that is not my main concern, sir."

"The recovery of your patient is not your main concern? Doctor, I'm more than a little confused here. Explain yourself."

The doctor cleared his throat. "She is not a normal human. She's a frankenstruct. A being made of cloned parts. To those who are privy to such knowledge, there are marks that reveal this. The PME are far advanced in cloning and genetics. Do you still want me to tend to her?"

"What?" Anger stirred in Theo.

"Ah." The doctor bowed his head. Clearly he'd realized his error. "Of course, some are quite happy to allow them a degree of humanity. And such opinions are not mine to judge. However, there is, sir"—the doctor coughed—"the question of the fine for aiding or harboring a frankenstruct. I believe it is ten thousand drachma."

Theo pressed his lips together. A trivial sum to him, but to the doctor it would mean far more. "I'll settle any such fines if they occur. But first someone would need to report that we have committed such a…transgression. None of my men here would do so."

The doctor blinked rapidly. "Thank you, sir. My lips are sealed, as you know, sir. I too am indebted to you for employment. I shall attend to her injuries."

"Do so."

From her dress this woman must be some sort of companion. Perhaps a sexual one? That the PME used frankenstructs as slaves was common knowledge, but to see one… Theo shook his head, bemused. She'd seemed so normal, so female, so very fragile. He'd wanted to stroke that porcelain-fine skin yet also to pick her up like some lost puppy and shelter her from harm. He smiled wanly.

The doctor was correct, though. Frankenstructs were illegal and to be destroyed on sight. He couldn't do that. He'd pay the fine if he had to. Money wasn't everything.

* * * *

Consciousness melted into being like clouds blown away by a cold and malevolent wind. Every jolt and swing of the stretcher Claire lay on vibrated fresh pain through her head and along her right leg. She gritted her teeth; almost everywhere hurt. Her first mission was off to an awful start.

Through the fringe of her lashes, she watched as two gray-uniformed men carried her stretcher into the grand foyer of an enormous dwelling. By letting her head loll to one side and then the other, she could see almost everything. As well as the stretcher bearers, two other men walked behind or at her side.

"I must advise sending her to the lockup cell, sir," said one.

The second man replied. "With the men? Dankyo, even for you, I find that appalling. The guest bedroom will do nicely."

Ah, she thought drowsily. This is the one in charge. The owner of this mansion, perhaps? She liked him more than the other, colder one.

At eye level, though she was the one moving, paintings seemed to bob past on parade, along with statues and fancy vases.

Though it felt as if someone had played drums on her body with a meat tenderizer, she marveled at everything. The men stopped and put her stretcher down with a small bounce at the foot of a wide curling staircase. A wave of nausea welled up her throat, then subsided.

"Are you certain of this, sir?" said Dankyo. The badge on his gray uniform announced him head of security. A house that needed a head of security—such ostentation spoke of wealth or paranoia or both. He looked…formidable.

Dankyo moved with grace despite his bulk. She narrowed her eyes further. To be discovered secretly observing him… She suppressed a shudder. He radiated danger.

"Yes, Dankyo," spoke the other, whose name she'd yet to hear, except that all addressed him as sir. His deep voice possessed an alluring rightness, a surety that whatever he said would be obeyed. Even the simplest of his words compelled her to listen.

This man had told the doctor to minister to her at the crash site, despite knowing she was a frankenstruct. His words had been peculiar enough to stand out from the painful throb of the merry-go-round of colors and sound inside her head. That any human would bother to do this for her was incredible.

She crushed the hope that bubbled up. Stupid to think he might care. Always there were reasons. Nothing came without a price, though usually the reward came after the task was done and not before.

"The telegraph has come back, sir," said Dankyo. "There'll be an army escort meeting us at Hoskitt in two hours, then an airship to New Baskerton. The survivors will be deported back to Merica. There's no point in putting her in the guest room. She can go with the men."

"She's not going, Dankyo. Be damned if I'm going to let the bureaucrats decide her future." Anger lent a hard edge to the words. "You know as well as I, they'll order her euthanized before they'll let her be deported. It's official policy. Take her up."

The stretcher wobbled under her and was raised in the air, tilting.

Euthanized. She knew what that meant: death.

Once she was well, she'd escape. It was her duty to. Where to, though? A notion crystallized. *Here I am, by myself. No Inkline. What if I go somewhere else and not back to the PME?* Like a dog chasing its tail, the idea went around and around. *What if?*

The headache stopped her pinning that crazy notion down. Later, though. She needed to figure this out.

On the floor above they took her into a room bigger than the one her entire training squad had slept in. A four-poster bed of brushed silver and bronze dominated the floor next to a set of four timber doors. The bronze and green stained glass in the middle section of the doors matched the green drapes of the bed and the bronze poles holding up the bed's canopy. Everywhere was opulence.

Claire forgot to pretend unconsciousness and opened her eyes wide.

"She's awake, sir." Dankyo's brown eyes glittered. "This room is not secure. A child could abscond. As your security advisor, I insist on some means of ensuring this...frankenstruct is still here on the morn."

His master sighed. "Your suggestion?"

"I'll arrange something, sir."

The men placed the stretcher on the bed then indicated she should roll off onto the bed. Gray-uniformed, with *Security* written on their shirt pockets, these must be Dankyo's men.

"Come on, love," the taller, heftier one muttered.

She winced as she shifted to raise herself on her elbows. Her red dress rode up, revealing three rows of black silk sutures on the outside of her right thigh. The room swam, turning the cream-striped wallpaper into a sea of milk.

"Here." Two warm muscular arms slid under her. One at her shoulder, the other just below her bottom—scooping her up and moving her onto the emerald satin bedspread.

"Sir!" Dankyo said.

"Calm yourself, Dankyo." The words were spoken from mere inches away. "She doesn't bite. Do you?"

Clear iron gray eyes stared down at her, though when she met his gaze, they darkened. She stared back. A shiver ran through her.

He frowned as if seeing her for the first time, and she wished she'd been able to hold back that shiver. It made her feel...vulnerable.

As her eyes slowly closed a shadow passed above, and something gently brushed across her forehead. His fingers, she realized. The touch of his warm skin against hers felt good, and the place inside where she kept herself coiled and ready to fight relaxed, soothed by the rhythm of his fingers. Blackness rolled in. Her last thoughts chased her down into the abyss. *Escape. Soon.* Though for some reason she couldn't remember why.

* * * *

The next day, she was left alone in the room apart from a burly woman with a face like a wax gargoyle that had squatted too long in the sun. Dressed in a floral gown, her brown hair in a bun, gargoyle woman occupied a leather easy chair, every inch of it overflowing with her flesh. Whenever Claire needed to move from the bed, the woman would scowl and grumble, only to heave from the chair and trundle over with the handcuff keys in hand.

The handcuffs must've been Dankyo's idea. One of her wrists was kept cuffed to the right hand pillar of the bed, and when she needed to go to the bathroom, the woman locked her wrists together. It made everything difficult, her arm cramping at times with it stretched over her head, and no one, gargoyle woman included, seemed to care that going to the bathroom was a laborious affair. She'd examined the cuffs. An ordinary pair she would stand a chance of picking, but these had some strange clockwork mechanism on each side. Still, a hairpin she found wedged at the back of the bathroom cabinet might be useful.

The little white dress they'd given her was already marked with blood. A bad color for concealment too. *One mistake from them is all I need. Once my leg heals, I'm gone. But where to? Have I got the guts to desert? I can't stay here.*

She remembered something about the Brito-Gallic league—how they hated the PME. Perhaps she could pass as human there if she was careful with how she dressed, at least until she figured out if frankenstructs were legal.

Yes. To the west, then. She breathed out slowly. Settling on a goal had eased the tightness in her chest. *To the west.*

The late-afternoon sun streaked in through the glass doors, and Claire was halfway to the bathroom. The outer door banged open, and two guards trundled in a trolley bearing an engine of some sort with wires at one end, a crank at the other, and ridges of machined metal going halfway to the ceiling in layers like a steel wedding cake.

What the... Horrible images crammed into her head—sharpened steel, blood, pain—the paraphernalia of torture.

She stumbled. Her injured leg caved, and she went to one knee, with her cuffed hands on the floor just stopping her from completely toppling over. Fiery spikes screamed up her leg. She stifled a gasp of agony. The room hazed.

"Here now." Quick solid steps approached her. Someone picked her up like a child and held her against their broad chest—the muscles and the scent of a man. Blinking to clear her vision, she let her gaze travel up to his face. The gray eyes she recognized.

"Good afternoon, *agapi mou.*"

That confused her even more. Had he just called her *my love* in Greek?

She screwed up her mouth. "I'm not your love. Put me down."

A smile tweaked the corners of his lips. "So you can fall over again? I think not. Where do you wish to go?"

She reined in her instincts—striking at his eyes would get him to drop her...and then she'd likely be shot.

Squirming didn't loosen his grip and only sent more pain spearing through her thigh. Fuming, she weighed her alternatives.

Very well. If he wants to carry me, that's his problem.

"Finished thinking? That scowl does not become you." He quirked an eyebrow.

This time she took a longer look—black wavy hair, a strong yet proportionate nose dividing his broad face, and black stubble on his chin. Her heartbeat accelerated.

"I was headed to the bathroom."

With that he swung slowly around, took her to the bathroom, nudging open the door.

Alone in the bathroom, with the door closed behind her, Claire felt tremendously relieved, as if she'd barely escaped a trap. That a man had touched her without her permission grated on her nerves, though he'd not done anything. She'd be more careful in future. Try to keep out of his way.

Except when she opened the door, she found him waiting.

"I can get back to the bed myself."

"Stubborn, aren't you? No. I'll carry you."

And he scooped her up again. She couldn't evade him, not with her leg injured and her wrists cuffed. The trolley with the strange machine awaited her at the bedside, as did an elderly man with thin gray hair. His neat suit and the stethoscope protruding from his jacket pocket marked him as a doctor. If this man carrying her hadn't made her nervous already, the machine surely would have.

She said a mantra to get her pulse rate down. *Why would they treat me as nicely as they have, only to torture me?*

"Perhaps if we exchange names, you won't feel so shy about being carried?"

Shy? She turned her gaze from the man holding her, to the machine, and back. *What is this device?*

"My name," he said, maneuvering around the machine and lowering her to the bed, "is Theo Kevonis. I am the owner of this house and the adjoining lands. I was at the airship crash, and I helped rescue you. I must tell you how glad I am that we did that." Very polite, but he hadn't let go of her wrists. The grip was loose, as if he barely knew he held her, yet when she pulled away, his fingers tightened and kept her cuffed hands there.

Theo? The thought struck her like lightning. Theo was a shortened version of Theodore. Her target's name. Inkline hadn't given her the surname. Surely, it would be an impossible coincidence for this to be the same man. Besides, Inkline was dead, wasn't he? Which meant her target didn't matter, one way or the other. Professional curiosity crept in, though. Could this Theo be important enough for a nation to want him killed?

"Where is your other man? The mean-looking one?" She inched up the bed.

"Dankyo? My head of security? I sent him away to help with the crash investigation. I'm sure, if he was here, he would have told me you were too dangerous to approach. Not that I would have heeded his advice. I've been looking forward to your company." He smiled down at her.

How did she reply to such talk? Dankyo would've been right, in a way. If she let loose in the way her ability and training allowed, she was dangerous. She said nothing—it seemed the safest choice.

"And this," he said, turning to the other man, "is the esteemed Dr. Eastway. Your name, agapi mou?"

He mocked her again. She shot a murderous look his way and was startled to see him grin back, as if they shared a joke. She tugged again, unsuccessfully, to pull her hands from his. Instead of letting go, he moved his thumb in soft circles at her wrist.

The feeling was disconcerting, awakening a tingle in strange places.

"Claire." She frowned, finding the pace of her breathing had quickened. "My name is Claire."

"I am pleased to meet you, Claire." Theo raised her hands and kissed the backs of her fingers.

Shock rendered her speechless. Her face heated. The casual application of mouth to skin unnerved her, almost more than a kiss on her lips. Inkline had accustomed her to that. She'd grown the equivalent of calluses in her mind.

"Dr. Eastway is going to use galvanic electricity to help heal your wounds. It's safe, though not yet a widespread device. We've tried it on many battle wounds. Doctor?" Theo gave her hand a squeeze, then stepped aside to let the doctor take his place by the bed. He went to lean against the wall between the chest of drawers and the bathroom.

"In case you're wondering," Theo continued, "the other survivors have been sent onward. I can't do the same with you because of our ridiculous law regarding frankenstructs. If I send you on, you'll be euthanized." He watched her carefully. "You understand? It's too dangerous to send you on."

She nodded. *Does he think I'll faint or something?*

She eyed him, then decided the doctor warranted more attention. Galvanic energy...electricity? Voltaic electricity she understood—it ran lights, small engines, powered some weapons. While she pondered this, she couldn't help, every so often, flicking a look at Theo.

He bothered her. *Threatening? Maybe.* But not, she sensed, in the way she normally classified threats. Though hard muscles glided beneath the cloth of his shirt, his strength didn't concern her as much as his aura of control.

Another glance and this time, she found him intent on looking at her. She fought down a blush, made herself look back at him for several seconds, before returning to the doctor. A mistake, there, perhaps, as left unchallenged, Theo's regard seemed to sear the surface of her neck and face.

This, her training had not prepared her for—she was meant to obey commands, to kill as efficiently as possible, and not face down men who simply stared. She found herself having to fight off an urge to ask him what he wanted of her. Even knowing he was on the wrong side didn't dispel this urge, though it made her more determined than ever to resist her impulse.

Although, really, which exactly was the wrong side? She'd never been asked which side she wanted to be on. In an offhand way, she'd been bred in a vat and created, like a vehicle made from spare parts—or as the other frankenstructs laughingly called the process, brewed and glued.

The doctor busied himself checking dials on the machine and setting switches. This man, doctor or not, bore a resemblance to Inkline—balding, cold in attitude. He made her want to sneak to the opposite side of the bed. Slowly, she forced herself to relax.

“Let’s see your leg.” Dr. Eastway grabbed the bottom of her dress and flipped it up, exposing the sutures on her thigh and the lower edge of her panties.

Damn him! She hissed and stiffened. Like all humans, he thought she was a *thing*. She sat up and grabbed his hand, bent back a finger to immobilize him. Almost...almost tempted into sharp time, so she could fracture that hand, and only stopping herself in the last second.

No. Mustn’t. That would be disastrous, to show them what she could do. “Take your hand off me!”

Chapter Two

The doctor froze. She'd snared his hand and looked likely to break it off at the wrist.

Striving not to smile at the man's predicament, Theo pushed away from the wall. He'd hoped the doctor wouldn't be quite so prickly.

"Dr. Eastway, Claire seems to be disconcerted by your bedside manner." *The wounds in her thigh are deep. This needs doing.* "Perhaps, Doctor, if you could instruct me? Claire, release him, please."

Claire stared at the doctor, anger evident in the rigid lines of her body. She glanced across at him, frowning. Slowly, she opened her fingers and let go of the doctor's hand.

"Thank you for listening to me. The doctor is a treasured member of my staff. It would have been a pity to have to punish you over something so trivial." He bowed his head a fraction and was glad to see the slight widening of her pupils.

Something stirred within. It was as if he'd been handed a gift all wrapped in pretty white paper. And this gift had such interesting skills—she'd immobilized the doctor very efficiently. Curious that. Why would a sexual companion have need of such skills?

The doctor snorted, massaging his fingers. "Yes, I can show you how it works. I must admit ministering to this particular patient holds little allure for me. The dials are set. It only requires placement of the electrodes around the wound."

On the other side of the bed was a dressing table with a delicate chair. He'd look less threatening if he sat, so Theo went around and snared the chair, deposited it next to the bed after swinging the galvanic machine out at an angle. The whole time, Claire observed, as if he were a snake about to strike.

He held up his hands, palm outward. "Are you agreeable, Claire? I'll place these electrodes. I promise you, this is for the best, though it will hurt."

She didn't react when he mentioned pain. Instead she looked at his hands, then at June, who'd sat impassively in her chair throughout the commotion.

"Would you rather June do this?"

When she shook her head, choosing him, it pleased him. She was, after all, a young and beautiful woman. But it was more than that—the differences between her and the women from his social circle intrigued him.

The facts in the senate report he'd read had added up to frankenstructs being human. Yet someone had messed up the final summary, and the law had been passed declaring them inhuman. It reeked of legal shenanigans or bribery. Whatever the reasons, the law was wrong. Claire was human. He'd stake his life on it.

What the report hadn't said was that frankenstructs were feisty and likely to bite your nose off if you looked at them the wrong way, or that they knew Greek as well as English, or indeed, that they were beautiful.

The chair withstood his weight, only creaking as he sat. He'd put it midway down the bed. Her thigh stretched before him, her dress again covering her modestly—though the thin white material left little to be imagined, the way it flowed over every contour and into every crevice.

He'd have to get more clothes sent up for her. Which brought to his mind the vision of her taking off the dress, then her underwear. Claire, naked, would be a wondrous sight, especially with some vivid red stripes to set off the alabaster skin of her luscious bottom. The curves of her breasts showing at the low V-neck of the dress hinted at tantalizing ripeness. From what he'd felt while carrying her, beneath the clothes was a toned yet well-rounded body.

She'd not been immune to his touch. The little signs of her body had betrayed her excitement—the widening of pupils, the fast pulse, the tensing of muscles. Perhaps, though, some of it had been fear? Not that he'd been unmoved himself. No perfume or makeup, yet she smelled and looked like a delectable woman. With his arms under her, he'd wanted to lean down and kiss that full mouth, to feel her whimper beneath him.

"Are you done looking?" A blonde lock fell across her eye, and she tossed her head, switching it away. "I think I can manage this placement of electrodes. Show me."

That she'd try, he didn't doubt.

The doctor stepped up and spoke. "No. You can't. The cuts aren't where you can see them properly. Here, sir." He handed one electrode to Theo. "A row along each cut, please. Five a side should do it. Make sure each goes in full depth."

The electrode tip was a tiny pin; from there the wire trailed to the machine.

Theo showed the tip to Claire. If he let her try to do this, the chances were she'd mess up the placement, and it wasn't worth the risk. Her cuffed hands hovered at her waist, ready, he felt sure, to lunge and grab the electrode if he did something she disliked.

He sighed. "The parts on this machine aren't easily replaced. I'm going to secure your hands to the headboard until this is done."

Anger flared in her eyes. "No."

"Think. I have several men out there who take my orders. I could have them hold you down. Or we can simply give up, and you'll have to heal at your own pace and maybe risk infection. Galvanic healing works, but it will be painful this first time. I've seen the doctor have to restrain men, veteran soldiers, to get this done. Choose."

He banked on that intelligence he'd seen in her. She wouldn't want his men holding her, and that left—

"Very well." Slowly she put her hands above her head.

So tempting, to watch the rise and shift of her breasts. No. This wasn't easy for her. It had to be done and he'd do it without sidetracking. A pity though. When hadn't he thrilled at the idea of a woman restrained to the headboard by cuffs? Mentally, he shook his head at himself.

He stood. "June, the key, please." He caught the tossed key, unlocked the cuffs, and relocked them with the joining chain threaded behind the metal lattice of the headboard, feeling the trembling of Claire's muscles as he did so.

"I'll be as quick as I can."

He carefully folded back the dress, just enough to see the three sutured wounds. Puffy, red, maybe some infection starting, and fresh blood leaked where falling had jarred the edges. The cuts were about six inches long. He'd forgotten the extent of the injury. Still, one treatment would do wonders.

"Ready?"

"Yes."

The first electrode pierced her skin, and she grunted at the pain, jerked on the cuffs. He watched her expression, waiting a moment until he saw her nod.

"Good girl." That drew a glare. *Touchy*. Jabbing her infected wound with a pin was okay, but calling her "girl" made her look as if she wanted to stick something sharp into him? Curiouser and curiouser.

As the doctor handed him electrodes, he slipped the pins, equally spaced, under the skin at each side of one laceration. "Doctor. Turn it on, please."

Green current sizzled for a minute across the first wound. He shifted the electrode tips, treated the second, then the third cut. Apart from gnawing her pretty lip and a few sharp intakes of breath, Claire didn't move.

She rose in his estimation yet again. None of the ladies, or likely even the lords he knew, would have borne this so stoically. Before he released her hands, he brushed the lock of hair from her brow. "Well done."

The startled, bemused look she shot him pierced his heart as surely as an arrow. His blood thumped fiercely. Here was a puzzle he wished to solve. A man's touch unsettled her? He'd thought her a sexual companion. The more he saw of her, the less likely that seemed. Who and what was she?

* * * *

The next day he returned to administer the galvanic treatment. The doctor, irked by all the goings on, begged off attending, though June stayed as a chaperone, sunken in her chair, observing without interfering.

Claire lay on the bed wearing a blue dress this time—one a little shorter than the red, with fabric as sheer as his housemaids could discover among the archive of clothes. A small trick—he wasn't completely deaf to Dankyo's arguments. Claire might be a woman, but her casual application of a fingerlock on the doctor spoke of some training. Escaping would be a damned sight more difficult in a flimsy dress. As an added bonus, this way he could admire her form without being too obvious.

During this treatment he left his hand on her thigh while he studied the wound. Her breasts rose a little quicker when she breathed, her lips parted, and the tiny hairs on her legs stirred in goose bumps.

Why this delightful reaction? Ah. Of course.

His fingertips had strayed a half inch under the dress and were only three, four inches from the apex of her legs. He slowly withdrew his hand, then casually laid it on her ankle, watching her as he traced circles with his thumb on her warm skin. Though she shifted her leg an inch away, when he put his hand back, she did nothing, as if hypnotized by the stroking.

The faint aroma of arousal came to him. She was wet. Desire had caught her up the same as him. His nostrils flared. She felt their connection. Manners said that he shouldn't take this further unless she assented, yet even so he let his fingers drift around her ankle and loosely hold her there—the first step of possession.

She would give that assent to him, and once he gained her permission, he didn't plan to do anything less than give her the most thorough ravishing any woman could experience.

Chapter Three

On the third day, he knew the pain would be light enough that he didn't need to fasten Claire's hands out of the way. When he strode toward the bed, she put her uncuffed hand above her head, joining the one already fastened there.

Her shoulder muscles slid, sculpted by light. Such a simple movement—yet the shift of curve on curve slew him. The widening of her pupils, the visible beat of her carotid pulse, the willingness, it all spoke to him of submissiveness. He caught his breath as his foot swung to touch floor. Need trickled, then poured into him. He wanted this woman at his feet, held by his will, wanted to wind his hand into her hair so tight she couldn't move, to tilt her head to one side and sink his teeth into her glorious long neck. It called to his blood. *God.*

The moment broke a second later. She stirred and took down her hand, her face flushed.

* * * *

Why do I have my hands above my head? Confusion swallowed her as Theo arrived at the side of the bed, all towering and male, those adorable black curls that begged her to twist them round a finger. She lowered her unsecured hand, speaking to cover up how lost she felt. “Good morning.”

What would it be like to wrap her arms around him, to smell his hair, run her fingers through those curls?

“Yes. It is.” He smiled. “This will hurt very little, and I don’t need to cuff both your hands.”

He sat, then efficiently inserted the first of the electrodes. After a minute or two of watching him work on her leg, Claire found calmness settling over her. The way he focused on her treatment and nothing else left her free to watch his every move without fear of being watched in turn.

The treatment over, Theo packed away the machine and its parts.

He took her hand in his, and kissed the palm—a simple possession of her hand. She wanted to pull away, and not, wanted that kiss again. The room vanished, and there remained only his hold on her hand, his gray eyes, the drumming of her heart.

“Claire?”

“Yes?” she asked huskily.

“May I have your permission to court you?”

A lightning strike might have had less effect. She stopped breathing and stared at him, knowing a complete dunce could see her reaction.

He ran a finger lightly from palm to wrist to arm. “If you don’t speak, I’ll take that as a yes.”

She swallowed past the dryness in her throat. “Why? I’m your prisoner, not your—”

"Lover?" He raised an eyebrow, and her cheeks heated. "I can't free you yet, Claire. I don't know enough about you. Let me into your world so I can decide what to do with you."

She laughed bitterly. "You wouldn't like my world at all. You're mocking me. I'm a frankenstruct. You don't *court* a frankenstruct!"

"I do what I like. You're putting yourself down. I won't have that. You are human, Claire, and I can see I have a job to do here in convincing you of this. Answer my question, please. May I court you?"

She stared. *He has a job to do...* For some reason that scared her more than anything else he'd said. She gathered her thoughts, acutely aware of how he still hung on to her hand.

"I can tell you about myself without you courting me." She shivered, though no breeze touched the room.

"True."

He agreed. The fluttering in her stomach subsided. Courting? She vaguely remembered notes about it. *Do I dare ask?*

"Um. What exactly do you mean by courting?" She had a hunch it wouldn't be simple or innocent or confined to merely kissing and exchanging compliments. Where he'd drawn the line on her palm, she couldn't stop feeling frissons of warmth—as if he'd dipped his finger in some unknown magic.

"Courting is a social ritual, where two people find out about each other. The boundaries vary." Though his words were oh so factual, with his fingertip he traced delicious looping curves on her wrist. "In some countries it stops at talking and kissing. In others...the couple may go further." He raised an eyebrow.

He was daring her—daring her to ask how far courting went here. In the face of his amused stare, her courage fled.

"Have you ever been kissed, Claire?"

She clenched her hands. All she could think was Inkline. Inkline making her stand there, slapping her, the pain. Slowly she pulled everything back into place, shoved away the memory of humiliation, and focused on the quiet man who sat by her bed, stroking her hand and uncurling her fingers.

"Yes. I have."

A line creased between his eyes. "But it's not something you liked. I can see that."

She looked to where June sat, except the machine blocked her view.

"June is discreet. Forget she's there. Kissing should be pleasurable." He slowly lowered his head and pressed his lips to her palm again, then to her wrist.

"Would you like me to show you?"

What a question! But he wasn't making her do it. She had a choice. With Inkline and the other trainers, it had been degrading and almost rape. Kissing for pleasure was something lovers did, and for a flustering moment she imagined herself in Theo's bed, their limbs entwined. *Oh my.*

Where had that come from? She'd seen two pleasure slaves demonstrate the sexual act, but she'd not actually *done* it, and...

She blinked. Moisture beaded on her brow. He hadn't moved since he'd asked her his excruciating question. Serenity radiated from him, like he had all the time in the world to wait for her answer.

"Yes," she whispered. Her heart fluttered like a lantern flame caught in a wild wind.

"Tell me if you want me to stop, Claire, and I will."

He rose from the chair so he could reach her, and then he pressed those firm lips on her wrist again. He looked up at her in between each kiss as he advanced, inch by inch, up her arm. Tingles washed up and through her body like a slow, inevitable tide. They rose up her arm to her lips, lingering and swirling like the last shallow wave on the beach, over her nipples, her stomach… She could refuse him—she held tight on to that thought—then the tingling reached her groin. She closed her eyes at that, reveling in the awakening sensation.

He kissed her shoulder and came to her neck. She sighed, tilting her head on the pillow, letting those warm lips close in on her and move along the line of her jaw.

"Claire?" he murmured. "Do you still want this?"

She opened her eyes to find his inches away. Was he doing this to please her, because he liked her, or did he aim to seduce her for his own ends and nothing else?

She shuddered and, half-dazed, studied him.

He tilted her chin, regarding her calmly, his irises a sea of ashen gray. How was that so? He was calm, when her heart beat so swiftly. She ached for those lips to touch hers.

"Yes," she breathed. His mouth descended on hers, his lips soft and sure, taking her whole mouth gently at first, then nibbling each part of her lip. Teeth and tongue played their part, goading her until she parted her lips and let his tongue inside. When she felt his hand cup her breast, then lightly caress her nipple, she moaned. His mouth plundered hers, and she fell away beneath him, laid out for him to take what he wished.

Her free hand clutched at his back just as his hand slid under her head and tangled in her hair, holding her still, keeping her exactly where he wanted her. And that was glorious, freeing her to enjoy the kiss, absorbed in the sensations. Her pussy dampened. The kiss became their universe, a unique creation, stretching on for so long that when he pulled away, their lips separating, his breath no longer hers...she knew a deep surprise and loss.

He stroked her cheek with the back of his hand. "There. Was that not worth it?"

She caught her breath, wondering at what he'd brought her, this gift of pleasure, then counted to ten. A smidgen of indignation crept back in. *Wait.* She was letting him play her like some toy, like a frankenstruct.

So she ducked her head away from his hand and adopted a frown, just enough to show she wasn't overwhelmed, or a fool. "That was...different."

"Just different?"

She searched his face for clues, but he remained unreadable. Deliberately so, she decided. His hand still rested over her breast. Her nipple throbbed, as if anticipating the pressure of his finger.

Two could play at that game. She gave back the same steady expression for several seconds, making her breathing slow, though most of the breaths were ragged. She should have said no, but…

I'm falling over my feet to please him. Lord. What irony.

Theo was rich, powerful, and seemingly infatuated with her. The sexual games between men and women had been hinted at in training. Was he playing her for a fool? She couldn't tell and held back a shiver. She had a suspicion his expertise extended into deep and dangerous waters.

Yet, would it hurt to go further, to see where this led? She'd bc gone soon anyway, and she couldn't deny how much he appealed to her. The sexual attraction was there, between them, saturating the air. If she could taste him in her mouth, smell him, if her nipple and mouth ached in memory of where his skin had been, would the same be true for him?

"Claire?" A twitch at the corner of his mouth told her she'd been contemplating too long. His thumb moved on her nipple, and she jumped. He smiled. "How was this kiss different?"

"The last man who kissed me"—she slid her gaze to look over his shoulder—"forced me. He was…" *No, hell, no, don't say a superior officer. He'll know I'm military.* "He was in charge of me, and I wasn't allowed to say no." Anger, sadness, humiliation—all vied for a place in her head, and she tensed. *Why in hell did I tell him that?*

"Look at me, Claire."

That familiar lightning connection surged in her blood.

"I will court you, but remember this. If you say *kokino*, I will know you want me to stop kissing you."

"Kokino?" She quirked an eyebrow. The Greek word for red?

Amusement and something darker glinted in his eyes. "Of course, that will also work on other activities we undertake together. Though I should point out that 'stop' and 'don't' and other sundry words are likely to only encourage me."

Despite lying there with one hand fastened to the headboard, she summoned up a little imperiousness. "Other activities?"

"I assumed, having gained your permission to court you, I will be instructing you in the nuances of lovemaking."

Her mouth dried. *Lovemaking? Ah. That definitely sounds like far more than kissing.* His words conjured indecent images. *Breathe. One. Two. Three. Slow and calm. Don't let him take over. I must keep my head and think.*

Already, he was taking liberties. Like Inkline, only...different.

"Lesson one." He pinned her free hand to the pillow beside her ear. She froze. With such a simple move, he'd knocked her into the dark, unfathomable depths. He wove his other hand in her hair, then eased himself onto the bed and leaned his weight on her. To free herself she'd have to do something extraordinary, and both of them would get hurt.

"Don't move," he rumbled.

She saw herself reflected in those eyes—caught trembling in a delicious cage. He slowly nestled his heavy thigh deep between her legs. She gasped at the wetness flooding her down there.

The command, the easy way he held her, both went straight to her center, paralyzing her, scaring her, but in a strangely exciting way. She *could* do something but chose not to. When a word meant freedom, she didn't need martial skills. She had the power to stop him. Yet, all she wanted to do was to wait, quivering, for his next move.

He kissed her, only this time his lips pressed harder, rougher, until she sank under the assault. She gasped at the thrust of his tongue and the nip of teeth. Writhing, finding herself trapped by his arms and body, sent her arousal soaring to new heights. Her nipples scrunched into tight pebbles. When his leg pushed rhythmically onto her mound, blood pumped into her clit until it stood up hard against his harder muscles. Moaning, panting softly, she melted into him.

Lord. What is happening to me?

He lifted his head, eyes regarding her this time with a hint of triumph. "Sometimes force can make things more enjoyable. Or so it seems in your case." He smiled. "True?"

She licked her swollen lips, feeling as if every part of her had been ravaged by the electricity from the galvanic machine. *Is it true? And if it is, does it matter*? He looked at her as a human. He kissed like some god come down from the heavens. Right then and there, she needed him so much. She held his gaze, feeling small and conquered and wanted.

He released her hand, rolled off her to the side, and waited. His arm draped heavily across her chest; his thumb idly traced the underside of one breast, making her aware of the power he had to hold her again.

He wanted an answer.

"I guess, it might be true," she said softly. She reached up and ran a finger across the stubble on his chin to the corner of his mouth. That she could touch this man, like this, stirred her and left her awash with wonder.

His eyes darkened. "You guess. I never like to leave a woman unsure about her answer."

With a directness that made argument seem wrong, he grasped her wrist and pulled her hand away from his face.

"What are you doing?" She tugged, though not enough to be a serious attempt.

He ignored her, shifted onto his knees, straddled her body. The circle of his fingers around her wrist, the way his knees clamped in on her body, and the weight of this solid man above her stole the air from her lungs. If she leaned up, she could press her mouth to his trousers and let her lips feel the muscle beneath. A sudden desire to do more than kiss stormed through her. She wanted to bite him.

Enough. That thought... She slumped back onto the pillow, shutting her eyes to comprehend the way he handled her, to smell his closeness. Countermoves raced through her mind and vanished. Within seconds he'd fastened her hands together above her head and flipped her onto her stomach. She turned her head to one side, breathing fast and shallow into the pillow and the side of her arm; then his hand came down on the back of her neck and held her there.

Pinned. His other hand flattened onto her lower back, weighing her down, sending heavy currents coiling between her legs. One of his fingers settled into the top of the divide of her ass, like an arrow pointing straight to her moist slit, to where she pressed into the bed. She groaned, tried to squirm. Her clitoris thrummed with excruciating *need.*

"Stay. Still."

The words stopped her. She wanted to obey, wanted his touch, and moaned her frustration into the softness of the pillow. How did this happen? How could he make her lust so fiercely with so little?

Silence throbbed past, slick and hot and wet, until the world was only him and her and what lay between her legs.

His hand slid a little lower. A soft noise escaped her lips.

"Have you a better answer now, Claire?" Then he clasped her neck tighter and wriggled that delicious finger he'd wedged in the split of her bottom.

Ohh. Either she gave in and told him the truth, or soon she'd be begging him to touch her, and she wasn't going to do that.

"Say you like it. Repeat my words."

Somehow, that made it simple. “I…liked it.” She breathed once. “Yes.”

“Good.” He let her go, lifted both his hands, and undid one of the cuffs. “I look forward to lesson two.” The way his voice dropped an octave made her lower body clench. But she didn’t move as the bed dipped, or even as she heard him walk away, open the door, and leave. The door clicked shut. She lay there, trembling, stunned, and wishing she’d had the courage to ask him for more.

Those other cursory lessons, of the darker skills some men demanded—she’d written them down in shorthand and giggled with her friend, Francine. She wondered what Theo’s lesson two would entail.

Then she sank her teeth into her lip.

What have I done? I must not lose myself in this, no matter what he says. I’m a frankenstruct, not a human.

Humans always end up hurting us. Always.

Chapter Four

On the chest of drawers beside her bed, she found a book about birds. Even with one hand above her head, she could turn the pages and read. Books were one of those rare pleasures she never got enough of, a way to withdraw from the world and simply enjoy the images that played out in her head. She read it from cover to cover and then began it again.

In the loneliest hours of the night, she woke to find her breaths chugging out of her like steam from an engine. Visions of paper flipping through the darkness dominated her thoughts—of someone burying a folder deep underground, in a cave where tree roots slithered like snakes. Feet scuffled at the periphery of her vision. It took hours, or seemed to, before she succumbed again to sleep.

The nightmare stirred up the darker places in her soul. What had happened yesterday was an aberration. She'd never received anything greater than a grudging respect for her usefulness from a human. The way Lord Kevonis treated her unbalanced her. And the way she'd reacted to him was unfathomable, even ridiculous. She squeezed her thighs together, shivered. Though even now, when she recalled the weight of his hand on her back, she yearned to feel that way again. Yet was it all just to get her into his bed? Or was it something more cunning? Perhaps he knew what she was, and was playing with her, to see what secrets she might reveal?

That morning, while in the bathroom, she tried the lock on her cuffs anyway. It would be handy to know she could free herself as needed. Another couple of days and she'd be fit enough to run. The Brito-Gallic League—just the thought of being free for the first time in her life, even if she had to disguise her marks, was enough to make her hand shake.

The hairpin snapped in the lock. She cursed softly, then attempted to get her fingernails around the prong of broken metal. It slipped and rotated and refused to come out.

She slumped against the wall, held the heels of her hands against her eyes. Not good. June would see she'd been tampering as soon as she tried to relock the cuffs. She'd call in the guards from the hallway. What if trying to escape meant he sent her off for euthanasia? Sure, Lord Kevonis had designs on her and wanted her in his bed, but he wasn't stupid. If she seemed a threat, she'd be eliminated.

She didn't want to die.

Someone knocked at the main bedroom door, and muffled words were exchanged. Footsteps approached.

"Girl!" June sang out. "Whatcha doing in there? The colonel wants to see you!"

Pressure built behind her eyes. A colonel? Well now, wasn't she lucky? Another hell-blasted military man, and what great timing. Theo had brought in someone to interrogate her after all. *Let me into your world so I can decide what to do with you.* She felt like blowing a raspberry. He was like all the other humans, willing to lie through his teeth.

She slid down the wall, bowed her head, and drew up her knees despite the fresh agony invoked in her thigh muscles. The tag ends of the stitches pricked the undersides of her arms. *Damn them.* She watched sourly as a thin line of blood trickled down the side of her thigh. Deep muscle aches she'd forgotten returned. The outer bedroom door banged open, and what sounded like a herd of guards tromped in.

"Where is she?" Dankyo. He was back.

"She's locked in the bathroom, sir, and doesn't seem to want to come out," June grumbled.

"There's no time for this. Get her out. Now. Take off the hinges if you must. Make sure she's cuffed, and bring her downstairs."

A few minutes later, the bathroom lock had been knocked loose, and two of Dankyo's gray-uniformed cohorts dragged her out into the bedroom. She didn't resist, much—just a few kicks to their shins for the satisfaction of hearing them yelp.

June stood to one side wringing her hands and making odd noises as if she wanted to say something but wasn't sure if it was her place.

"No more of that, girl, woman—whatever you are!" The taller guard kept a tight hold on Claire's upper arm. She kept her face rigid. "June, there's no time for whatever you were supposed to get her dressed in, but can you clean up the blood?"

June wrinkled her mouth. "Sure, I don't know what Mister Dankyo thinks he's doing. I can tell you now that Lord Kevonis won't be happy. Here, let me brush her hair as well."

"Just the leg, June. Been told to bring her straightaway."

June grunted, and something shifted in her face, relaxing so the creases became less deep. "Let her go a bit, Harry. Can't you see she's scared?"

Scared? She wasn't scared...much. Claire made sure nothing showed. Made herself hard as steel. Be nothing. Say nothing. These people were no better than any others.

Nevertheless, Harry's grip loosened. "Here, let June clean that."

With a wet cloth, June carefully wiped away the blood.

The gentleness of her touch confused Claire. One minute Dankyo was instructing them to haul her downstairs like a piece of luggage, yet these two, Harry and June, were being nice?

"Come on, love," said Harry. "Can you walk down the stairs?" The corners of his mouth curved up, barely—as if he was unsure if he should smile.

Shocked, Claire stared. She'd grown accustomed to Lord Kevonis's forward ways—after all, he had designs on her body, but were his men insane as well? Nobody smiled at frankenstructs.

In a large niche halfway down, beside a turn in the stairs, a sculpture caught her eye—two naked figures. A man, his hair like coiling serpents, embraced a voluptuous woman, her back arched, and the head of his erect phallus peeked out between their bodies.

"That's a nice piece of art," said Harry, at her shoulder.

She'd been standing there slack-mouthed for several seconds. *Art*? Flustered, she averted her gaze and continued on.

She was led through folded back timber doors to a balcony tiled in granite and suspended at man height above the outside gardens. Theo sat in a wide rattan chair, leaning with one elbow on an armrest and talking quietly to Dankyo, who stood at his shoulder.

Dankyo, as always, somehow radiated both impassiveness and threat. But it was Theo who drew her eye. She'd not seen him at a distance before. His wide, sprawled pose brought to mind pictures of kings ensconced on their thrones—about to dispense justice, declare war, or with regally raised eyebrow, receive the obeisance of a slave.

Her senses pricked to a higher level. Her skin seemed made newborn, so she felt every featherlight movement of the air. The fragrance of flowers came to her. They twined and dangled from the high trellises enclosing the balcony. She judged Theo half a head taller than Dankyo, though he was leaner, with that strong Grecian nose dividing his face. Black stubble shadowed his chin. Those short bristles had rubbed against her fingers and felt exciting and raw. The curls of hair on his forehead reminded her of the sexually aroused man in the sculpture she'd passed on the stairs. Heat flushed her cheeks.

On the long table before Theo were platters of food wafting delicious smells across to where she waited, swaying slightly, between the two guards. Breakfast was overdue.

Dankyo looked up and came to her.

She glanced uncertainly at Theo, frowning. Where was this colonel who wished to see her? Then Dankyo drew near, stopping half a yard away, with his fingers tapping against his blue trousers.

She'd seen a tiger once, outside the fence of the training camp, and its walk was like Dankyo's, all spring-laden power and casual ferocity.

"Have you checked her, Snow?" asked Dankyo.

Harry stiffened to attention. "No, sir! Uh, sir, for what would you like her checked?"

Harry Snow. She filed that away along with June's name. Knowledge was power.

Dankyo's nose wrinkled, but he simply shook his head and walked around her. His hand snaked out, and he grabbed the manacles, raising her hands.

For the first time she saw mirth in his eyes. "She's been poking at these. Have you been trying to escape?"

She smiled thinly back, determined not to show he was hurting her arms.

"Dankyo," Theo drawled. "Leave her be. Unless she's a danger to me, let her sit."

"She's tried to get the cuffs off, sir." Dankyo swung around. "Perhaps it might be safer for you to dine alone? I can take care of her."

"Ah, Dankyo. I know your maneuvers too well. Safety is important, but I would rather speak to her myself. Claire." He crooked a finger.

Though suspicion narrowed his dark brown eyes, Dankyo stepped aside to let her pass. "Of course, sir."

Theo regarded first Dankyo and then Claire as she walked to him and halted before his chair. He had his feet planted in that wide-based manly way. As if he brushed her with the softest of feathers, she felt the drifting path of his gaze upon her skin. It annoyed her. He'd said she was human, yet he looked at her as if she were a thing. Her mouth twisted.

"What is it?" he asked.

She hesitated. Thinking it was one thing, saying it, another.

Theo relaxed back into the chair. "Tell me, Claire. Now, please."

"You look at me as if I'm an object."

He nodded. "I don't think you're an object, Claire. I'm looking at you that way because you're a desirable woman."

She hoped desperately that the somewhat strangled sound in her throat hadn't carried.

He barely spared her a glance. "Dankyo, you know I gave instructions as to Claire's apparel at breakfast. Fix that and the cuffs. And, Claire…"

"Yes?"

"No more escape attempts, please. I have your best interests in mind. If you abuse my hospitality, I can't say where that will lead exactly, but it won't be anywhere nice. Understood?"

He expected her to honor such an agreement? How quaint. If he was going to suddenly shift from showering her with compliments to veiled threats, that was fine with her. It affirmed what she'd dreaded. She was only a convenience to him.

"Understood." *Perfectly understood.*

"Dankyo. Fast as possible, please. Follow my orders next time."

She would have grinned at Dankyo's discomfort, but it would have been stupid to rile him further.

"Harry." Dankyo gestured. "Carry her."

To her amazement, she was carried swiftly back upstairs over Harry's shoulder, and the cuffs were removed. She was allowed to bathe, albeit with June watching every move and two guards outside the door. Twenty minutes later, she was clean and dressed in a yellow silk calf-length dress, her hair combed and loose over her shoulders and her hands resecured with a set of padded cuffs. A quick examination confirmed the same locking mechanism.

The house guards escorted her downstairs and into a rattan chair at the opposite end of the table from Theo. Dankyo, as before, stood beside him.

A trio of sparrows flitted across, inches above the table, chasing each other with loud indignant chirps before zipping out through the dense wall of flowers to the open air. It was so beautiful, so peaceful, and if not for the four attending house guards and Dankyo, it would have been an intimate and hidden affair.

Yet, this was so wrong. This was a breakfast for the rich and idle. She didn't belong here.

Chapter Five

At the other end of the table, Claire looked around at the table setting, the birds, at anything but him. Theo frowned. He drummed his fingers on the white linen tablecloth next to the senate report and the broadsheet from New Baskerton. Today's paper, yet, after all these days, it held no news of the Pancontinental Mexican airship. Which meant someone high up was keeping it under wraps.

Spiro, his manservant, backed onto the balcony, pulling a serving cart laden with freshly cooked sausages, poached eggs, mushrooms, and bacon. Tilting an eyebrow he waited for instructions, all attentive in his starched white pants and shirt.

"The lady first," Theo said.

The graceful line of Claire's neck drew his eye lower to where her breasts swelled above the bodice of the yellow dress. A petite chin, curved and kissable mouth, a turned-up nose. With her straw blonde hair feathering her shoulders, she looked as pretty as the little doll his sister, Mari, used to play with. Only this doll he wanted to play with—really wanted. He shifted in his chair, rearranging trousers that were suddenly uncomfortable.

Then why am I sitting here merely having breakfast with her?

Right now, Claire looked bewildered as she surveyed all the food piled high on her plate. While Spiro served him, she picked up her fork and knife and tried to cut the food. The linking chain of the handcuffs clinked against the edge of the plate.

The contrast of the circlets of metal against a woman's skin never failed to get his blood humming. A delectable woman, restrained at his breakfast table, one of his favorite scenarios. He imagined clearing the balcony of staff, stripping her, laying her naked across the table. Those pretty white wrists lashed above her head, legs spread wide for him. His member pressed hard against his pants.

Yes. A breathtaking thought to start the day with. Now all he had to do was get her to agree to such arrangements. He had a feeling that would be difficult—she had a ton of feistiness and anguish all bundled up inside her. No wonder, though. Spiro's voice brought him back to reality.

"Sir? Will that be all?"

"Yes. You may go, Spiro. You also, Dankyo." He gestured in dismissal. "And the four guards, please."

"That may not be wise, sir." Dankyo flicked a look at Claire, his eyebrows scrunching together. "You don't know what she is capable of."

"True, but she's at the other end of this table, and she's cuffed. I think that is sufficient, don't you?"

"Ah—" Dankyo's mouth writhed as if he struggled for words.

"Go. That's an order."

When the balcony was clear, he rubbed his brow. Damn. Why was he so tongue-tied? What was there to converse about with someone who had no family? What would it be like to be her? Lonely, surely?

The senate report on frankenstructs detailed their assembly from cloned parts—a deliberate ploy so the PME could say they weren't human and thus use them like any other piece of manufactured equipment. They credited a Dr. Frankenstein with the breakthrough. A straight clone would be irrefutably human. Such a clever technicality with such sad results for someone like Claire.

Something should be done, but what exactly?

He had access to higher echelons of power. Dammit, he *was* a higher power, if he chose to get involved. Politics meant doing. This would be a fitting first foray. *Note to self: fix this ASAP.*

A small portion of egg flew from her plate and landed on the table next to a little vase of peonies. She put down the cutlery, her hands disappearing beneath the table, and stared fiercely at the plate as if it held something poisonous.

When he cleared his throat, she glanced up at him, and just for a second he saw the smallest line of watery reflection at the corner of one of her eyes. *A tear. Lord.*

Dankyo might think him mad. Common sense said to keep his distance. Yet the memory of her body under his on the bed called to him far more than any sensible decision. He'd already pushed this further than he should have. Common sense could go hang.

He cleared his throat again, put his hands to the edge of the table, and shoved back his chair. As he walked up, bearing his plate, her amber eyes grew rounder and darker until he thought he might fall into them and never emerge.

"May I?"

He indicated the cane chair at the corner, next to her. When she nodded he lowered his plate and sat, so close that if he put his elbow down and laid his forearm flat, he'd have his hand in her meal.

Nicely close. If it bothers her, all to the better. He might not want to hurt her, but a bit of anxiety added spice.

"You've not told your man, Dankyo, have you? That you're courting me?" She scowled, then held up her wrists and shook them, jangling the metal. "And why these, here? Is it so you can laugh at the way I cut up my food?"

"As to your first question, no, I've not told him yet. I will. As for those, I don't trust you enough to take them off." He settled his shoulders in a comfortable spot against the chair.

The aroma of sausages reminded him why he'd moved. He took up his knife and fork and eyed her plate. You didn't cut up someone's food without asking. Not in polite company.

"Would it help if I cut up your food?"

She pulled back, eyeing him. "Perhaps. Where is this colonel? I was told he'd be here."

That was sufficient for him. He started cutting. "I am the colonel. It was my Air Corps rank. Some of my staff like to use it still."

"I see."

She watched while he sliced, as if she'd catch him doing something wrong. He kept going until her entire plate of food was in smallish pieces, then speared a piece of sausage with her fork and held it up.

"Here."

Hesitantly, she brought her hands up and took hold of the fork, her fingertips brushing against his where they wrapped about the utensil. The touch blazed a path to his groin. Her fingers were so slender and delicate. He didn't let go completely, curling one of his over the top of hers and trapping them there.

He held his breath, fascinated to watch the shift of emotion across her face. Her nostrils widened, a blush crept onto her cheeks, and those gorgeous plump lips separated slightly in arousal...and from something so simple.

This wasn't just any woman. In her eyes, he glimpsed at times a deep sadness before it vanished, buried beneath ever-present layers of wariness.

He had a hankering to pierce that shield she carried. There were easier conquests, ones no one would raise eyebrows at or gossip over. Courting a frankenstruct might hobble his political career before he even got it off the ground. So why did he feel compelled?

To the devil with self-analyzing. He wanted to do this, so he would. He ran his fingers lightly down the side of her hand to where the metal circled her wrists, and hooked the chain when she pulled away.

* * * *

Claire scowled back at Theo, trying to mask the confusion as he stroked her wrist with one calloused finger. She tugged again but he merely regarded her impassively, as if appraising her. Heat surged through her. The world got strangely smaller.

This was more of his *courting.* Of course, she could pull free, if she wanted. Break his fingers, maybe, before his guards got to her. Or even say his silly word, kokino.

What an idiot she was being. Hadn't she decided to show some self-control? If only she didn't feel that quivering sensation down below. One finger on her wrist, and she was losing it. If he kissed her hand as he had the day before, or—she swallowed—if he held her down, she might simply melt.

He released her.

Focus. Calm. Her heart settled. *Thank the Lord.*

Quietly, she forked up a piece of fried mushroom and put it in her mouth, chewed it. Eating gave her time to gather her scattered thoughts. *Logic. Calmness. Breathe slow.*

He said he didn't trust her. Logically, for her to gain his trust, she'd have to answer questions about the airship and her reasons for being on it. Perhaps he waited for her full recovery? Stupid, though. She'd been instructed in the art of torture and interrogation—best to act while the subject was weakest.

This courting business was the passing fancy of a rich man with nothing better to do than ignore the advice of his own security advisor. Mentally, she curled a lip. Why had she been disconcerted by his touch? Her body's chemical balance must have been disturbed by the shock of the crash. Theo was no more dangerous to her than a pussycat, and she would do well to remember that.

The fork tempted her. She must smuggle it upstairs. It would make a superb lock pick. She should be putting more effort into her escape. Another couple of days and she'd chance it. She'd have to go on foot at first—vehicles would be easily tracked. Though maybe a steam cycle... She needed maps. There should be a study or an office somewhere.

A movement drew her from her reverie. She left off aiming the fork into her mouth and swung her gaze back to Theo.

He'd finished eating and leaned both elbows on the table, watching her. Her heart accelerated. *Just a chemical imbalance. That's all. Pussycat.*

Why then did she wish she could inch farther away, yet also want to lean in closer?

The irises of his eyes were more beautiful than she had thought possible. Sea gray specked with flares of gold that made them glow when the morning sun glanced in though the trellis. Above those eyes, his brows boldly followed the line of bone.

What piffle was she thinking? He was just a man. The color of his eyes meant nothing.

"Claire?"

She drew in a controlled breath, felt her ribs expand.

"Yes?" She sat up primly.

Her plate was empty. The fork scraped across the white china. She laid the silver pronged utensil on the tablecloth—near the edge, where a subtle brush of her wrist would topple it over. Get this fork up to her room, sharpen the end tine until it became flexible enough. *Yes. That's the spirit.*

"Coffee?" he asked, cocking one of those elegant eyebrows.

"What? Oh, yes, of course. Thank you."

His servant had left. The folding doors leading back into the house proper had been shut. What little she could spy, through the fringe of plants, of the outside lawns was an empty green expanse. Suddenly, this breakfast area seemed far too isolated.

Theo tilted the gold-trimmed white pot and poured. Steam and an enticing bitter aroma rose from the dainty matching cup.

Training had covered all this. The use of the correct tableware. Small talk. How to smile and say *thank you*. Only it wasn't the same. With this man across from her, an undercurrent colored the simplest of things. Her cup wobbled when she raised it.

All the signs of arousal... She pursed her lips. Ridiculous, but she couldn't deny the dampness in her underwear, or the way her heart beat double time when he spoke to her or held her.

The froth on the surface of the coffee seemed a safe place to look. As the level in the cup sank, a memory crystallized. The cup wobbled again, rattling when she placed it in the saucer. She remembered when she'd felt a little of what he awakened in her.

Part of her training had been interrogations practice. The realness of the pain had been frightening...yet, when she'd been bound to the chair with her hands at her back and her feet tied to the legs, she'd found it exciting. The powerlessness had made her feel so *alive.*

"Claire?"

She snapped her eyes open.

"Are you all right?"

"I'm perfectly all right, thank you." How dare *he* appear so unruffled?

"Truly?" Such a warm voice, deep enough to swim in.

Time to go, before he addled her mind even more. She dabbed her mouth with the napkin, put her hands to the table to steady herself before she pushed back the chair.

"Stop." The word lashed out, freezing her. Startled she looked up.

She'd trained for this, over and over. Rapid decisions in the face of adversity. Yet...her mind emptied. Before she could decide what to do, he snared her wrists and pulled her down onto the table. Her elbows slid, plates bumped out of the way as he stretched her arms out in front of her. She turned her head, found herself face-to-face with him, jerked at her wrists, and couldn't budge. Her talent lay in speed, not strength.

"Let me go!"

The danger was back in those gray predatory eyes. She lay helpless, half across the table, feeling her breaths come faster and faster. She daren't blink. The table pressed against her waist, and Theo's lips were mere inches away. With his other hand, he found and twined a piece of her hair around his finger.

"Ahh. How curious," he murmured, twisting the hair a little tighter. Then, as if she were something remarkable that needed fixing in his memory, something he'd never seen before, he examined her, inch by inch.

When she tugged against his hold and found herself still held fast, heat flooded her. The chair wouldn't move back. He must have hooked it with his foot. He leaned in and wound another curl of hair onto his finger until it pulled at her scalp. Beyond the bitter richness of the coffee, she smelled the cologne she'd come to associate with him—a dark, masculine aroma that made her imagine the grinding of cogs and engine parts.

This isn't inescapable. If she struggled, she might near upend the table. If she screamed, *someone* would come running. He waited, holding her, gray eyes watching, as if some choice teetered in the balance. She tensed again. His grip adjusted an infinitesimal amount on her wrists, as if to say *I have you.*

Yes. You do. Everything about him enveloped her, made her crave exactly *this.* His possession. In her mind something relaxed; the balance shifted. She welcomed every way he could touch her, the heat from his body, the atoms of his breath. Everything.

As if he sensed her surrender, she felt the warm shift of air as he exhaled. Then his lips met hers, kissing her ever so gently.

The touch quaked her to the core. She shut her eyes, wanting only to feel. With each press, his mouth ventured more—harder, more urgent, drawing each lip under his teeth, then releasing it, parting them and pushing, until his tongue slipped warm into her. Beneath the coffee flavor, he tasted strange and foreign—exciting.

She had his tongue in her mouth, and the way she lay, her breasts half-swelled from the bodice of her dress. If he touched her there... She moaned into his mouth.

He pulled away. The loss made her ache for his lips on hers again.

"Better," he said. "Much better. An obedient woman. It suits you." He let go of her hair, ran his hand under her chin.

She should move. Resist. All she could do was blink up at him, then jam her eyes shut and shudder.

Timber grated on granite as he moved his chair closer to the corner. Without freeing her, he reached under the table. His fingers touched her dress, then inexorably inched the fabric up past her knee, along her thigh, upward. Her heart hammered. There was bare skin under those fingers. Where was he going? Not there, surely. Not here, at the table. She opened her eyes and found his waiting for her. He smiled back, smoothed those fingers higher to the juncture of her thighs.

"Open your legs, Claire."

She shook her head, trembling.

"Am I hurting you?"

Heavens, no. This feels so good, so dark and wicked. Can anyone see? She chanced a look. Beyond the veil of flowering wisterias, nothing stirred. Though her stitches ached, with every new sensual advance on her body, the discomfort shrank further into the background.

"Claire? There's only us. Open your legs."

She swallowed and slipped out her tongue a second, then gave in and parted her thighs, groaning as he slid his hand under the edge of her panties and onto her wet cleft. When his hand pressed again, she opened her legs more. His thick fingers trailed along, dipping in here and there, just enough to part her swollen lips. Hot sensation pulsed. She clenched down there, inner muscles acting of their own accord.

I can't stop him. Not now. That thought made her muscles spasm again, her pelvis nudge forward. *Touch me. More. Deeper*.

Panting, struggling not to writhe, humiliated by this consuming *need*, she moaned quietly.

"So wet." Amusement tinged his voice. "So very nice. I'd bare your nipples as well, and taste them, but I doubt you're ready for that much exhibitionism. Are you?"

She couldn't answer; the sensations made thought impossible.

With his finger, he found the entrance to her, fingertip pressing barely in, then out again, sending fiery pulsations to her clit. He put his forehead to hers and waited like that while his finger moved in and out and in... She gasped.

"Mmm. I love hearing you." He kissed her forehead. "This is lesson two, by the way."

Vivid, delightful ideas inundated her—his mouth, his tongue *there*, licking her. She'd used her fingers on herself, and it had never felt like this. Everywhere throbbed to the beat of her heart.

His thumb weaved in rhythmic circles around her clit; then another finger and another joined the first, delving in a little farther each time. A ring at the base on his finger let her gauge the depth. Slipping, sliding, deep, shallow. She could hear the liquid noises, her panties so wet the air cooled her. Her clit rose up into a tight ball, expanding, blood thumping through it, and so sensitive she bit her lip when his thumb brushed her.

Now his thumb rolled over the center of that nub, up and down, smearing her juices. Her pussy tensed around those invading fingers.

"I wonder, will you come for me, Claire?" Theo whispered.

She stared, dazed, into his intent eyes, barely comprehending, wanting that rhythm to take her to the edge. More. Her hips jerked to get closer, but the table's edge stopped her. Her wrists were pinned, her body held in exquisite limbo.

"There's no one here to see. Except me. Just don't squeal too loud."

Then his thumb skated onto her clit, pressing in time with his fingers. Again. Again. She sucked in a last breath, held it, straining, until at last a tumult of ecstasy rolled through, shaking her like a diamond jigsaw into a million brilliant pieces. Slowly the world calmed, and she found he still held her wrists. As he removed his fingers down below, his thumb grazed her clit, making her shudder in the flare of another shock. She panted, head down on the table, feeling the linen against her skin.

He released her wrists and carefully turned her head to face him. "Well done. You're the first woman to come at this table."

His eyes smoldered. She couldn't conjure up a single coherent word and stayed put as he ran his finger along the line of her jaw and across to tantalize her lower lip.

"If you lie there much longer, I'll be tempted to tie you to the table legs and try buttering your ass instead of the toast."

My God. That spurred her into action, and she sat up. She straightened her dress, finding it difficult to meet his eyes. *I shouldn't have done that.*

"I'd be delighted if you'd sit on my lap a moment." Theo wiped his fingers on a napkin—skin shining with her arousal—then leaned back, sprawling with his arm propped on the back of his chair. "No?"

"No." She vigorously shook her head. What had she done? That didn't feature in any of the books on ladylike manners she'd read. She'd had an orgasm at the breakfast table.

If he commanded her to sit on his lap, she wasn't sure she could say no.

"Perhaps next time?"

She blushed. "There won't be a next time! You"—she cleared her throat—"caught me unawares. I should not have let you do that."

"Oh, and why is that?"

She stared at him. Anger took over from indignation. "I..." The heat on her cheeks upped another few degrees.

"Claire. You didn't do that. I did. There was nothing to be ashamed of. " He sat forward. "I think that settles it."

She shook her head.

"If it is anyone's fault, it's mine. I have a foible—I like making women, some women, do what I want them to. You happen to be delightfully susceptible." His eyes glinted mischievously.

But it was too easy to imagine Inkline sneering and insulting her. *Slut* would be his favorite word. She was nothing more than an animal.

"Claire," he said more sharply, "you did nothing wrong!"

He didn't understand. Hell, she wasn't sure she did.

Furious, just plain blindly furious, she yanked on the tablecloth, upsetting china and cups, then shoved back her chair with a squeal of its legs on the tiles, and a *bang* as it tipped over.

"Didn't I? Well, someone did!" She spun around, prepared to march off.

Dankyo skidded onto the balcony, followed closely by the four guards. He flipped the cover off his holster.

"Wait!" Still in his chair, Theo held up a hand. "Stand down, Dankyo." He ran his palm over the top of his head. "Sit, please, Claire. I can see there are misunderstandings I should clear up."

"No!" She flounced her skirt out from where it had wrapped around the chair. "No. I'll not stay. I have nothing more to say."

That infuriating combination of reasonableness and... She set her mouth firm, glared at him again. And pure goddamned *maleness* would unhinge her if she stayed a moment longer. She could even *smell* the difference between him and other men.

She turned and sailed toward Dankyo, who'd stopped halfway to the doors, clearly appalled that anybody would defy his master. When she went to brush past, he put out his arm and barred her way. Harry and a second guard moved to back him up.

"Claire"—Theo's voice remained even—"I may comprehend your reasons, but I will not have impoliteness at my table."

Fuming, she put her head down a moment before turning and walking back to him. "You comprehend my reasons? I doubt that. Very much."

He rose. She looked up, disconcerted, having forgotten his height. "I require an apology."

She nodded, dry-mouthed, finding she'd lost track of why she'd become so angry. She was an assassin, a trained killer, and not his rag doll to be ordered this way and that. Her anger should surely be at herself, not at Theo. Or, was there no one to blame and get angry at? Was Theo right?

"I'm...sorry, Colonel." And she was, in a way.

He leaned in, whispering in her ear, "Thank you."

The gentle stir of her hair beneath his sweet breath sent a mesmerizing signal through her flesh. Her knees threatened to give way.

She stepped back onto someone's toes. "I'm...ah... Thank you for the breakfast." Cheeks hot with embarrassment, she swung around and set off blindly for the stairs.

Once she had Dankyo and his guards in tow, her mind calmed, and by the time she'd reached the bottom of the stairs, she allowed herself a small smile and a mental pat on the back. She had the fork tucked into her underwear. That was her practical side. The other side of her, where those words of Theo's fluttered round and round in the back of her head, well, she'd think of that again, later, when she was alone.

Chapter Six

The sound of her sharpening the fork against the metal hinges of the bathroom cupboard would have been impossible to disguise if it hadn't been for the regular firing up of some engine on the estate. The cacophony drowned out almost everything at least three times a day.

When an airship arrived that evening, she watched Theo march out to it with a retinue of four men. Dankyo trailed along last in line, like some prehistoric, overmuscled rear guard.

The dire red airship, emblazoned with a black rose and its name, *Final Rebuttal*, rose into the cloud-strewn purple and orange sky, floating away to the purr of its propellers like some giant bee.

Both men were gone. She smiled bleakly. He'd gone without saying another word to her.

No lady would have let him be so rude to her at the breakfast table, you silly git. Whatever made you think he really liked you?

* * * *

As the airship reached cruising altitude, Theo left the helm to Captain Muir and headed for his study.

The *Final Rebuttal* showed her age in the worn spots on the brass of the metal apparatus about the ship, in the frayed patches on the Oriental carpet in the gangways and the creaks and groans from the envelope as she went aloft. Not fast enough or well-armed or armored enough to be a warship, but she was his.

Almost every part of this ship stirred memories. He took pleasure in the solidity of the oak door to the study as it silently swung beneath his hand. Dankyo stalked in behind and closed the door. Warm colors surrounded Theo: the plush red of the curtains over the portholes along the far side melded with the golden colors of the timber of the desk and the framework of the leather-upholstered chairs.

"A brandy, Dankyo?" He lifted the cut-glass decanter from the tray on the occasional table.

"No thank you, sir. On duty." Dankyo stood like another piece of furniture—solid, unmoving, unemotional.

"Dammit, sit, man. There's nothing for you to do for four hours. One small glass won't disable you. I give you permission to relax." He poured a half inch of brandy into two glasses, handed one to Dankyo, and sank into the giving leather of the desk chair.

For a moment Dankyo looked lost; then he took two stiff steps and settled gingerly into the only chair in the room that was bare timber. He sipped. "Very nice, sir."

The coolness of glass against Theo's hand contrasted with the rich burn as the alcohol surged down his throat. "Skol. So"—he stretched out his legs, crossed them at the ankles—"what do you think of our Claire?"

"Our?" If anything, Dankyo sat up even stiffer and straighter. "Sir. Permission to express my opinion?"

Theo cocked an eyebrow. "Go ahead. You always have that option, man."

"We have coddled this woman for several days, and still we know nothing about her apart from her name and that she is a frankenstruct. She was on board a PME diplomatic vessel. I have my doubts about that ship, as well as doubts about who this woman really is."

"Hmph." Held at eye height and jiggled, the liquid in the glass swirled like an amber sea in the bottom of the glass. "I like her."

"That is hardly a professionally assessed fact," Dankyo said indignantly. "Sir."

"I know that." Theo studied the distorted figure of his head of security through the glass. "I admit we need to find out more about her. I shall be careful. But I still like her, and from what I've seen, she likes my attentions."

"In my book, sir, being careful means keeping her ten miles away from you."

"Ah." He grinned, knowing his next words would unsettle Dankyo.

"I have plans for her. Have you heard of shibari, Dankyo?"

Dankyo raised both eyebrows a fraction of an inch. "Sir knows it is the ancient Oriental art of rope bondage. Might I also add that though I thoroughly approve of tying the woman up, in the interests of security, I do not believe she is a pleasure slave." He carefully placed his glass on the spindly table near his chair. "Although sir's pleasures and hobbies are not mine to comment upon, I doubt she will be agreeable."

"We shall see." Theo tossed back a large gulp of brandy. "If nothing else, the pursuit should be invigorating. Hmm. There's a store on Pannier Street. I should pay a visit. Hinchcliff and Co."

Unfolding from the chair like some mechanical being, Dankyo rose, straightened his trousers. "I must resume my duties. Might I make one last candid observation, sir?"

Theo waved casually.

"Sir, ahem...caution is advisable." He stared fixedly at a portion of the wall above Theo's head. "I believe...the young woman has you by the testicles, sir."

It took all Theo's willpower not to choke on his last swallow of brandy. "Well then, I can only hope and pray."

* * * *

Servants brought several new dresses for Claire to select from, and the next morning the handcuffs were supplemented with a long chain running to the bed's column. Finally she could move about on the bed. The ache in her shoulder muscles went away.

Were these rewards Theo's idea? The long steel chain ran cold across her hand like a silver serpent.

Did they not wonder how dangerous such a thing might be? She could have strangled June if she'd wanted to—not that she would. With small gestures and kindnesses, the woman had become more than a mere jailer.

Inkline would have told her she was weak, and that this, the Hellene Nation, was the enemy of the PME and so therefore all its people were her enemy. Inkline could go to hell, if he wasn't already there. She'd make her own decision.

Besides, June didn't have the key anymore and had to call in a guard to free her from the cuffs. She didn't want to hurt June. Killing anyone no longer seemed right.

Soon after she woke that morning, Harry walked in with a box of books. Blearily, she watched as he lowered it to the floor. "The colonel is to be away a few days, and he thought you might like these. He told me to say *enjoy*. You do read?" Harry scratched his head.

She slid up onto one elbow, stared dumbfounded from Harry to the box. How had he known? June must have told him. The twinkle in the woman's eyes as she shuffled about arranging ornaments said it all.

"I do read." Her heart did a little skip of joy. They both seemed to be waiting for something. "Uh. Thank you?"

Everything was in there. A whole world of inventiveness. Books about cooking. Archaeology books on diggings where the layers revealed the crushed remains of strange four-wheeled vehicles, their owners entombed within. Books about pets. Stories about murders or monsters or choosing men to marry. Those last, she left in the box.

For hours, engrossed in reading, she forgot to sharpen her fork.

After a lunch of roast meat and salad, eaten with her fingers—oh, if only they knew it was too late—Claire sat cross-legged on the bed, facing June. She arranged the blue skirt of her dress over her knees. The sutures barely bothered her. Tomorrow, she'd be healed enough to escape to the Brito-Gallic League. To freedom.

She sighed. If only she didn't have this niggling, horrible thought at the back of her head that somehow this was wrong. Yet what could be wrong with freedom?

A half-knitted garment lay on June's lap. She peered over a pair of spectacles at Claire, though her hands continued clicking and clacking the knitting needles. "Yes?"

More potential weapons, Claire noted. The bone point of the needles would go into an ear or an eye with ease. Ah, these were stupid, stupid thoughts.

"Why?" A tendril of her hair tumbled before her eye. She pulled it out straight and turned it round her finger.

"Why what, dear?"

Dear. Again. She closed her eyes. How could they treat her like this? As if she was normal?

Though the cuffs on her wrists said otherwise.

"Why are you treating me so nicely?" She stared at her fingernails, then dared to look up at June.

June snorted. "'Cause you're only a young woman. Not some monster. Ah, don't look at me all googly-eyed! If the colonel says you're right by him, then you're right by me too. 'Bout the only one in the house you gotta watch for is Mister Dankyo. But then he's paid to be suspicious as all hell." She raised her hedgelike eyebrows. "'s that good enough for you?"

A lump had formed in her throat. Claire found a spot on the skirt to rub at. She blinked at June then nodded, not trusting herself to speak.

* * * *

Pearly fingers of moonlight edged across the bedspread, slinking through the top clear panes of the doors as if to beckon her to the world outside. She lay awake, mulling over why she might stay and what else she might do.

The words Theo had said held a promise within them—that she was desirable and a woman, and not merely a thing. If they were true, she might be somebody for the first time in her life, a whole person. But if they were lies…if they were lies, her worth could be contained in a gutter.

Could she stay here? How? She couldn't cook or knit or tend gardens. She could kill. Sure, and that was so damn useful right here and now. Tell Dankyo that and she'd be in a grave faster than a bullet could sing through the air. The center of her grew heavier and heavier. No. An assassin would never be greeted with open arms, and a frankenstruct assassin? Huh, she carried her own death warrant if she told them what she was.

She sighed. She could kill or she could, apparently, enthrall Theo with her womanly ways, and from what he'd done and said to her at breakfast, that meant ending up in his bed. He'd told his staff to take care of her. What was he thinking?

But, oh, he was so gorgeous and did such wonderful things to her. When he was in front of her, she felt wanted. When he wasn't—

Heavens, I can't stop thinking of him.

She squeezed her thighs together and felt the swell of lust. Her body wanted her to stay. She hugged herself and lay there for ages, imagining how things might go if, for once, the world turned her way.

Three in the morning and a new guard arrived, his boots thumping on the floor and awakening her. She asked to go to the bathroom. The thin woman released her from the bed, and in the quietness of the predawn, as she crossed the room, she heard the guards talking.

"You know why the colonel's away?"

Someone murmured something.

"Yeah, well, I was told the truth. Ain't saying who told, but they're bringing back a government interrogator…for her. He'll be taking her away."

All her future imaginings turned to ashes. She faltered.

The air itself tasted bitter in her mouth. Her heartbeats thinned and beat like a dying bird's. The night air wrapped so cold about her fingers, toes, and throat, she almost forgot to breathe.

So, that was that. She'd work on the fork this morning and today, then leave at night. No use staying any longer. It had indeed been lies. She was hollow inside, empty as a scraped-out gourd, and felt so terribly lost and betrayed.

Chapter Seven

Nighttime was always best. Making it across the open space surrounding the house would be difficult in daylight. At night it was mostly dark, except that every so often they fired up some sort of searchlight.

The fork did its job well. Half an hour or so of maneuvering the tine inside each lock, while listening for telltale clicks, and she was free. The lock at the end of the long chain proved even faster to pick.

She'd meant to leave June out of this; only, as often happened to plans, it went wrong. The skinny woman fell ill, and June had to do double duty. From the snoring, the long hours had taken a toll. It occurred to Claire to wonder how uncomfortable it must be to have to sleep in that chair, especially for someone as bulky as June. The moon hadn't risen yet. She studied the room. The outer door—closed and locked. June, sleeping in the chair. She rolled over and looked at the balcony doors. Black outside, for the moment. Nothing stirred bar an owl hunting and a few crickets down below in the gardens.

Pillowcase in hand, the cuffs muffled by the cloth, she crept over to June and swiftly gagged her by stuffing the pillowcase in her mouth. She had it fastened in place and the cuffs and chain holding her in the chair before June properly awoke. The sheet tied her feet to the chair. June's eyes stared accusingly over the top of the gag.

Sorry, Claire mouthed.

Clothes were a problem. In the drawers were only underwear and nightclothes. The cupboard held dresses. Until she could steal something better, the aqua silk pajamas she had on would do.

She crept to the balcony doors, snicked them open, and folded them back. The dew-wet tiles on the small balcony chilled her bare feet. To her dismay, the *Final Rebuttal* squatted there before her. The outside searchlights came on, throwing stark shadows and blazing yellow light against the house. She took a slow step back and shrank into the blackness of the door opening.

Give them time. They'll turn the lights off eventually.

Theo and Dankyo might have returned. *Doesn't matter*. Her plan was unchanged. Once past the house defenses, she'd head west, and if this place was where she thought, she'd hit the border within a day.

A sucking noise drew her attention to the room. *June*. Something fell with a *bang*. The side table, she guessed. The outer door rattled. "Key!" someone yelled. The noise stopped. June wasn't breathing.

Run? Go over the railing and hope to get away in the confusion, and let June be? It'd kill her. *How to strangle effectively*—the facts from the training session flashed to her. *Doesn't take long to die without air*. To her own surprise, she didn't hesitate, and sprinted for

June, hurtling the bed in a stride and ripping away the gag.

Nothing. No breathing.

With June tied in the chair, it was difficult to get her breathing again. She took in a lungful, put her lips over June's, and blew. *Once, twice.* The door rattled; the key must've jammed. June breathed, took in two long breaths, then opened her eyes and muttered a black curse at Claire. The door thudded open and rammed into the wall with a crack.

She smiled weakly. "Good. You're alive."

Then the light came on, and chaos rained down upon her.

Harry wasn't on duty, and these men had never had dealings with her. All they knew was she'd gotten loose and that she'd tied up and maybe hurt June. The first of them came at her with a knife.

Sharp time kicked in. Time slowed, though her muscles did their usual and obeyed her commands with a speed that bewildered the guards. She curved stiffened fingers past the knife, whacked the first guard in the Adam's apple. The second went over her planted ankle as she pulled him off balance using his own momentum. He went headfirst into the timber side of the bed. The third came in with gun drawn. Training took over. The knife and a knitting needle lay on the floor. She snatched them up, lunged, and nailed the needle through the flesh of the man's hand, between the long bones of the palm into June's chair. With him shrieking and the gun falling, she turned to the door.

By then there were three more guards surging into the room. She cocked her hand back to throw and sink the blade into the middle guard. *Harry*. She halted, appalled at what she'd nearly done, cold metal poised in her fingertips. Harry stood there stunned, but his left-hand partner flung his knife, and the other man charged at her like a bull at a cape.

Even she couldn't do both, so she caught the knife as it plunged spinning at her throat, and was flattened by the charging guard and sent sliding half under the bed, her neck wrenched painfully as it hit the bed leg.

Within seconds there were three guards holding her down. Her head ached from being shunted into the bed, and her hands were clamped behind her back. Dimly, she heard Harry taking charge and calming them down.

Lord. What had she done? Everything is what, she wearily told herself. I've done everything wrong.

* * * *

Theo stalked into his outer study, straight past the oak desk and Dankyo, his three guards, and the woman. Claire knelt, tied hand and foot, beside them. He flung his gray frock coat on the leather sofa, let it slide to the floor. The silence stretched as he pretended, with chin in hand, to examine the wall behind the sofa. He rubbed at stubble, knowing his eyes were sunken from lack of sleep. They all waited for him to do something, to command, and for once he was dumbfounded.

This woman he'd trusted, despite Dankyo's advice, had betrayed him, almost killed several of his people. How long had she been planning this? *Right under my nose. Damn. How did I get this so bloody wrong*? Yet something inside him still urged this ludicrous decision, still wanted…yes, to somehow pull her from the fire.

What could he do? She'd left him with little option except to send her off to be assessed and sentenced by the paper pushers in the capital.

If I have to do this, God forgive me, at least let me be as sure as I can be. I need facts, not emotions.

"Report, Dankyo." He didn't turn around.

"The frankenstruct attempted to escape, sir. She subdued and tied up June. The guards realized something was wrong. When they entered the room, she attacked them. Two guards were injured, and I believe June almost died from asphyxiation."

"Ah. I see." The heavy feeling in his stomach spread, mixed with anger at the damage she'd done to his people.

"My advice, sir. Hand her over to the authorities. It's clear—"

"I'm sorry." The words were so quiet, Theo almost missed them.

He spun on his heel, staring down at Claire and seeing only the back of her tousled fair hair. Slowly she lifted her head until she met his eyes. The anguish on her face would have matched his own if he hadn't schooled his reaction. Had some common sense finally sunk in to whatever mess lurked in her head? Even now, he couldn't help but note the beauty of her form. Only it was clear that her sensuous, toned body wasn't just for show.

Her mouth quivered, as if there might be more she wished to add.

“What did you say?” he asked gently.

She swallowed. A tangle of sweat-sodden hair fell across her forehead. He restrained himself from reaching down and brushing it away. “I said I’m sorry.” The redness around her eyes deepened. “I didn’t mean to hurt anyone. Just wanted to get away. Please tell June, I didn’t mean to—”

“Sir,” Dankyo interjected. “This is unnecessary.”

“Wait.” Theo held up his palm.

A guard cleared his throat. “Excuse me, sir. I’m Harry Snow. Could I say something?”

“Yes.”

“Uh, just, well there’s more to it. She coulda knifed me, and she didn’t. With her speed, she had me, and she didn’t do nothing. Plus June tells me the girl came back to help her when she choked, an’ she got her breathin’ again. And though she did stab Gary through the hand, he was going to shoot her. It’s a tiny wound.” Harry grinned. “He’s quite chuffed that he has a knitting-needle wound to show the girls, sir.”

Theo raised an eyebrow, felt a flare of curiosity and relief. “Dankyo?”

As always, Dankyo’s flat-top hair was razor sharp, and his black shoes shone like the deepest lake at midnight. Slowly, he shifted his large feet until they were precisely shoulder-width apart, clasped his hands behind his back.

“Ahh. It is substantiated. It is true, sir.” Dankyo grimaced, then pinned Theo with his steady gaze.

"Nevertheless, the woman is dangerous, and I cannot have her anywhere on your property. Her speed was phenomenal. Three men report seeing her catching a thrown knife in midair." He glanced at Claire, who'd subsided onto her heels and seemed to be more interested in the carpet than anything else. "Surely, you won't contemplate anything other than removing her?"

"No?" He looked down at her again, bemused. Hard to believe she'd done all that. "Leave me, Dankyo. Take your men."

"Sir!"

"Leave!"

Dankyo came as close to glowering insubordination as Theo had ever seen. "Very well. Though sir might do well to recall what I said on the airship."

They left quietly.

He went to the desk and perched half his weight on it, let his feet take the rest. His white linen shirt felt sticky against his skin; the gray trousers he'd worn for the high-altitude flight prickled him with heat. He wanted nothing more than to get changed, but he sat there and waited. Out of the two of them, Claire looked far worse. An abrasion darkened her temple. Her pajamas were ripped at the neck, and the back was spotted with blood.

Though Harry's words had roused a hope that he might salvage her life, a spark of anger held him back from making things too easy. Dankyo had a good point. How dangerous was she to him and his people?

"Claire? Are you wounded? There's blood on your back."

"No. Bruises only."

As she raised her head, the slow glide of the muscles of her neck made him imagine the taste of her skin. He saw himself sinking his teeth in there, at the soft juncture of neck and shoulder, the bitter taste of her sweat, warm against his tongue.

Then the hurt on her face clawed at him.

He sighed, slapped both hands flat on his thighs. "Why? What were you doing? Where were you going?"

"Back to where I came from." She spoke in a monotone.

Incredulous, he leaned down and put his hand under her chin. "And you want to go back there? Because I thought it would be the very last place you'd go."

She moved her head, trying to get loose, and only succeeded in plastering more stray hair to her cheek. "No," she croaked, pain stirring in those golden brown eyes. "But there's nowhere else for me. For a frankenstruct."

He stroked his thumb across her lower lip, marveling at her softness. "Well then, why did you try to run? I had meant to find a place for you here."

"Lies. I overheard the guards. They said you were bringing back an interrogator. That he would take me away."

"No. Never. That is the lie. You heard gossip. I'm back. Do you see an interrogator?"

With his hand on her, she couldn't hide the tremor from him, couldn't hide the flicker of hope in her eyes, though it quickly died away. She closed them.

"If I could take back what I did, I would."

He murmured, "And if there was still a place for you?" Before she could answer, he threw in another, harder, question. "But first I need to know what you are. You're not a common soldier. Are you some sort of bodyguard?"

A long pause, and then she quietly said, "Yes. I am."

"A bodyguard. Hmm."

If a bodyguard, then perhaps her employer had been an important personage.

"You're really a bodyguard? I don't want any more lies between us, Claire. And, why are you so fast? Even better, how are you so fast?"

"I'm a bodyguard, but—" She shook her head.

"What is it? I won't think any less of you, but I need you to talk about this. Secrets are not an option, Claire."

She said nothing.

"Give me something here. My security head is outside champing at the bit to get me to wash my hands of you! And frankly, Claire, I don't want to do that. Talk to me."

She sighed, blinked up at him. "I...don't know how. I guess it's something to do with how they made me. The parts they used. I can only do it for a short while. We called it sharp time."

He exhaled in relief. *Getting somewhere, finally.* Seemed like the PME had more of a head start than anyone had thought. They were making frankenstructs with extraordinary abilities.

"Sharp time? Fitting. Now tell me, how do I know I can trust you? Because that's the crux of it all, isn't it?"

Ah, that got her attention. Claire wriggled, and he released her chin, then heaved himself to his feet. Briskly, he went around the desk and pulled out the top drawer, where he kept a ten-inch Tung steel knife and a six-shot revolver. He slid the knife from the sheath. "I can cut you loose, or not. Which is it to be?"

As he walked to her, he watched her expression, wanting badly to see honesty there. He'd judged men all his life, and a woman was no different. Well, a little different. He followed the smooth curve of the pajama jacket where it cupped her breasts. With her hands tied at her back, her nipples pressed forward against the silk.

"What am I to you?" The sheer earnestness of this reply jolted him. Her eyebrows tilted up, then back down, as if she struggled to control herself. "Am I a person or a thing?"

"I could never think of you as a *thing*. You're you. A human being. Why?"

"Because..." Her voice cracked. "Because, if you make me a person, I swear to you, on anything you like, that you can trust me to the ends of the earth." She hung her head, a curtain of blonde hair falling across her face, but not before Theo saw a tear spill from her eye and trickle down her face. "Besides, I never wanted to hurt you anyway."

Shaken, he put the knife on the carpet, not wanting to accidentally injure either of them. If that wasn't the truth, he'd retire to the mountains and become a hermit.

"Claire," he murmured as he put his arms around her, holding her tight to stop the trembling. "I can't make you a person. You've always been one. Now, sit still, love, while I cut the ropes."

This was going to be a minefield. People would need to know about Claire and the way the PME were creating them. How to do it without her getting hurt, though—that was the big question.

CLAIRE HELD STILL, her thoughts tumbling fractured through her mind while he sawed through the ropes. She'd given in to him then, without even trying to resist. Told him her deepest thoughts, and she didn't really know what he wanted of her. But, oh, it felt good to trust someone, just like he wanted to trust her. Tears flowed down her face. She didn't care if he saw.

The sickness in her belly vanished when the last rope parted. *Rope. That day with Inkline*—She shuddered. With her limbs free, she tried to rise, only to find her feet had become numb weights.

"Here." Theo scooped her into his arms and took her to the leather sofa, then knelt and massaged her ankles. Amazed that he would do this, she barely noticed the fizz of pins and needles through her flesh.

At last he stopped with his hands still surrounding her right ankle, a strange look on his face.

She blushed and found herself fixed in place by his eyes, though she couldn't say exactly why. The heat from her cheeks seemed to surface elsewhere, lower down. He released her leg and moved to sit beside her, the couch sinking under his weight. His arm slipped along the couch behind her. The solid length of his thigh against hers felt good. The aches of her body sank to a dull background. Temples drumming with each heartbeat, she turned to look up at Theo.

"Perhaps, this is too soon?" he asked, moving in until his mouth and hers were less than an inch apart. "But you do owe me a kiss."

"I do?" she squeaked.

He studied her. The balcony at breakfast had been secluded, but here, they were alone in a closed room. No one was going to walk in on them. She already knew she had trouble saying no to this man. The beats at her temples thudded louder.

Wanting to see where this would lead, yet afraid to, she went to lean away, only to find his hand cradling the back of her head, holding her there. His grip tightened, and he kissed her, delicately as a butterfly landing on a flower at first, then pressing closer. He explored her mouth, caressing every part of it with tongue and lips. She answered with her own lips as if it were some deadly duel with weapons, until something, his thumb perhaps, circled her nipple through the silk. The myriad of blossoming pleasures, the ache in her loins, and the taste of his tongue—together these crumbled her defenses to nothing. She lay there, barely able to respond, feeling herself slide down the couch until she lay beneath him, moaning and holding on to the solid muscles of his upper arms as if they were the only thing that could stop her drowning under the onslaught.

Chapter Eight

"Claire?"

She opened one eye to find Theo looking down at her. Panting and unable to find a single word for her tongue to use, she lay there under him, held down by his heavy body. He leaned in and kissed the tip of her nose. This was like being in a cocoon. His thigh pressed in, spreading her legs. One of his arms nestled beneath her; the other was... *Oh.* She shut her eyes again. His other hand he'd inched under her top and run smooth and warm across her stomach. Fingers cupped her breast, then brushed over her nipple. When something hard rubbed along her mound, she couldn't stop herself from straining upward until her bottom lifted off the couch. She wanted more of that feeling.

"You like that." He smiled and kept his thumb playing with her nipple. "And I thought you'd be too sore to do anything more than kiss."

Find some words, Claire. "I heal fast." There were aches, but none worth cataloging. "This is more than kissing."

"A little more. Do you want me to stop? From what I've been told, you should be bruised in half a dozen places."

"No. Don't stop." Ah, if he stopped now, she'd surely die. "But...I've never had sex." She waited, nervous, a bit afraid of what he might say.

"You haven't? You're a virgin?" Theo chuckled. "But then, I don't plan on having sex with you. I want to make love to you." Leaning in closer, he licked her earlobe and murmured, "I want to use you all up until you're limp. I want you on your knees begging me to lick you and fuck you. Most of all, I want to restrain your beautiful body with ropes, pin you to my wall, and do whatever I want to you."

Ropes? No. Though the rest—

Held dumbstruck by a mix of excitement and fear she'd not known before, she stared back, mouth parted. An image came to her, of Theo standing over her, using his hands on her body, and more—those diagrams of sexual positions made real and multiplied by a thousand. Oh, yes, she remembered them, and how she'd experimented with her own fingers.

But, being tied up with rope—she shuddered, remembering that winter's day, three years ago. Being tied to a chair had been sinfully enjoyable...until Inkline got involved. She could handle most things but not that.

"What are you thinking, Claire? I've scared you, have I?" He sighed. "Say something. I'll go as slow as you want me to. Go only as far as you want to go."

She wriggled under him, a little desperately.

"I think maybe—"

His hand—she'd not been following what he did—his hand slipped beneath the untied waistband of her pants and between her legs. His finger slid along, around her aroused clitoris where it poked up, then farther, finding the wet lips of her vulva. He kissed her again, moving his tongue inside her mouth. She forgot her words—couldn't think and feel this at the same time.

"Where else can I taste?" he murmured.

He kissed his way down her body, from the side of her neck to breast to stomach, then tugged her pants and underwear down to her knees. Only now, he positioned his legs until they gripped her outer thigh like a soft vise. She tried but couldn't move either leg, for the other was wedged against the back of the couch. Then, *bliss* as he applied his wet, warm tongue to her clitoris. She forgot all about moving.

She anchored her hands in his hair and pulled him to her. Fingers plied at her nether regions as he played her like some glorious instrument. She plastered herself to his mouth as close as she could get. Sobbing and moaning, she came near to breaking through to the stratosphere. The sucking and licking, the fingers inserted and thrusting in her moist flesh, it sent her higher, higher, until at last her body filled to the top and rocked into gasping oblivion in a convulsion of ecstasy.

When she opened her eyes this time, Theo loomed above.

With his arms propped to either side of her, he simply said, voice deep and soothing, "That will do, for now. I didn't mean to frighten you." He kissed her once. "I said too much, perhaps. Seeing you, beautiful, sprawled here like this, under me, is like drinking fine brandy—heady and exhilarating."

She tried to slow her breaths, felt a delicious shiver run from her spine to her center. His words amazed her. He'd called her beautiful? Then he turned her to face outward so he could squeeze into the space between her and the back of the lounge. They lay together, breathing as one body.

With his arm over the top of her, his larger fingers wrapped round hers and holding her hand snuggled by her side, she looked out at the study through half-closed lids. She idly surveyed the immense desk and the airship-shaped table lamp, embellished with steel and gold, the plush blue carpet, the door opposite that she'd entered by...and the haphazard pile of cut rope. There was her hard, dangerous, friendless past, where she'd never known a man who didn't aim to hurt her or use her for his own ends. Here, with Theo, was her future—a novel sensation. For once, she rested safe in the arms of another. *Glorious.* She let out a long, contented sigh.

Nothing, she decided, would keep her from it.

The clock on the wall ticked ponderously through the minutes, and she felt the slow slide of her consciousness into sleep.

"Should have turned off the lamp," Theo muttered. "It's only three in the morning."

She wriggled a little closer to him, if that was possible, settling the hard length of him into a more *interesting* position against her bottom.

"Do that again," he growled, "and I may decide you're well enough for further endeavors."

For a threat, it was an enticing one. She had an inkling Theo wouldn't let her stay a virgin for much longer. *Oh my.*

"Would you like to talk?" He kissed her nape.

Would she? She brought his hand up till it was before her nose. Playing with his fingers, she tried to organize her thoughts.

He drew his index finger down her nose to the tip, then traced across her lips. The scent of her body lingered on his skin.

"Well?" he asked. "What are you thinking?"

Fear nibbled at her, swirling murky tendrils through her stomach—like a monster hiding below the surface, waiting to lunge at the smallest sign of weakness. Theo was a person, a human—something she wanted to be, yet would she ever really *believe* herself one? What he'd done for her, being so gentle, so loving, and trusting her against Dankyo's advice to the contrary, when he didn't have to risk himself...it seemed so far above what he had to do. He could have raped her. Could have left her tied up and done whatever he wanted to...but he hadn't. She turned her face into the upholstery and felt Theo gently twine her hair around her ear.

He could have thrown her to the dogs. The undercurrent of gossip said such things sometimes happened.

"What's wrong?" Theo tugged on her hair.

"Nothing."

Right now, everything was so wonderful, yet how well did she know him? One misstep and perhaps he *might* throw her to the dogs, or to Dankyo. She walked a tightrope over a chasm that went straight to hell.

But she *liked* it here. She liked Theo, and, oh, what he conjured from her body, she liked that too. This was the man she would have wished for, if she'd ever dreamed of rescue. Her notion of traveling to the Brito-Gallic League in disguise, hoping she could survive there—a half-baked fantasy, a dream. Here was real.

Yet, already, she'd lied to him, saying she was a bodyguard. If she told him they'd trained her to kill, it might turn him against her. No. She could never tell him. She drew in a deep, shuddering breath and choked out the words, "I'm sorry. I don't know *how* to talk about things. I *can't*!" Though she strained to stop herself, her body shook.

"Shh. You don't have to talk. Oh, Claire, whatever is wrong, I'm sure I can help you fix it."

Which, of course, only made things worse.

"Come." He heaved himself off the lounge and hauled her up after him. "This couch is far too uncomfortable." He tucked his arm around her. "We'll go to my bedroom."

That set her heart pitter-pattering all over again. Her untied pants threatened to tumble to her ankles.

"Wait." She secured them with a bow. Theo took her hand, squeezed it.

When he reached for the doorknob and turned it, she tensed. Outside would be others, people who would look at her and wonder what had gone on in this room. Though she'd rather face swords and bullets, she squared her shoulders. Let them wonder.

Theo never wavered. Either side of the door were two guards, and down the hallway sitting on a timber bench beneath a triptych of oil paintings were Dankyo and two more guards armed with repeater gauss guns. They all leaped to attention. Did Dankyo never sleep?

"Sir!" He stalked toward them, his black stare flicking from her to where Theo draped his arm around her and back to Theo. "Is this advis—"

"Yes. It is," interjected Theo.

Dankyo slowed then stopped a yard away. His hand went to his belt; he drew an inch of his sword from the scabbard and bowed slightly. "Perhaps sir would like my resignation? I no longer feel I am able to fulfill my duties regarding your safety."

"No." Theo's single word crackled with menace. "I do not wish your resignation, Dankyo. I wish your compliance with my orders."

His eyes on Theo despite the bow, he blinked for a moment or two, then straightened. Dankyo slid the sword back into the scabbard. "Of course. Sir. I always have your safety and best interests at heart. I apologize absolutely for my behavior if it offended you."

"Thank you. Claire is not your enemy, Dankyo. Is that clear?"

"Yes. It is clear. Sir."

"Good. Go to bed, Dankyo. These two guards only for my door."

But even she could see the reluctance in how Dankyo responded. And when Theo turned and headed down the corridor, she watched the glitter of hate reappear in Dankyo's eyes. With her hand held by

Theo, she had no choice but to follow, though it felt as if someone aimed a rifle at her back, so vehement was Dankyo's gaze.

Up the curving flight of stairs they went, past the sensual sculpture that had caught her eye an eon ago, along the curved passageway overlooking the foyer, to a double set of doors made of timber and riveted metal.

Just inside the doors was a minifoyer. Paintings hung on the walls. A display cabinet was filled with objets d'art. The middle shelf held an oversize pistol she didn't recognize with a bronzed revolving barrel and a blue steel grip.

Theo tugged on her hand.

The bedroom was enormous. Two standing voltaic lamps graced either side of a large four-poster bed with posts of ebon and brass inlay. The red and black oriental quilt had been folded back in preparation for sleep. This was a man's bedroom. No flimsy designs or pastels, no delicate ornaments, everything looked solid and perfectly capable of withstanding a rocket attack.

She stood there, unsure of where to go, as Theo went to a red lacquered suitcase sitting on a low table, clicked it open, and rummaged inside.

To her right, golden curtains framed a curved window jutting out past the line of the outer wall like a cockpit on a gyrocopter. The glass was sectioned into four pieces by metal rods. She strolled over. Outside was the airship, a giant darkened balloon outlined in moonlight, anchored by ropes to the grass.

The lamps in the room extinguished. Glass and metal reflected moonlight; the room was a soft, silvered darkness. Measured footsteps came closer. Theo hugged her from behind, his chin beside her ear, surprising her a moment, until she remembered how much taller he was than her. Her eyelids lowered a little. Excitement stirred the hairs along her arms. *What is he planning?*

"Beautiful, isn't she?" He ran his hand down her side, the silk softly hissing, then he tucked a finger into the pajamas' waistband. "Almost as beautiful as you. I thought you might like to change into something more interesting."

She caught his hand before he slipped it farther inside her pants. *More interesting?*

"You want me to stop?"

"I don't know."

"Let me show you. If you want me to stop, you know what to say. Yes?"

She swallowed. "Yes."

He freed his hand, undid the tie. The pants fell to her ankles in a susurration of cloth. With his lips kissing her jawline then the hollow of her neck, he crept his left hand down the opening of her shirt, popping the buttons one by one. Transfixed, she let him, only tilting back her head to offer her neck.

"I find…" he said, biting her and licking down the side of her neck. She shuddered, and her pussy clenched. Instinct owned her. She sighed and moved her buttocks back against him, feeling that hardness again. *What would it be like to have a man inside me*? "That your strength appeals to me."

"My strength?" He shifted behind her, pulled her head onto his shoulder, and slowly kissed up to her cheekbone and across, then near each eye, making her shut them. She kept them that way. Without the distraction of sight, every touch seemed more potent. And he touched everywhere, as fleeting as a firefly, grazing his fingertips on breast and belly and thigh, then below her nipples, close enough to arouse them to hard points. When he stepped away, she swayed, lost without his caresses.

"Yes. You're strong, self-contained. Aren't you, Claire?"

She shook her head. "Maybe." Right now, she didn't want to think.

"Except now, with me. Controlling you, like this, means so much more. Keep your eyes closed."

She did, feeling the seconds ache with promise. That he liked her strength was somehow...intoxicating, because already, she liked the idea of surrendering. *What will he do next?*

"That's my girl. It's not that difficult, is it?" His voice teased her, amused yet filled with a fierce satisfaction.

"No." She craved his touch.

Ah! Something—his finger—had touched her hip, and he circled her with an unhurried *thump-tap* of heel and toe on the timber floor, as he ran that finger around her waist. The shirt, fully open, slipped from her shoulders. She felt the light brush as her underwear slid down to join the pants at her feet; then his hand, first at one ankle, then the other, made her lift each leg in turn. The pants and underwear were whisked away. She could hear herself breathe.

"Stay there," he said.

She could smell him.

She almost opened her eyes to say something, but instead balanced there. Why she obeyed him, she wasn't sure, but it satisfied something primal, something deeply sexual. And letting go like this made her feel safe.

Anticipation strung her insides tight. She yearned for further caresses. Her cleft swelled.

"Here. Raise your feet." An article of clothing, both silken cloth and something harder, slid with muffled clicks up each leg. Theo arranged it about her torso, cool beads shifting across her breasts until the garment fitted snugly on her body. Something narrow settled between her legs. She gasped at a throb of pleasure as his fingers played in her moisture. A few more adjustments and he led her off to one side. A light flared on. "There. Open your eyes."

In a tall mirror, she saw herself, dressed in a black corset paneled with satin. Coming down from a halter, pearl ropes fanned out over each breast with her nipples peeking out between. A tiny skirt of chiffon, divided at the crotch, barely made it as far as her upper thighs. Lines of seed pearls undulated down the satin, and a string of larger pearls dived deeply between her legs, emphasizing the split lips of her sex. She could feel it run up between the cheeks of her bottom at the back. Even as she looked, she felt a renewed throb, for every movement she made, from breath to heartbeat to shift of feet, moved the line of pearls and rubbed against her clit.

In the reflection, she saw Theo beyond her shoulder, bare-chested, the ringlets of his black hair stark against his forehead. He raised a satin and pearl choker and positioned it about her neck, clicking it into place. “And these,” he said, holding first one wrist and then the other to snick matching black satin bracelets on her wrists. “They suit you.” From the hardness, metal lurked beneath the black cloth.

Where the choker and bracelets rested on skin, her pulse rose, thumping, to the surface and reminded her of where she was, who she was with, and especially, how dangerous this could be. But…she trusted him.

To her surprise, her throat still worked, though the words seemed to stick to her tongue. “How did you know my size? Where did this come from?”

“Bought while I was away. I have a good memory, especially for someone as striking as you.”

Which meant, he’d planned her…seduction, while she’d been planning escape. She leaned back against him, fascinated by the allure of the woman in the mirror. The heat from his body soaked into her like a glass of wine. She lifted each wrist and examined the bracelets—identical, and each with tiny loops of steel projecting from them.

“That’s for a chain to pass through,” he whispered, mouthing her nape. “Does it bother you? Think, before you answer.”

“Yes…” she said slowly, fearful of being again restrained in cuffs.

“And yet?” He pressed a hand against her stomach, holding her against him, making her feel the rigid line of his cock. The pearls slid in her juices, pressing, rolling over her clit and anus. She let out a whimper. "Ahh. You feel them working on you." He chuckled. "And yet?"

And yet the idea of it, of being restrained by Theo, held a strange and deadly fascination. She shied away from that thought and shook her head. "And nothing."

"Aah. I can see my first project will be to get you talking more."

She stood there in silence. The fear she felt came intertwined with lust in almost everything that Theo did to her. Taking her by the shoulders, he moved her to face him, gray eyes inches away; then his mouth descended, covering hers, devouring her. She breathed in his breath, letting him do as he willed. One broad hand held the base of her neck; the other splayed over the curve of her buttocks. His fingers wrapped around the pearl rope running between her legs, tightening it. Desire ran rampant through her, surging higher with every tiny movement of his lips on hers and the rub of the pearls on her pussy and nipples.

When she put her hands to the belt of his pants, he reached between their bodies, snared both her wrists, and pulled them round to the small of her back where he held them with one hand. Again, the pearls shifted. She bit her lip, a moan escaping her as she arched.

Eyes shut, she heard a soft animal-like growl.

"Claire, if you're not damn careful, I'll eat you up."

What? She opened her eyes a slit, still panting, to see that he'd stepped away a little, angling his stance so as to observe her.

His gaze brushed her, lingering on her breasts before he locked on her eyes. "Last chance. Do you want to stop? Are you too sore? It might cause me irreparable harm, but I can stop." Then he eyed her darkly, as if he'd liked to do exactly what he'd threatened to—eat her up.

The pain of the bruise at her neck had faded to nothing in spite of the choker. With her whole being, she yearned for more of him. He inflamed her past bearing, and knowing that he watched her swept her excitement to another level.

She licked her lips, aware of her wrists still caught behind her and the display of her body. God, if he didn't do more than this, she'd surely burst.

"No," she said huskily. "Don't stop."

"Please?"

Ah, how he tormented her. "Please."

"Over here then." Still gripping her wrists, he urged her toward the bed, to kneel by the side of it and lie facedown across the quilt with her bottom up. He spread her hands, palm down, over each cheek of her buttocks.

"Don't move," he whispered in her ear, "and I won't have to tie you."

Tie me? She almost let go at that. Was this what she wanted? But he held his hands over hers a moment. She stayed there.

"Good."

His fingers trailed over the backs of her hands, over the ends of her fingernails, and down her thighs. She quivered, sucking in air through the quilt bunched beneath her mouth.

"Spread your legs, Claire."

She shifted them, feeling even more exposed, a breeze caressing her engorged labia. He traced down the line of pearls, reached her wet cleft, and followed deeper, where the pearls seemed to have sunk into her flesh. Slick and wet. The scent of her lust reached her. Slowly he went farther until he reached her clit. He circled it, teasing, making her shift her bottom to place the finger just *right*.

"No." To her shock, he smacked one cheek of her ass with the flat of his hand, just missing her fingers.

Oh. A wave of pleasure from the smack vibrated through her lower body. She froze and took a piece of quilt between her teeth.

Her taut nipples throbbed as they pressed into the bed. She heard him kneel. The end of a finger pressed against the entrance to her vagina, slipping in, then the smallest distance out, over and over while something, a finger and thumb perhaps, clamped softly on her clit and began to squeeze and release in exquisite rhythm. Two, then three of Theo's fingers eased into her entrance, stretching her. Each thrust slid farther inside until her body climbed, brimming with tension, to the peak. The fingers slid all the way in, the finger and thumb squashed down tighter and faster. She wanted to move but mustn't, couldn't. Her clit became a swollen nub, bursting, wanting that last press. She shook and exploded over the edge, crying out into the darkness of the quilt, convulsing around his fingers.

When she'd quieted and her heart had climbed down from the heavens, she found her hands at her sides, tangled in the quilt.

She heard Theo move behind her and the slither of cloth falling to the floor.

He leaned his whole body on her, his erection hard against her back. “I think you’re wet and open enough now, darling. If it hurts too much, say so.”

She took in a deep breath, then nodded slightly. Trepidation caught hold of her. This was far beyond what she’d gleaned from anatomy books and demonstrations and gossip. He moved the moistened rope of pearls to one side, then placed his hands over her wrists where they rested at her side and held them down.

This time it wasn’t a finger at her entrance. The blunt pressure of his cock strained at her vulva all the way round, evenly—tight and slowly inching inward through her juices. Holding her breath, she concentrated, wanting to remember this…this stinging, almost painful, stretching feeling of delicious fullness. When she thought his cock could go no farther, he waited a few moments, then withdrew to the entrance and back in, only deeper. Again, the hint of pain, and yet—*Oh, that’s good.*

His thrusts strengthened bit by bit until they jolted her, sending her body along the bed. He slowed, rocking back, then building in tempo again. She groaned as his cock seemed to swell inside her, his balls slapping against her clit. That expanding ebb and flow of pleasure returned and overwhelmed the last vestiges of pain. She writhed, or tried to, her wrists twisting under the heavy pressure of his hands. Her clit ground against the pearls as she whimpered, wanting, desperate for more of everything her body was feeling. His last thrust slammed against her flesh, holding her down.

Oh. Yes!

He released into her, his ejaculation spurting inside, his cock so far in, so deep, his balls jammed against her. Ecstasy fireballed, reverberating from clit to core and back again. Flattened between the bed and his body, she gasped out her orgasm, her bottom straining to arch, every muscle taut and shaking her into a thousand white-hot pieces.

Chapter Nine

The soft click of a door and the murmur of voices broke through Claire's dream. The same dream she'd had before, of something buried deep in the earth and footsteps sounding, just off to the side, where she couldn't see.

Strange, that she'd slept so soundly. Normally, the smallest noise or even change in smell would awaken her. Yet while beside Theo, in his bed, she'd felt so content, so safe, she'd sunk down into a level where nothing disturbed her.

The dream footsteps had merged into the sound of real ones approaching on soft flooring. She lay on her side, covered with a sheet pulled up to her waist. Through her eyelids, she saw a shadow arrive, then loom closer. She tensed until the heavy scent of the shadow told her this was Theo.

Theo: male, glorious, and last night they'd made love. More accurately, he'd possessed her body and done what he'd wanted. Delicious. Remembering *everything* made her feel like wriggling.

The familiar throb returned to her groin.

Lips softly kissed her bruised ones. "Time to wake," Theo said. "It's past dawn." The sheet slipped away as he smoothed his hand down her arm to the dip of her waist.

She rolled over onto her back and smiled up at him. The neck of his silver-gray dressing gown showed a tempting V of bare chest. When in her life had she ever woken up with a man hovering over her, his eyes simmering with lust? She reached with both hands and pulled his head close again, kissing him back, enjoying the yield of skin on skin.

“I could eat you,” she whispered.

“Aah, but that’s my job. We need to get this off you.” Moving the hand on her stomach lower, he tugged at something. A jolt of pleasure ran up from her pussy.

She glanced down and saw the satin corset, his hand tucked into the pearls dipping between her legs. “I’m still wearing—” She blushed.

“Yes.” He grinned. “You are. You dirty woman. But I like it. Come!” He took her legs and pulled her to the side, until she had to sit up or risk falling to the floor on her bottom. “Up, up, up! The bath is filled with hot water. There’s soap and fresh towels, and…I’m going to watch.” He paused and eyed her upper thigh. “Those stitches look ready to come out. That’s a better result than the galvanic treatment usually gives.”

The skin beneath the line of black sutures was pink and clean.

“I heal easily.” Yet it stirred her to unease. Here was another thing that made her different. Nothing could ever change her nature.

The bathroom was on a scale with his bedroom—large and luxurious. Two bronze sculptures of flamingos guarded a huge round bathtub with gold feet. Half the tub sat embedded into a raised tiled area coming out from the wall. She'd never seen anything like it.

At first, Theo sprawled on a red divan, watching with hooded eyes as she stripped off the corset, bracelets, and choker. Feeling suddenly shy, she stepped into the steaming water.

Though the heat made her gasp, she quickly lowered herself. The bubbles in the water clung to the sides of her breasts.

A thought struck her. "Who filled this?"

"Kirsten. She takes care of my room. You'll meet her eventually. Why?"

She sank deeper, head back; water lapped at her ears, muffling sound. "She didn't see…anything?"

"Like your half-naked body?" he drawled, then rose from the couch and walked over. She felt like some water creature eyeing a predator. "I threw the sheet over you."

Efficiently, he shed his dressing gown. His erection stood out as proudly as the one on the sculpture on the stairs, the muscles of his stomach and chest rippling as he moved. That telltale arrow of hair led the eye to his groin. Trying not to stare and only partly succeeding, she moved to one side, sending water sloshing. Every movement of Theo's signaled determination—she had a suspicion no wasn't going to work at the moment.

With the water around his thighs, he looked like some god risen from the depths of a sea.

Seeing his gaze drift lower, she looked down to see her exposed breasts shining with moisture and bubbles. “Um. I thought I was getting clean?”

“You look very clean to me. Come here.” He beckoned, then sat on the edge of the tub. His cock was straight and thick, and almost long enough to touch his belly button—she’d had that inside her last night?

Any thought of not going to him vanished. She waded over on her knees, sliding across the porcelain. She couldn’t help looking at him, at his cock. Last night, buried under the avalanche of her awakening feelings, she’d barely had time to study his body.

“Put your mouth here,” he said, rough-voiced. He wrapped his fist around his erection.

She stared at those gray eyes, at the desire and *command* in them. He knew she wouldn’t refuse. Not when he said it like that. She licked her lips. *What will it taste like*? The end of it was just the right size to slide into her mouth. She put out her hand. The bulbous head smelled fresh and felt soft, with an exciting underlying hardness. He’d bathed already, she realized.

He watched as she put her mouth to the head, then hesitantly engulfed more of him. Her saliva made his cock slide sweetly. It sent a shiver through her, desire flaring between her thighs as she recalled the feel of him, how he’d filled her. When her lips met his hand and she licked at him, swirling her tongue around his cock, he groaned.

“Slow,” he croaked. “Seeing your mouth wrapped round me—”

He released his cock and held her head, guiding her movements, then reached down. The unexpected pinch of fingers and thumbs on her nipples shocked her. She couldn't move; the world became nothing more than her mouth with him inside, her nipples, and what lay between her thighs.

Theo chuckled. She blinked up at him. "You'd better let that go before you bite me."

His cock glided from her mouth, leaving it strangely empty and her lips swollen. Salty precum had leaked onto her tongue. He joined her in the water, then moved her so she faced away.

"Sit on me."

Oh, now that appealed to her. He wedged her feet half under and behind his so she couldn't slip in the water. With his hands guiding her, the tip of him probed at her entrance, then pressed on in, sliding slowly, like an airship docking into its moorings, so far up inside, her throat closed over again.

"Ah-unhh." She clamped her eyes shut. Squeezed, down there, tight. If she died right then and there, she'd be happy.

"You're easily pleased," he whispered. "Now stay there. Don't move." He nibbled at her ear while playing gently with the areolae yet never quite...*touching* them. "Stop wriggling," he commanded, biting her lobe, hard.

Oh. Even his bite sent electricity through her, lighting her up everywhere that counted.

Impaled, she panted. How could he make her feel like this? Aching, until it took over her every thought, until all she wanted was to move? The loss of control, the presence of someone who could make her do what he desired, it intoxicated her as nothing else ever had.

"Now?" she begged, gasping as he twitched inside her, and her flesh answered.

"No." He stroked her neck. "Today, this will be all we do. Day after tomorrow, we're going on a picnic, where I intend to make love to you, and you are going to let me do whatever I wish."

"Outside?" she asked, frowning. Whatever he wished? "No tying me up?"

"Perhaps."

"No," she said firmly.

Just as firmly, he tweaked her nipples and bit her neck. She almost came.

"Saying no is not allowed. Not yet. Wait and see." He put a hand under her bottom, one finger slithering wetly between their bodies to the entrance to her anus.

"Hey!" she muttered, squirming, but he held an arm under her breasts and gently wormed the finger inside.

"Saying no might have consequences. Like your little ass here being next on the menu."

She said nothing, absorbing the strange new sensation, head lowered, eyelids half-closed. It was different—odd, yet nice. Her nerves registered his cock, then his finger. She couldn't seem to stop feeling them both. Now one, now the other. *Mmm.* Her clitoris twitched, engorging.

Theo kissed her neck and then pulled finger and cock out of her as he pushed her up and off his lap. The sudden change made her whimper. He stood. "I'll find your clothes."

While she washed off the bubbles and toweled dry, Theo brought in a set of clothes and laid it out on the chair. In the time she had to herself as she dressed, she questioned what had come over her. Why did she let this man command her? Inkline had done that, and she'd hated him for it. With Theo, it was entirely different. As if her needs were his own, he made sure she reveled in everything they did. Except for when he simply did what he wanted. She smiled. Like he just had. Which strangely pleased her even more.

The plans she'd made of merely pretending to Theo that he had the upper hand had faded away. She didn't want that anymore. She wanted this, the relationship they had.

They breakfasted at a table set up before the large window in the bedroom, with morning light slanting in across the dishes and glinting off the silver cutlery.

"There's one requirement that I have to insist upon. I agree with Dankyo that you must write out for us exactly what you know about frankenstructs and the PME. The smallest detail may be important."

She slowly spread butter across a piece of toast. "I can do that." She smiled. "In triplicate if you like."

"Good." Theo put his hand atop hers on the table and squeezed. His touch and mellow baritone distracted her, and it was a moment before she registered the next words.

"There's nothing more I want you to do today except rest, and tomorrow you can go to visit June. Maybe I'll see about showing you around the estate."

"Oh." She swallowed a mouthful of toast, then looked up anxiously. "Is she okay?"

"Yes." He patted her hand. "Dr. Eastway looked at her. No ill effects."

"I'd rather go to her today." Funny, how attached she'd become to the lady. She didn't even know what her real job was here.

"No. You caused quite a ruckus last night." He dabbed at his mouth with a napkin. "I want to make sure everyone knows your place on the estate before I let you loose on them."

She cocked her head. "My place?" She supposed some might resent her. Were there others like Dankyo, who would hate her?

"Yes." He studied her, waggled his head. "Your place. Simple. Under me."

"Oh! Now that's—"

"True?"

Heat slowly crept up her neck to her cheeks. In a way, it was true, she guessed. *Oh, heavens.* It appalled her and thrilled her all at once. But saying it out loud. *No.*

"Can't say it to me yet? Never mind. I'll have you doing it soon." His eyes danced; then he leaned across the table and kissed her hard and slow until her head spun.

Resting, doing nothing more than sitting about, left too much time for thinking. Theo went missing soon after breakfast.

To occupy herself, she did sit-ups and watched the men and women walking about outside. She thought about examining every inch of Theo's room—the closed drawers and locked cupboards tempted her. Opening most of them would be easy. Making sure Theo never knew she'd done it wasn't so easy.

Oh, but it was so, so tempting.

After chewing on her lip awhile, she left them alone.

By the time he returned late that night, she'd done two hundred and fifty push-ups and three hundred sit-ups as well as fifty of every other exercise she could remember. She'd gone through the katas of Judo, Kendo, and Karate.

The first thing Theo did on his return was sniff the air.

"What have you been doing? Bath. Now."

Horrified at his expression, she scurried to obey.

When he entered the bathroom, she was under the water with just her eyes and the top of her head above the water.

He eyed her. "Are you pretending to be a crocodile or a seal? Because I think I like mermaid better. Perhaps I should check if you've grown a tail?"

To her disappointment, when he slipped into the bathtub, he only cuddled her in his lap. "Remember," he said, licking the very tip of her nose, "we're not making love until I take you on a picnic. And thank you for not prying into anything of mine. I like that I can trust you."

"Um. You're welcome." The simple compliment made her feel good—weird but good. She nestled up to him some more and laid her head against him at the snuggly juncture of chest and shoulder. She inhaled. Warm and lemon-soap fresh and extract of man. Yummy.

The next morning he slapped her bottom to wake her. Again, she'd slept through him rising.

He smiled, slung a frock coat over his shoulder, and ran his hand through his dark curls.

"Sorry. I'll be distracted again today. I have another trip to town in a week or so. Political stuff—and I have to smooth some feathers first by telegraph. I'll arrange for Kirsten to start you on a tour of the estate, in...three-quarters of an hour?" He raised his eyebrows. "I'll catch up with you once I'm done. Try not to trip over Dankyo. The man is very protective of me, and it'll take a while before he accepts you."

Claire nodded. "I understand. I guess I'd feel the same way if I were him."

Kirsten? Ah, yes. The girl who looked after Theo's bedroom. He trusted her to look over his property with no more than a serving girl as company? No guards? It gave her a ridiculously happy feeling. To be trusted so graciously in return made her feel like lying down at his feet. Trust inspired loyalty. It was infectious. Now she knew why he had such a tight cadre of people around him.

"What should I wear for this tour?"

He pulled her into his arms. "Something that you like. Have a look in the wardrobe." He softly kissed her mouth. "I've had some more clothes put in there. Kirsten's a lovely lady. You'll find June at the nursery. Enjoy yourself."

"I will." She touched her mouth where he'd kissed her as he strode to the door.

She found a little red knee-length skirt, all ruffles and lace at the bottom, and a fitted bodice top to go with it. Twirling in front of the mirror made the skirt flip out to expose an indecent amount of leg. It was sexy and surely naughty, but when she thought of how Theo would approve, it made her warm inside.

Kirsten knocked at the bedroom door a few minutes later. In a plain blue and white dress, with her brunette hair secured in a bun, Kirsten looked happy and young enough to brighten any room. Claire compared her muscular figure with Kirsten's—next to all those curves and softness, she was an overgrown warrior woman.

This woman had makeup on too. Did Theo expect her to wear makeup?

That, of course, was exactly her problem—she didn't fit in here. She stood out like a sore thumb. Not feminine, and she certainly wasn't going to be a house guard.

"The colonel said I was to give you a grand tour." Kirsten pursed her mouth. "I'm not sure what that is...but we could start in the kitchens? Tell me if there's something you'd rather see."

"Oh. I have to see June. But the kitchen sounds good."

They walked on in silence. Kirsten didn't seem to mind and bounced with each step. What had she in common with this bubbly woman?

"Here's the kitchen," announced Kirsten, flinging open a white door off a hallway near the foyer.

Though the estate must house at least a hundred men and women, Claire was surprised at the size of the kitchen. The noise hadn't carried into the hall, but the banging of metal pans and implements, the hiss of fires and ovens, and the chatter of the kitchen staff filled this room up. She wondered how their heads didn't burst.

The aromas of roasted meat and vegetables mingled enticingly with mysterious herbs and spices. Inside a massive steel glass-front oven, a pig rotated on a spit. Her mouth watered.

By the time she and Kirsten emerged from the kitchen into the hallway, they'd been fed several pastries and tidbits of meat by the head cooks, Jonathan and Maria. Her stomach gurgled from the unexpected fullness.

They continued on to a two-story open area studded with pots overflowing with pink blossoms. A set of white doors led outside. This would be the back of the mansion.

Claire licked a smear of liqueur off her finger. "I thought it was bad to have two head cooks. Isn't there a saying about that spoiling the broth?"

"Um?" Kirsten screwed up her face. "Is there? Who cares? As long as I get fed. Come on. I'll show you the gardens."

Once past the doors—three broad stone steps led down from a rear colonnade—Claire paused. This was the first time she'd been allowed outside the mansion. She'd been prepared for some hostile looks, yet every member of household staff had been friendly. It must be because Kirsten was by her side.

For two or three hundred yards, a sea of grass stretched, pure green and mown to within an inch of the earth. Past that, eight low whitewashed buildings interrupted the flatness. Automatically, she put each of them into place on the map in her head.

"This way." Kirsten beckoned to the left.

After checking the rows of vegetables with the ancient head gardener, George, Claire gained a new respect for gardeners. She'd planted seeds and watered and even had a try at swinging a hoe. June was George's wife. She emerged from a small greenhouse and stood with arms akimbo, tut-tutting while shaking her head slowly at Claire.

"Oh, June, I'm so sorry for what I did. Will you forgive me?"

June sighed, wrinkling that squashed nose of hers. "Course I will. Come here, girl, and get a hug. It'll make us both feel better."

Tentatively she walked up and put her arms around the woman. She was big and round and smelled of freshly baked bread and oranges. And except for Theo, she gave the best hugs ever, even if she was six inches shorter.

"Thank you," Claire murmured. This was all so strange—lovely but strange.

Next stop were the kennels, but along the way, Claire found herself looking at her hands. They ached in new places from the rough handle of the hoe, and she'd raised a sweat from the effort. The smell of fresh soil and the sight of the green seedlings half uncurled in their seedbeds made her think of life.

If I ever have to leave, what am I going to do? Every hour she stayed, made her want even more to stay. Would there come a day when she'd feel safe enough to tell Theo what she was and why she'd been on the airship? *Hi there. I'm an assassin, and I may have been assigned to kill you*. Maybe there just wasn't a right way to say that. And maybe her secret was buried so deep in the PME military archives that no one would find out. If she left here, she'd miss more than Theo. There were things to do here she'd never imagined were worthwhile attempting. Gardening, of all things. She smiled a little sadly.

Kirsten pointed across the open lawn. "That's the barracks over there and the firing range and Henry's vehicle depot."

A vehicle depot? Her professional curiosity prodded at her. "What sort of vehicles?"

"Oh, Henry has the steam limousine and a little fast car thing, and then there's the landships."

"Landships? As in mobile armored vehicles? With cannon and tracks?" Her voice peaked. "Whatever for?"

Kirsten turned and did a dancing backward walk. "Don't know really. Ask Dankyo or the colonel. Say…" She blushed, her cream complexion reddening markedly. "What do you think of Mister Dankyo? He's rather cute, isn't he?"

"Cute!" What did she say to that? "Um...I suppose he's quite handsome." *And intimidating and angry.*

"Handsome!" She giggled. "He scares me half to death but yeah"—she cocked her head—"I wouldn't mind his arms around me. But, don't you tell him I said so! Swear you won't!"

Claire shook her head. "I won't. Never." *Lord. I have a hard time not getting shot by the man whenever he sees me, let alone talking to him.*

"Good. Phew. That was just girl talk, you know?"

"Sure."

Now, that really nonplussed her. Girl talk—she'd only ever come close to that with Francine. She sneaked a sideways look. Maybe they could be friends, even if Kirsten was bubbly and didn't understand Dankyo should only *ever* be touched with a long pole.

In another of the low white buildings, in a cramped office beside the kennels, she met the kennel master. His desk was covered with books, pens, and paper.

"Hello! Mr. Theo!" The kennel master was short, with thin tangled hair, and faded clothes. Behind him, through a shut paneled door, came a cacophony of howls and barks.

"Morning, Filip."

Claire turned to find Theo behind her. He rested his hand on her shoulder. This casual possession of her body made her look sharply at him.

He brushed her cheek with his knuckles. "Miss me?"

She took a quick breath. Where he'd touched tingled with heat. She paused, chagrined at how much he affected her. "Yes."

"Good." His eyes softened.

That pleased him. Knowing that made her giddy.

"Kirsten. You can go back to your duties. Thank you, dear."

She curtsied. "It was a pleasure, sir." She nodded at Claire and left.

"Such a good time this is, Mr. Theo! The bitch, she is whelping soon! Tomorrow maybe." He sniffed through his squashed nose. "And this is Claire! I have heard of you from June." He bent and took her hand, kissed the back.

"Oh. Have you? I'm pleased to meet you, Mr.—"

"Filip! Just call me Filip. Come! Look at my babies."

His babies, as he called them, were wolfhounds. Behind the door, in a long narrow room split into runs, dogs ran back and forth, barking and whining. At the first run, a bitch with teats almost bursting with milk rested on a purple pillow. Her big eyes looked up at Filip with adoration as he jumped the little gate, then stooped to pat her.

"Soon, hey, Angeliona?" He peeked at Claire. "She's my favorite. I'll be watching her all night to make sure her little ones come out all right."

She nodded. Angeliona unraveled her long legs, heaved onto her feet, then padded over to the gate Claire leaned on.

"She wants a pat, Miss," Filip said.

The dog's head cleared the waist-high gate easily. Her shaggy brown coat felt rough under Claire's palm.

"You are beautiful, Angeliona," whispered Claire, squatting to pat her some more. "May you have many bouncing puppies." The dog rested her chin on the gate, then slurped her warm tongue along Claire's arm. Her doggy breath was sweet if reminiscent of fresh meat. Had she'd chosen to rise up on her hind legs, the wolfhound could have put her paws on Claire's shoulders.

"I see you like my dogs." Theo's words brimmed with laughter. He gently rested his hand on Claire's head, then took hold of her shoulders and tugged her upright.

"Am I another pet?" she asked wryly, turning in the circle of his arms.

"Perhaps. Time to do some work. You promised to write out everything in triplicate. Remember?" He kissed the tip of her nose.

"Oh. Yes." Anxiety jolted her. She needed to distract Theo—before he figured she was worried. She tilted her head down, leaned into him. "What if I only do it in duplicate?"

"Are you tempting me? I might have to spank you. Come."

Simply waving a good-bye to Filip, Theo headed for the door.

Spank me? What have I gotten myself into?

She caught up to him outside. "I wanted to stay a bit longer."

"Hmm." He smoothed back the hair straying across her face, pressed her against the white wall, crushing daisies underfoot. The ridges of the stonework etched into her back. The hard bulge in his trousers pressed into her mound until she could feel him throb under her. He kissed her, tongue tip anointing her lips then he nibbled her lower lip before he moved his mouth over hers.

"Mmm. This is nice," she managed to whisper.

"If you'd"—another small kiss—"stayed a minute longer, Filip might have had a heart attack."

"Why?" Her eyelids fluttered, and she fought not to writhe against him.

"Squatting on the floor, like that, I rather think he received an eyeful."

She snapped open her eyes. "Oh. I'm not used to skirts."

Another, harder, kiss ground against her lips. When the pressure of his body lifted from her, it took a moment before she realized he'd strode onward. Mouth open, she counted to ten before following.

Two of the manor staff walked across the open ground. Neither cast the slightest look in her direction, though surely they'd noticed the kiss.

"Why didn't you say? Filip will—"

"Don't concern yourself. He'll probably just adore you even more than he already does. Men are like that." He grinned. "He could see you liked the dogs, and that puts you way ahead of most to start with."

"Oh." She took hold of his elbow. "Why do you keep wolfhounds?"

"It's a tradition with my family. They also patrol with the house guards, and since we pasture a few sheep to the north, they help to deter the wolves. Sometimes, when my schedule permits, I hike up there to help out. Though it's an indulgence Dankyo detests."

"Oh. Dankyo does detest a lot." She cast him a sideways glance. The easy lope of his long legs spoke of an active man who did more than sit at desks. "I'd wondered how you kept fit."

"There's also a small gymnasium in the manor, and I swim when I can." He laughed. "Why? Would you like to join me? I could do with some competition." His tone and the challenge in his eyes suggested more than merely keeping fit.

A thrill spread from her pussy, radiated down her thighs. *Keep walking; this is nothing.*

"Perhaps I would. No horses?" She kept her head down, walking on, thinking cold, clear thoughts, determined not to let her body take charge.

"No. There's two steam cars in the vehicle depot. And the gyro, of course, if I need something faster. Why?"

She shrugged. "I just thought horses were what you had in places like this." Her gaze took in the estate.

He laughed. "Mmm. Maybe I'll get a stable going, then. I do ride." He eyed her. "You also?"

"Um. No." She cocked her head, squinting under the midday glare. "I would like to learn, though."

"I can just see you with the wind in your hair and a horse between those long legs of yours." They'd reached the back steps. He put his hand to the small of her back. "Though I can think of another animal that would like to ride *you.*"

She frowned as a servant trotted down the wide stone steps, inclining his head to them. "Shh. Someone will hear. Does everything have to be about sex?"

"It's the novelty, dear. Give me a decade or two. By then you might be boring as mud."

"Oh!" She bit back a horrified retort. He was teasing her about making love. Yet that he could be so easygoing captivated her.

Once inside the study, he pulled out the chair before the desk. "Sit." He waved a hand at a stack of paper on the desktop. "Paper, pen. I'll send in some food later. Maria told me you ate lunch already. If you want, I can arrange for a stenographer and you can dictate. Or would you rather write this yourself?"

She slid into the chair, flattened her palms on the desk. Leather and fresh paper smells abounded. The last time she'd been here, Dankyo had delivered her trussed up like a chicken, waiting to be slaughtered. She swallowed.

"I can do it myself. What shall I write?"

He reached out and traced the outside and inner whorls of her ear, and she half closed her eyes at the delicate sensations. "This isn't a test, Claire. But you have to be fully honest. You're from the PME, and though you mightn't be privy to the plans of their war cabinet, whatever you tell me will be a big help. We need information about the frankenstruct program. Please, dredge up everything about your past that seems relevant. Can you do that?"

She stared into those cloud gray eyes, summoned her best anti-interrogation skills, and wholeheartedly said, “Yes.” She was lying. But she had to. Even though it scored another claw mark on her heart.

Chapter Ten

By early evening she'd covered twenty pages with the close, tiny-lettered writing she'd been taught.

She sat back in the chair, raised her arms, and stretched until her muscles and eardrums thrummed with shifting blood. Well. That was her life up to a few years after she started on the assassin program, only she'd started lying when she came to her fifteenth birthday—said she'd gone into a bodyguard line of training. The skills were similar; she'd only fudged a bit. If it didn't need a lie, she told the truth. The ability of every frankenstruct she knew of was detailed, except for Francine. She just couldn't bring herself to do that. Besides, Francine was more a scout than an assassin.

She picked up the pen, tapped it on the paper. She could leave a hint about the assassinations. The more she pondered it, the more she wondered who the PME wanted her to kill.

Quickly, she lifted the pen and scratched in a last paragraph, hinting at those rumors without saying she was an assassin.

There. Done.

* * * *

Theo sat at the end of the long trestle table and surveyed the boisterous end of the evening's meal. Most of his people were here, apart from those on guard duty and a few other essential tasks. The conversation had grown louder and merrier as wine circulated. Along the horizon yellow and orange washed across the sky. Two bonfires crackled in pits to the side.

At the start of the evening, Claire had been given a place beside him. He'd watched her sit prim in her long sea blue gown, all goggle-eyed through the first course. Since Jonathan was next to her and opposite sat Kirsten and Maria, she'd soon thawed out. He intended her to be drawn out by these most friendly of his staff, expecting to see her enthralled by stories of cooking disasters and triumphs, girly gossip, and fashion. Instead he got…hell, he got this…

Claire stood in a small group of mostly men. The blue dress clinging to her curves and the low neckline surely strained some of the men's eyes. Oblivious, she took Kirsten's hand and showed her, yet again, how to throw a knife. Kirsten flung the blade. This time it clunked into the log she'd aimed at. A squeal of feminine glee split the air. Kirsten jumped up and down laughing, then hugged Claire.

"I did it!"

Theo chuckled and stretched his legs out across Claire's vacant seat.

On this warm night cicadas and crickets clicked and chirruped. With autumn here, they'd soon be silent. The olive crop had been poor. *Perhaps I should get the south field—*

"Sir?" Dankyo deposited himself on Kirsten's chair. It creaked.

Theo looked pointedly at the protesting chair. "You need to lose weight, man?"

"No, sir. I'm at my ideal weight. It's only the weight of muscle."

"One of these days, you'll learn to take a joke." Theo took a sip of his red wine, sighing at the flavorsome burn in his throat.

"I recognize your jokes, sir. I just refuse to take part in them."

"Uh-huh. What's bothering you?"

Dankyo slid a wallet of papers across the table. Theo glanced at them. Claire's story.

"Finished reading already?"

"Yes." Dankyo leaned back, making the chair groan again. "Some of it seems...odd. The last paragraph is the most disturbing. Mass assassinations?"

"Mmm. My thought also. Get this copied and off to the right people tonight. I need Claire's original. I think I can use this to push that bill through. We can pressure the PME with this. Get them to call off any attacks. Right now they're vulnerable to trade treaties and vetoes."

Dankyo nodded. "So you still plan to get the Frankenstruct Bill repealed."

"Hell, yes. It's a damn injustice. Then we can squeeze the PME with the benefit of a higher moral stance. As it is, we're not better than them. If the PME free the frankenstructs, I can guarantee most'll up and leave. Slaves never have liked doing what their masters want them to."

"Oh?" Dankyo lifted his eyebrows, sniffed. He jerked his chin sideways. "Except that one?"

A personal question? From Dankyo? Theo tried not to show his amusement...and amazement. He looked at Claire. "That's different. Contrary to what you believe, Dankyo, it is a consensual affair. We both enjoy the exchange."

His cock hardened just at the memory of their last *exchange*. So much more to show her too. He inspected Claire's figure, from those full breasts down over where the dress material swayed and outlined her stomach and buttocks—all the way down her legs to the perfect sweep of calf muscle. As if she could feel his gaze on her, she turned and smiled warmly, then walked over with Kirsten in tow.

"Really?" said Dankyo.

Surprised at Dankyo's late reply and the peculiar tone, Theo looked at his head of security. Dankyo watched the women.

No. My mistake. He's watching Kirsten. Well, well. Looks as if the man is flesh and blood after all.

As the women approached, the hip-tilting allure of Claire's walk and her lilting voice drew a smile from him. So many little things made her who she was—not as blatantly feminine as some, but underneath was a simmering sensuality.

Kirsten took a seat next to Dankyo. To Theo's amusement the man stiffened—though most wouldn't have seen the difference.

“Claire.” Theo snagged her waist, curving his arm about her and pulling her toward his lap. She resisted, ending up standing at his side with her arm braced on his neck.

A little line creased between her eyes. “Um, there’re people watching.”

“So?” He increased the pull of his arm, and she gave in, sitting, with a bump, on his lap. “Better.” He made sure to not let go. “What is wrong with this? Sitting here?”

She mumbled something.

“Are you embarrassed to be seen with me?” He might have laughed, except he didn’t want to give her the wrong impression.

“Not exactly.” She frowned again. “I just thought a bit more dignity was in order.”

He chuckled. “Dignity? It has its place, but we’re lovers, and I want to be able to touch you, hold you when I feel like it, my dear. I want you to feel the same way.”

He rubbed his hand down her back, enjoying the warm contours at her waist before venturing lower. He could rest his hand on her bottom all day. From the way she wriggled, Claire liked this too. He nuzzled her neck, bit down.

“Ow.”

He watched her take one small shuddering breath. “Relax, darling. No one here thinks any less of you.”

"Sir." Dankyo rose. "I'll speak to you later of some other concerns." He scooped up the wallet of papers, raked a last black glance over Claire, and left.

From the way Kirsten followed his weaving progress between the little groups of people, there was chemistry going both ways. While he was distracted, Claire hopped off his lap and stepped out of reach.

"I'll, uh—"

"Claire. Come back."

Kirsten watched, wide-eyed.

Walking backward, Claire retreated. "I'll get some more wine."

He rubbed his chin. He wouldn't chase her down, but this needed changing. She should be happy and comfortable around him in public. Teaching her that would be interesting.

"Shall I go get her, sir?" Kirsten asked. She sprang to her feet, then tugged her skirt free from the chair.

He eyed the half-full glass of wine already in front of him, drummed his fingers on the table. "Go to her if you wish. Don't make her come back. I'll deal with her myself, later."

"Oh." Her hand tightened on the skirt. "Yes, sir."

He grinned as Kirsten scampered off. The woman was no doubt imagining far worse punishment than he intended. A little awe and fear didn't hurt. He was the lord here. Claire would soon find out that meant more than obeying him in bed. Not even Dankyo was allowed to refuse a direct order.

Chapter Eleven

Next morning, Theo reminded her of the picnic. Claire bathed, wondering where the gyrocopter was stored, then dressed in the clothes laid out on the bathroom divan.

Dark gray leggings went under a strapless white bustier that fastened between her breasts with gold hooks. Next, fitting snugly over the top, came a maroon leather jacket with a flared bottom and a flock of straps and buckles down the arms and front. Completing the ensemble were ankle-high black boots, maroon gloves, a pair of gleaming brass goggles, and an ivory and gold hair clip to hold her hair in a ponytail. Goggles swinging from her hand, she went in search of the gyrocopter.

The bathroom door swung shut behind her with a soft click. Instead of going left along the little hall to the bedroom, she went right toward a heavy steel door that had always been locked. The door swung smoothly open on four oiled hinges.

In the middle of a wide room, a gyrocopter sat on a circular platform, which had a low metal railing curving around its periphery. To the right, timber doors had been pushed back, and a rectangle of startling blue showed the day to be spectacular and cloudless. Theo stood a few yards away at the near wall, turning a crank. By clicking on a ratchet mechanism, he slid the gyro's platform toward the opening.

Theo wore a hedge green leather coat, along with black boots, gloves, and tight black trousers. A wide belt held a stumpy Gerwelt, pistol and a knife was sheathed at the opposite hip.

He smiled at her. "Here, help me wind this thing out."

A bedroom with a gyrocopter launch pad. How delicious. She smiled back and went over, anchoring her hands on the end of the handle and leaning into the turn. The platform wound out faster.

With a *clunk* the platform reached its set position, projecting out the side of the mansion. They strolled over. Claire exhaled as she put her boot on the polished timber slats. It echoed but barely swayed. Beneath was a two-story drop; above was sky.

The gyrocopter had two seats, one behind the other, inside an angular glass cockpit that was open at the back. The steam voltaic engine at the rear started easily when Theo cranked it, coughing out a thin stream of smoke, then sputtering, before settling into a contented purr. A spider web of polished rods formed a golden curved tail, and above Claire, the two tiers of gyro blades slowly picked up speed. All in all it resembled a supersized mosquito with the throaty sound of a contented cat. Tucked and strapped into a wicker compartment behind the last seat were a picnic basket and a pile of cushions.

"Shall we?" Theo offered her his hand, and though she had no need of help, she rested her fingers in his before climbing in.

Once seated, Theo increased the throttle and shouted back, "Seat harness on! Goggles on! Bugs get past the screen sometimes!"

The goggles were brass with silver inlaid stars, quaint, yet functional. She slipped them over her head and did up the buckle, then found the four straps of the seat harness and buckled them also.

The machine lifted off with a blast of power that pushed Claire into her seat. She gulped to subdue the crazy stew of excitement rising in her stomach. Below, men scurrying about the perimeter of the airship shrank rapidly to antlike figures. The land seemed to flatten as if made into a giant green-hued map. A distant river undulated in reflective blue loops like a jewelry snake.

The wind was cold, leaking in the side of the goggles and making her eyes water. She adjusted the leather strap.

"Where are we going?" she cried, but Theo only shook his head. With the noise of the engine and the wind blasting past their ears, she doubted he'd heard a thing. She leaned back, grinning. The view alone would keep her occupied for eternity. Airships were never this exciting.

When at last the gyrocopter descended, she peeked over the side, and her heart plummeted. A long smudged shape lay across the scorched ground near a gash in the land—like a gargantuan beast struck dead by flame with only blackened bones remaining. This was the airship crash. A hundred questions rushed gibbering through her mind. Most of all—why had he brought her here? Did he suspect she had lied?

The bump and shudder as the gyrocopter landed and the engine shut down did nothing to pull her from her bewilderment. Her knuckles showed white where she gripped the back of Theo's chair. Metal ticked as it cooled. She unclipped the seat's harness and hopped out. Adjusting the skirt of the jacket gave her time to gather her wits.

There might be nothing to this. Just some morbid curiosity. But she didn't believe her own logic. She pushed up the goggles, put her gloved hand over her eyes for a moment to compose herself, then swept back some straying, wind-shredded hair.

The fall of the airship had plowed up the ground in great furrows. No rain had fallen to encourage new growth, and the brown earth, torn and raw, seemed to Claire as terrible as a bleeding wound. The stench of fire clung to the place. Sweat trickled down her back. Before this crash, she'd been a possession of the Pancontinental Mexican Empire, a thing to be ordered about by Inkline and others. Cold prickled among the sweat. She tugged off the gloves, then tucked them into a pocket.

"This is where we found you," Theo said in a low voice. He pointed at a sail of crumpled metal with the Mexican eagle emblazoned upon it. "Over there."

"How many...survived?" She faced the place of her rebirth—this womb of death. She knew none of the others on board, but she remembered the cries and screams that night. She pressed her hand to her stomach.

Death was never pretty or easy. Yet she prayed that Inkline had died in the most horrible way. She shook her head. A lump of charred timber tumbled when she accidentally kicked it. Ash puffed into the air.

"Six survived, including you." He regarded her steadily, with a faint aura of concern.

This is not the time or place to fall to pieces. She cleared her throat. "Do you know their identities?"

"Why? Is there someone you're particularly concerned about? I have the names from all the bodies—eight of those. Military or government diplomatic neck tags on all of them."

She suppressed a frown, kept her face still and unreadable. "Inkline. Was there an Inkline?"

"Yes. One of the bodies."

She closed her eyes.

"Claire?" Fingers under her chin. She opened her eyes, looked into his narrowed gray ones. "What is it? A friend?"

What should I say? How much can I—

A crease marked his brow. His grip tightened. "The truth, Claire. I can see your mind churning."

That sent an alarming bolt of fear through her. She'd kept herself so close—sure nothing had shown.

"Dankyo has suspicions, and we don't need to feed them. Is there anything you've not told us about this crash? Who was this Inkline?" He released her.

He's dead. Inkline is dead. I'm free, aren't I? Weather this interrogation, and it's finished.

"It was in the report I wrote, wasn't it?" *Oh. Wait. I left him out. Didn't want to write about something so close to the assassination plot. What did I say?*

She made herself smile, in a twisted way. "He was my employer. In the Diplomatic Service. I hated him." She looked at Theo square-on. He *couldn't* know exactly what she thought. She'd skim the truth. "I hated him with every ounce of my body." Her voice shook, and she let all the years of anguish, sadness, and fear flavor her words.

"If he was here right now, alive, I'd be sorely tempted to put a knife in him. There. I've told you. But"—she slowly turned, surveying the crashed airship—"why I was here...I cannot remember. I'm sorry. I have no memory of why I was here." She leaned into Theo, muffled her voice against his warm chest. "I'm so sorry."

He wrapped both arms about her, hugged her close. Kissed the top of her head. "It's over. He can't hurt you any longer. Is that all?"

She nodded, her hair making rasping sounds against his jacket.

They stood together for a while. Time flowed past like a languid river, washing away all her past, all the torment and pain. *I'm free.* She let Theo's presence melt through her. For once, she didn't mourn the loss of a family that had never been—an ache she'd always carried inside her. Theo was more than enough.

"So," Theo said. "You were Inkline's bodyguard? He was a diplomat?"

She nodded. If she could have hidden inside his jacket, she would have.

"Then that's all we have to tell Dankyo. I'll let him continue his investigations. Maybe concentrate on this Inkline. Something must have stirred up the Brito-Gallic League, for them to attack this ship. There's...only one other question I have to ask, because Dankyo will raise it, and I need him to believe in you as much as I do. So, here it is. You'd never do anything to hurt me, would you, Claire?" His embrace didn't change in any way, yet he held his breath. Claire's heart stuttered.

"No! Of course not. I would never hurt you."

"And my men, the people who work for me? I am their protector as much as they are mine."

"No. Truly, if I could, I'd not hurt anyone, ever again. You do believe me?"

He took a breath. "Yes. I do. That's all I needed to hear."

He patted her hair for a while longer. She cuddled in and let the tension in her muscles soften. *Safe. I'm safe.*

Theo opened his arms and let her loose. "Come. Back to the gyrocopter, and let's do something cheerful. I'll go downriver toward the coast. There's a good private spot I know of."

Having restarted the gyrocopter, they boarded it. The land fell away from them. On the eastern horizon a great line of steel gray clouds hunched like a monstrous beast. Claire watched the airship's remains dwindle. With Inkline dead, surely any assassination plot would fail. It couldn't have been *this* Theo. He was important, but not *that* important. Even if it was him, she'd never let anyone near. Never. She'd know another frankenstruct in an instant.

The alternative was revealing everything to Theo—what she could do and what they'd wanted her to do. It had the potential to destroy this fragile little world she'd found. The gyrocopter whirred on, blades whistling, cutting the air into a million turbulent pieces a few feet above.

Visions flickered in her head—of the airship from above and the fig tree with the tangle of exposed roots. Of roots snaking along the ground, clawing aside dirt, flinging papers into the air that fluttered back to earth in a burning rain. Her dream. She'd seen this one every night. Smoke and fire and falling and...

She remembered the crash. The aftermath, lying under a weight of hot metal and debris. Cold ground by her side. Blood in her mouth. At the base of the fig tree, Inkline furtively carrying something yellow...something yellow. Her assignment folder.

The purr and whistle of the gyrocopter yanked her back to the present.

Sweet heavens. She'd seen him after the crash, alive. Inkline was alive. Claire sank her face into her palms, peering through blurred fingers at the back of Theo's seat. *What can I do? Inkline never gives up. He'll return and find me and make sure my assignment is carried out. He'll drag me back to the PME.*

It was that simple. The tipping point that drove her into the flesh-numbing air of a black reality. She remembered Theo's last question and replayed his response. He hadn't quite believed her. No matter what he'd said, she was sure he doubted her, and now it seemed he might be right. For if Inkline gave her a direct order, standing in front of her, she didn't really know what she'd do. Disobeying him seemed incomprehensible.

She crunched her fists until the fingernails bit deep into her palms. When she opened her hands, on each palm was an irregular line of bloodred crescents.

No. Stop. Hadn't she learned anything these last days? She was stronger than she'd once thought. She could do this. She could refuse Inkline if he turned up. Just because she never had, didn't mean she couldn't.

How ridiculous—to cave in when she'd not seen Inkline for days. But she had been living inside a fantasy. She'd wanted so much to be somebody, she'd blinded herself. Only now she could see through the cracks in her bubble of glass. Something would go wrong, eventually.

She lifted the goggles and wiped at her eyes. She needed to be vigilant, in case everything disintegrated around her.

Curls of Theo's black hair stuck out at odd angles where the goggle strap mussed it up. Hand trembling, she stretched and touched it, letting a curl run fluttering in the wind across her skin. A plan? Should she assemble one? Maybe tomorrow. Right now she wanted to live, to enjoy the moments she had.

Theo reached back over his shoulder and found her fingers. "Everything good back there?" he yelled over the engine noise.

She swallowed, clearing away the obstruction in her throat. "Sure! There's nothing wrong!" She held on tight to his gloved fingers an extra few seconds, memorizing the feel of them, before letting go.

Chapter Twelve

Theo watched the landscape slowly change. The windswept high plateau sloped down to the river. The water tumbled through a ravine, then emerged onto the plain, widened, and slowed. Farther west, past a lake of blue-green depths, the river slithered to a sunlit archipelago at the edges of the sea.

"Down there!" He pointed at a clearing, reducing speed to steer the gyrocopter in to a gentle landing on the northern bank of the river. The coughing engine frightened some long-legged cranes. They flapped skyward, legs scraping a line of turbulence in the water. Forest crowded the opposite bank and surrounded the clearing they'd landed in.

He swung out and dropped to the ground. Claire slid off her goggles, then took his offered hand. Once her boots touched ground, he reeled her in, wrapped her in his embrace, enjoying the curve of her ass against his gloved hand. His other hand held the back of her neck in the V of thumb and fingers, his ring finger lightly playing with her nape hair. Her neck stiffened at first, then softened. Her rich amber irises widened, and her hips angled against him. Her acceptance of this act of possession pleased him.

Back at the airship crash, he'd sensed she wasn't revealing everything. When he demanded truth, she still held back. Maybe not a straight-out lie, but close. The important answer, that she'd not hurt him, he believed. Now he just had to coax it all out of her, and he would, else the only alternative would be sending her away. God, he didn't want that. Once he pinned down whatever she hadn't told him, he'd get to take it out on her ass, and that made it all the more enticing—figuring out the almost lie.

For now, he had to soothe her. She was wound up tighter than a clock spring.

He leaned in and kissed her fiercely, snuggling his hand farther down her firm bottom, pressing in along the crotch seam of the leggings, as his tongue penetrated between her lips. She relaxed into his arms, a satisfied hum sounding deep in her throat.

He pulled away, casually undoing the ivory hair clip and shaking loose her shoulder-length hair. "Let's get this picnic organized." He tapped the tip of her nose.

Claire's gaze took a moment to focus. "Oh. Yes." Clearly his kiss had done more than stir her a little. He wondered how far he would be able to entice her today.

The soft grass near the bank was a good spot for the picnic rug and cushions. He twisted open the catch on the basket, folded back the lid, removed the strawberries and cool yogurt, the honey, pastries wrapped in a cloth, and more. Underneath the food lay a flask of wine. Claire hovered nervously. Picnics were obviously another novelty for her.

Even better. He liked the idea of drawing her out, introducing her to new things. His servants were always doing things for him, and doing this for Claire was pleasant—no, more than that, it satisfied something inside he'd not known was there.

"Now..." he announced with relish. "First some food. Then we are going to talk and learn about each other." He sat down, legs crossed.

"Why?"

"Because we know next to nothing about each other. I've read what you wrote, but that's dry stuff. I want to hear it from your mouth. You like the idea of there being a place for you here. Well, this is one of my requirements."

She raised one eyebrow in that cute way she had, but she joined him. At first she sat like he did, with her legs crossed—a position you could rise from easily, if need be. She surveyed the surroundings, going from the butter and bread knives to the pistol at his belt—all the potential weapons. He didn't doubt she knew exactly how many steps it took to reach the gyrocopter or the forest line. Battle ready, Dankyo would call it. If she was guarding him, he'd approve, but in a consort—

Then she saw him watching her, as she watched *everything* else. He shook his head, slowly, in dismay. She shrugged and moved those long legs around until she sat with them tucked up and angled together to the side. He inclined his head.

That she'd understood him was nice, but even better was the trust implied in the way she'd relaxed. A fierce satisfaction overcame him. *Re gamoto*. He could get used to having a woman on hand who could swap from personal bodyguard to sexual submissive in the blink of an eye.

"Have you tried these before?" He took up a small platter. "Baklava. Almonds, honey and crushed walnuts layered in fine pastry. Delicious." He offered them to her. While Claire picked up a piece, he uncorked the bottle and poured them both a glass of retsina. The surprise on her face when she bit down made him grin.

"Good?"

"Mm-hmm. Yes!"

The retsina was made on his own lands. Not the most revered of wine varieties, but this year's had turned out nicely. From the way she sipped, screwing up her mouth a little when she thought he wasn't looking, Claire hadn't tried much wine before. Slowly the retsina and the food did their job, and the tension left her face and shoulders.

"You must be curious about me. I know I am about you, about your life before this. Unless, that is, you already know who I am?"

She shook her head. "No. We—I wasn't told much about your country."

"Well, I own many many acres of land, different properties. I am a rich man—purely by virtue of my birth." He grimaced. "I try not to abuse my power. And truly, being rich does give me power. I plan to do more than simply live on the surplus. I have a right to a seat in our House of Lords. You understand?"

"Yes."

"But, also a part of who I am is that I like to be the dominant partner in any sexual relationship. This you must understand too, by now?"

"Uh, yes." She took a measured swallow of retsina, looking at him from under her eyelashes. Her hand didn't visibly tremble, but the surface of the retsina did.

"From what I've seen, you're happy with that?"

She said nothing.

"You're very red, Claire. A beetroot would be put to shame."

"I'm, uh, happy with that." On one side, she curled her hair back behind her ear. He waited until she stopped fussing and put her hands in her lap.

"Good." He let his own pleasure show through in his tone and noted her blush fading. "Because, this isn't about me only. If you're not happy, then I'm not. I may like holding you down when we have sex...or restraining you in other ways"— *ahhh, good; that made her breathe even faster*—"or sometimes even turning your bottom red with a paddle, but I want you to find joy in this." He made himself sit still, despite wanting to reach out and fondle her.

"Um"—she swallowed—"I'm not keen on the restraining, or the, uh, paddle, and you know ropes are out."

"No? I think perhaps it's too early to decide that. When the moment arrives, yes? Then we'll see if you feel the same way. And that is one of my rules. I get to decide how far we try to go, because I don't think, Claire, that you really know yourself."

At that, he picked up the cloth that had held the pastries, reached across, and slowly looped it around the hand she leaned on. Then he kept her hand pinned there to the ground, with the cloth wound tight, while he cupped his other hand beneath her chin. He watched her for a long moment. Her eyes were on his, her nostrils flaring. He moved in and kissed her thoroughly. When he pulled away and dragged the cloth from around her wrist, her lips were parted, and she looked like she'd fall over on her back if he pushed the slightest amount. *Superb.*

"Your lips are swollen, Claire. And I know that if I touched you between your legs, I'd find you wetter than that river behind you." He narrowed his eyes but kept the warmth of approval in his tone. "That was restraint. You liked it. I had thought we'd already established this."

After a second, she gulped. "I did...like it. But that was different. I could have gotten myself free."

"I don't doubt you could have tried and maybe succeeded. But you didn't. You enjoyed being held down. It's not necessarily about being overpowered; it's about relinquishing control. There's always an out. For me, there's a thrill in knowing you're giving me that power."

He made his voice stay utterly steady, imprinting on her that this was fact. "The greater the restraint, Claire, the greater the enjoyment will be for you. When you trust me enough to hand me complete control, I'm going to tie you up in rope. I love the stark beauty of rope on a woman's skin. I'm going to tie you up so thoroughly that you won't be able to stop me from making you come, over and over."

She froze, and he could see that both fascinated and shocked her, as her throat and mouth worked with little movements.

He smiled. "This is not meant to be algebra. If you'll let me, I'll take you on a journey, one you won't easily forget."

She shut her eyes, opened them, and fixed him with those golden irises. "Mmm." She steepled her fingers together. "But what if I want to stop or take a different path to the one you're on?"

"I'll always take into account what you want done to you."

"Done to me?" The words twisted into a squeak. She shook her head as if perturbed at the betrayal of nerves, then cleared her throat.

His gorgeous bodyguard was unsettled, if aroused. *Good.*

"Just remember, I'm the one with the ultimate say. And I guarantee, you won't always, one hundred percent, like what I do. But that adds to the fun."

She shot him a suspicious look at that. "A last thing to remember, and this is important. I have rules. I have to. It's not just you and me—there're hundreds who rely on me, look to me for leadership. I can't have you questioning me in public. If I give an order, I expect to see it obeyed. I'm speaking specifically of last night when you walked away from me. Do that again and there will be consequences. On the other hand, if you want out of this, I'll endeavor to find somewhere you can live without the PME coming after you. Is that all clear?"

"Um. Yes. It's clear."

He let her think about everything he'd said, in silence. For a while they sat together, finishing off most of the delicacies and listening to the wind rustling the tree tops, and the plop of water as fish searching for bugs popped to the surface.

"Now, I'd like to hear about you. Something that's not in that report."

He took a sip from his glass. "Come, tell me something? Anything. I'll listen."

"This isn't what I'm used to."

"What? Bodyguards don't get to talk? Do you have friends?"

She shrugged.

"Right." He suppressed his annoyance. How was he going to get her talking? She was so different from his previous consorts.

He began to clear away the food, and after a moment, Claire joined him at his side. They put everything back into the basket, except for the bowl of strawberries, which he whisked from her hand.

"Now. We're going to play a game. Sit there. Kneeling." No dalliance this time; he made that a command.

She opened her mouth but did as he asked.

He waited until she sat with knees together on the plaid rug, stretching those leggings in many appealing directions.

"You said that you'd not made love to a man before?" Red spread across her cheeks. Still so easily embarrassed by sex? "So, I was your first lover?"

"Yes."

"Then, I'm honored that you gave me that privilege. And I hope I didn't disappoint you."

"Ah." This time he got a smile back. "No, Theo, you definitely didn't disappoint me."

For once, he was the one in shock. She'd smiled at him *and* called him Theo.

"Good." He put a wicked twist to his own smile. "I'll have to make sure my record stays impeccable. Give me your hand."

With only the slightest hesitation, she extended her arm. He turned her hand over, then stroked her palm.

Fascinated, he watched the shifting colors in her irises, like clouds and sunlight passing through.

"I said I wouldn't tie you up with ropes yet. I also said that ropes aren't the only form of restraint." He kissed her palm, then gave each fingertip a brief touch of his tongue. *Ah, yes. Her eyes widened the slightest.* He curled her fingers into her palm, let go of her hand.

She blinked at him, the tip of her tongue coming out and resting in the middle of her upper lip. Clearly, she was thinking about his words. He'd like to suck that little pink tongue into his mouth while he kissed her…or have her lick his cock.

"What are you planning?"

"You'll see soon enough."

She shut her eyes. The sunlight haloed her hair in gold. She was so beautiful. Yet, he thought wryly, he valued the smile she'd just given him more than the prettiness of her hair.

"Sit up on your knees, Claire," he said softly.

Slowly, she did so.

"Straighter. Good. Now, I'm going to answer your questions, and you will answer mine. If you answer me, I will reward you with an instruction, and some food." He plucked a strawberry from the bowl.

"What?" A tiny crease appeared on her forehead.

"You'll see. My first question, and I'll warn you in advance—this means those leggings come down—tell me your earliest memory." He dangled the strawberry. The lure, of course, was not the fruit.

"Wait. So, I have to answer you, and then you'll make me take off my clothes? And if I don't answer you? What happens then?"

"I'm not sure. Perhaps, I'll spank you...perhaps not. Depends on how much you've said. Do you want this to go further or not?"

Her eyes looked fathomless as pools, yet deep down, he glimpsed a rising swirl of desire. He waited, grinning, the strawberry rotating on its stalk where he held it between finger and thumb.

He'd tried just plain asking, and she'd still held back. Dankyo was right. He had to know more about her. If she couldn't handle honesty, he'd be better off sending her away, no matter how that tore him apart. With his political connections and all those under him, there was too much at stake.

He aimed to make this talk fun. And with this game, he'd blurred the lines of who held the reins and who did not. He made up the rules and the consequences. She had the choice of opting out.

"I..." Claire opened her mouth a few times, ducked her head.

Ah. She'd decided to participate. He studied her sweet body. The anticipation might just kill him.

"My earliest memory? I remember running down a forest pathway. My friend, Francine, ran beside me. We used to play hide and seek. She was darn good at that. Too good." She raised her head, stared at him, as if daring him.

As if he'd not follow through. He put the strawberry to her mouth. She parted those soft lips and sucked in the redness, chewed and swallowed. He let his finger trail into the hole created by those lips and imagined his cock there. "I think, after all, you should do this. Pull them to your knees."

And at last, *finally*, she was talking.

She put her hands to her waist, and slowly, teasingly, she shimmied the leggings down until they bunched at her knees. No underwear. The golden triangle of hair greeted his gaze. Now that was worth seeing.

"Your question?" He found another strawberry.

"What happens after?"

"This time it's a secret."

"Hmph."

He cocked his head. How he liked messing with her. One of the perks of being the dom. Keeping the submissive off-kilter was at least half the fun. Too predictable, and things got boring. He never, ever, wanted boring. Neither would she.

She sucked in her bottom lip. A nervous habit. One he could count on. The more he understood her, the better. "You won't tell me?"

"No." He shook his head.

"Then I should make it a hard question. Why did you not listen to Dankyo when he told you to...dispose of me?"

Oh, now that was some question.

"Because, though I listen to Dankyo, I trust my own instincts even more. I don't think, even now, that you're a danger to me. How could anyone who'd do this be a risk?" He smiled. "Take off your bustier."

He fed her the strawberry and ate some fruit himself while she opened the buckles on the jacket to get at the bustier, then undid the gold hooks and took it off. Her breasts, round and inviting, swung free. The nipples shrank, wrinkling up into perky pinkish buttons.

"My question." He found a small bunch of red grapes, examined Claire, naked apart from the opened jacket, all the way from her knees up. Too tempting. He put a hand above the twisted cloth at her knee and ran it up toward the delicious territory between her legs where the light tuft of pubic hair came to a point.

* * * *

Claire found her breath stilled in her throat as she waited for his hand to get to where she wanted it to be. Her clit and vulva had acquired heartbeats of their own. Yet he didn't caress her there; instead his fingers combed lightly through her pubic hair while the fingers of his other hand traced their way to an areolae...again, not quite touching the center.

"Claire?"

She opened eyes she'd not known she'd closed. Damn, the man was smirking at her, or near enough.

"What are you most afraid of?"

She flinched, felt herself come down from the isolated world of pleasure she'd inhabited.

"Claire? I understand that's an even harder question than yours." He put a hand on her knee. She focused on that. "Maybe, just this once, I'll let you reserve that one. Answer later. Would you like a different question?"

Would I? But I'm afraid of so many things. Myself, to start with. This was a trade-off. Hand him her heart and soul on a platter, and he'd what? Give her great sex? No, she belittled what he offered. "Claire?"

She looked at him. Kind, gentle when she needed him to be, twice her body weight, and he wanted to tie her up and spank her. *Whew.* And just the thought of that made her squirm, made her want to both climb all over him and run the opposite way.

"You'll give me a different question?"

"If you want. But you get to answer it later today." His hand on her knee squeezed.

She screwed up her face. "No. I'll answer. I understand why you need honesty. Even if I hate talking about things like this." She huffed. "I guess…I'm afraid of being lost, of having no home, nowhere to go. Of not being me." She couldn't keep the misery from her words. This topic was so close to the core of sadness in her. Even in the midst of desire, she felt the worst of it. *And now, I'm afraid of losing you, because really, what I just said makes me sound like the most useless sort of person.*

His arms enfolded her, and he pulled her tight into his chest. "Thank you," he said softly. "Shh. It's okay."

He didn't think she was something awful? She crumpled a bit and slid her arms around him, put her face into his shoulder. Solid. Nice. For a while it was enough to sit and be comforted; then slowly she remembered her ass was bare, for Theo had glided his hand down, feeling her between the cheeks of her bottom.

"Hey," she whispered huskily, turning her head up.

He kissed her. A slow, steamy kiss that warmed her from her toes to her pussy and left her thighs quivering.

"Enough of this." His voice rumbled deep. Suddenly she was aware of everything, her skin so sensitive, and every detail before her sluiced sharp, as if ice water had been thrown on her. From the way he glowered, Theo had plans. Devious ones. *Oh, dear.*

With a last pat on her bottom, he drew away. "No more questions. Not from me, though Dankyo wants you to elaborate on that report, and you will do that." He ended on a stern note. "But now, straighten up and keep your arms by your sides. Don't move."

Dankyo, oh damn. She could handle him. But this was going elsewhere. Where *Theo* wanted, and she was sure he meant to do more than hold her with a dish cloth.

Confused, quaking inside, she straightened as he'd commanded, rising up on her legs from where she'd hunkered down while they'd cuddled. The bumpy ground under the picnic rug poked into her knees. *What did he have in mind*? At least, she noticed with relief, there were no ropes.

He pressed her chin up and rearranged a part of the jacket. She couldn't see exactly what, but, straining her eyes, she saw him unclip something and remove a piece from the middle section; then the front straps were pulled in snug across her front.

Aha. Now she knew why the thing had so many buckles and straps going in every which direction. Devious indeed.

"This garment is from the same place as the corset you wore last night."

"It is?" She tried to look down.

He caught her chin, stopped her. "Uh-uh. No."

Just that...*holding* made her clit warm a degree more.

Metal jingled, and the edges of the jacket pulled together, tightened around the sides of her breasts, squeezing them together.

"The pressure, though light, will increase the pleasure you get from *this*." He brushed a nipple, and she jumped.

"You may look."

What did he do? Two buckled straps crossed tightly over her chest. One cut above and one below her breasts, squeezing them together between what remained of the left and right flaps of the jacket, making her breasts look and feel far plumper than ever before. Her nipples scrunched up hard as pebbles. It wasn't just the feeling, as if her breasts had become small balloons; it was the look of it and knowing that this was how he wanted them to be. Exposed. Emphasizing her sexuality.

She breathed faster, deeper.

"Now, some more food." He retrieved a grape, bit the red globe open, and pressed the cut surface to her nipple. She gasped. Cold, and it made her nipple protrude even more.

He watched her, crinkles appearing around his eyes.

He liked doing this to her, and that made her even hotter…knowing, feeling his approval. Then he leaned in and kissed her, sucking her lower lip into his mouth while that grape scooted in cool lazy circles across her nipple. The fingers of his other hand skirted her clit and made their way along her wet slit. She lost sight of him, knew her eyes closed as sensation swallowed her. Her nether lips parted under his finger. Swelled. Behind her eyelids, her world had gone muted yellow, but she knew he watched. He kissed her again. The smell of her arousal mingled with the sweetness of fruit in his mouth.

His tongue swept into her mouth, played slippery warm games with her tongue. Lust ripened. Her breasts, squashed up into firm melons, thumped with blood, as if she'd grown new nerve paths. Her moistened nipples felt so tight they might have been forged in iron. The brush of his hand or shirt on her made her utter little uncontrolled noises of pleasure.

He backed away a small amount, leaving only that finger in her cleft. She thrust to gain more of his touch, needing that pressure. She looked up, saw him. Always, he watched her, carefully, as if she was something precious.

"Don't move." He swiped that finger, slick as treacle, along her labia and past her clit, took it away.

Ah!

Swaying, she fought to steady her breathing. The sexual games were intoxicating.

He bowed his head until he was close to her cheek again. "Time for a distraction." He moved lower. His wet mouth fastened over her nipple and sucked it in—liquid heat spread like fire. Her bound breasts, her clit, her cleft—all throbbed in time to the suction and licking of his mouth.

She stiffened, bowing her back and hissing though her teeth, her hands instinctively grabbing hold of his biceps and digging in with all fingernails.

"Better," he added. "Much better. There's no point in coming all the way out here and remaining sad for the rest of the day, is there? You, my dear, need sex." He tweaked her left nipple. "Yes?"

She couldn't deny that, not when it seemed he'd connected every part of her with electrified wiring and turned on the power. Her body *hummed*, waiting for his next move. "Mmm."

"Excellent." His gray eyes glinted. "Put your arms together behind you. Clasp each forearm at the elbow with the other hand. Now, dear."

Oh, heck.

Whatever he wanted, she knew it would set her alight. She did as he asked, and he went around behind her. Holding her arms there, at the small of her back, made her breasts push out even more, making them protrude so much she wondered they didn't pop from the tension. If there were birds and bees out there, she couldn't hear them. The thump of blood in her arteries and heavy sigh of her lungs had come to the fore. And the clink of buckle and slide of leather fed into the growing tightness along her arms, from wrists to elbows, where they lined up against each other. She couldn't separate them. He was buckling them together, no other explanation possible.

More straps. Restraining me.

Lord. This, then, was the control he'd spoken of. Not utter and complete—she could move—but closer than he'd taken her before. Every part of her sang like a soprano on the highest note and came alive. Theo bit her neck. Electricity swept sizzling through her, from top to bottom. *Yes. Oh, God, yes...*

"Hinchcliff and Co. do make very nice clothing. I think you'll agree?"

She half-groaned out her reply. "Yes."

She looked down at herself, where her breasts jutted out, and felt wetness seeping from between her legs, near where her buttocks rested on her heels. She was naked except for the jacket and pushed-down leggings. The buckles above and below her breasts made them and her nipples stick out and ache. She struggled a bit, tried to free her arms. Nothing gave.

Heat pulsed, vibrating from everywhere, becoming one unified throb that threatened to turn her into jelly. Theo resumed biting her neck. She couldn't do anything to stop him—even her legs were trapped by where the leggings were wound around them at her knees. She panted, wanting him between her legs.

"You tied me," she blurted hoarsely, amazed at her own reactions. Why, oh why, did this make her so *hot?*

"Not really. No ropes."

Mmm. But almost the same. He'd found a middle ground that she liked. She knew he wouldn't hurt her, trusted him not to—maybe that was the difference?

He set her straight, held her shoulders a second or two to make sure she balanced properly, then moved away and lay down.

With his eyes lit up with amusement, Theo rested on his elbow regarding her. He was still clothed, though his erection pressed at his pants hard enough to show a clear outline.

"This is so much better. Ropes are nice, but I think this could be worth exploring in the future."

How casually he assumed power. She wanted him so much, and he lay there—cool and calm.

She remembered where they were. "Mightn't someone see us?" she said thickly. *What is he doing over there*? She wanted his touch.

"No. And if they did? Would you mind?"

"I...don't know." She shocked herself with that answer. If someone saw her, like this, exposed—oh, that excited her even more.

He rose to his feet and efficiently stripped off his clothes, removing his trousers last. She couldn't help staring at his erection, recalling what it had been like in her mouth. Her pussy squeezed as he walked toward her, the hard muscles of his chest, abdomen, and thighs shifting enticingly.

Why she wanted this, she didn't know, but the allure of being restrained was obvious now, even to her. Her body heat climbed to inferno level.

"I'd like to put this"—he put his fist around the base of his cock—"in there, inside those soft lips. Wet your lips and open your mouth."

He wanted to...fuck her mouth. She squeezed her thighs tight together, swept her tongue over her lips, and opened her mouth.

The soft tip of him nudged her and then pressed in until the hardness of his shaft entered. She moved her tongue around, feeling him out, welcoming him in. Then she felt him slide farther, farther, and the tip touch the back of her throat.

"I'll be gentle." His voice was tight. "Ahh, yes." A thrill ran along his penis, and she felt it twitch. He halted.

Even with her hands strapped behind her, she felt in some control of his pleasure and explored him, swirling with her moist tongue.

Steadily, he thrust in and out of her mouth, gripping her shoulder and head. She tasted saltiness and the sweetness of the grape juice from where his fingers had touched his cock.

He slowed, drew back to her lips with just the head inside.

"Enough." He withdrew, his cock popping wet from her mouth. This time, he was the one gasping. She looked up at him from beneath her brows and lazily curved her tongue across her lips. Daring him.

"Ha." He laughed throatily. "You're getting too cheeky. Your turn."

Returning with the cushions, he dumped them at her feet. The strength in his arms surprised her as he tilted her back, arranging the cushions under her neck, back, and bottom until her lower body arched upward, her arms trapped under her, though padded by the soft cushions. He'd slipped her leggings lower, wrapping them about her ankles like soft manacles. If she'd felt exposed before…now she was blatantly on display. Coolness licked her skin.

Openmouthed, lips bruised, tongue still remembering his taste, she stared at Theo standing over her and wondered what he meant to do. Whatever it was, she could barely move in any direction.

She shivered and felt a fresh tide of moisture flood her pussy.

He spread her knees so her legs opened. "Stay like that, Claire. I want to see all of you."

He put his hand down there. Two of his fingers touched her turgid lips, moving her juices along her slit, then over her aching clit. She gasped and tensed. His fingers lifted away, and she heard him kneel by her side, then felt his fingers anointing her nipples with her own juices, his hands wrapping around each swollen breast as if they were fruit he could pluck.

She strained, lifting her head to watch for a few seconds. All she could see was her squashed-together breasts and Theo.

He rose up from his knees and kissed each nipple, laying his warm tongue on each, then licking across. So sensitive—she groaned and felt the tiny bumps on his tongue trail over her. She flopped her head back and thrust up her groin. Releasing one breast, he found her pussy, one finger slip-sliding inside her to its full length. Her muscles clamped on him, pulsing at the slide and tug. His other fingers, she lost count of how many, pressed in, stretching her.

"Ah. Ah." She moaned to the sky, mouth so open her jaw hurt. "More."

He lifted his lips from her breast, his fingers slipped from her pussy. "No talking."

"Uh." Blindly, she nodded agreement. Anything to get him to resume all the things he did to her body.

The renewed rhythm of fingers and tongue brought her, shaking, like the ratcheting upward of a chain, to the sweaty hot edge. When his thumb slid onto her erect clit, she thrust the tip of her tongue out. The slickness, the slip and slide inside, and the gentle twirl of thumb on her clit... With a small gasp and a scream, she let go. Exploding pleasure welded her body into one rigid arch of muscle, her pussy locking tight on to his fingers. *Yes!*

Sunlight blanched like white fire through her eyelids.

When she felt her heartbeat slow and her lungs calm, she opened her eyes to a slit to find Theo smiling down at her.

"Now that was something wonderful to watch. Happy?"

The words to answer him were lost in a dazed jumble in her mind.

"My turn," he said with a predatory glint in his eye. Again he arranged her body, turning her over so her ass was in the air, her face on its side against a cushion. "How are your arms? Sore? Numb?"

Half-lost in memories of orgasm, she opened and closed her hands, abruptly reminded of the grip of buckle and leather around her. Nothing gave. Nothing seemed numb. She chose not to speak and shook her head. It would be sacrilege to speak. Her temples still thudded with the pounding of blood.

With an open hand, he slapped her bottom, sending a jolt of pleasure to her loins, and she grunted, unable to stop the instinctive arch of her bottom upward. Already her body stirred.

"I'll take that as a *yes, I'm perfectly happy*?" He put that hand back and massaged. "Your bottom is so nicely made for smacking."

She knew she should glare back at him for that smug tone, but couldn't—her body quivered with expectation. Ahh, that a simple smack could do this to her. She wished he'd do it again.

She buried her face in the cushion, blocking out light and turning the world into one of pure feel and smell. And the ripe, rich smell of lust thickened the air.

His hands gripped each cheek of her ass; then instead of his cock, something flicked across her sensitive clit and up along her slit. His tongue. Her fists clenched and loosened. With his tongue playing slither and glide across her labia and clit, slowly, he drove her back into arousal. Whenever she tensed as if about to come, he drew back for a few moments, until she was biting the cushion in frustration, her fists closed, her bottom straining up for more.

She lost track of how many times he did this, and then, to her surprise, instead of his tongue, the blunt stretch at her opening told her his cock demanded entrance. With a body-jarring *thump*, he went all the way in—a savage thrust into her wet tunnel. She gasped. *Oh. My. God.* And again. His flesh slapped against her, stretching her vagina fully at the zenith of each thrust. She lay there accepting everything he gave her, loving it, wanting to take him in to the very limit.

The cushions rocked under her to the movement of her body. She knew she grunted and moaned with each lunge, but nothing mattered. If anyone saw, she didn't care. Something grabbed her clit. *Ah*, his finger, his thumb, and they squeezed in time to his thrusts.

Too much. She crested a wave about to break, gasping, poised and straining, at the very heart-pounding edge.

With one final push, his cock pulsed, and he came, erupting into her. She opened her mouth and screamed into the cushion at her own release. She lay there, almost mindless, shivering and throbbing now and then from the tardy yet delicious spasms in her womb.

When he pulled off her leggings, undid the buckles at her back, and rolled her over, she let him, so limp and exhausted, she could barely raise a shaky hand to wipe the tangle of hair from her face. Theo kissed her softly yet thoroughly.

“There, my love,” he said. “Let’s lie here a while. When you’re ready, we’ll swim.”

He pulled her in close to his side, cradling her in his arms.

Chapter Thirteen

Theo ran his hand along the sweet undulations of Claire's waist and hip before tucking his arm over her and cupping the roundness of her breast. He smiled at the signs of exhaustion—the rise and fall of her chest and the urgent beat of blood at her throat. Underneath her skin, Claire was all woman, and he enjoyed arousing her, but even more so, he loved coaxing her along the path toward submissiveness, her natural inclination, and that she resisted a little, every step of the way, just made it tastier.

Sunlight gilded the tiny soft hairs at her nape. He drifted his fingertips across them just to see her quiver.

"Uh-uh. Don't," she whispered, crunching her neck to escape. "That tickles."

"And this?" He used his teeth on the same spot.

"That, I'd like more of." She curved her neck the other way, exposing it.

He chuckled. "Perhaps later. Are you rested enough for a swim? Can you swim?"

She sighed, hard. "Yes."

"What is it? Hmm? Memories? You've not yet told me enough to satisfy my curiosity."

No answer. He pinched her side, and when she only squirmed, he pinched her nipple, held it.

She jerked, then pawed at him, remaining silent, so he held on longer. Eventually she gave in. “What?

“I need an answer.” He released her nipple.

“We’re not still playing that game?” she said, tersely. “You said that Dankyo would handle this.”

“He can get the details. This is personal. You and me. An answer, Claire. We need to be honest with each other, and I suspect there is a great deal you haven’t told me. But you will. I won’t, can’t, tolerate dishonesty or evasion in an employee or a mistress.”

That brought on another silence. He could almost see her mind ticking over. Stunned, certainly. She hadn’t realized how much he’d guessed. This had to come out sometime.

Still silence. Perhaps a reminder was in order. He shifted his hand, wormed it down between them, found her little nether hole, and inserted the tip of his finger while securing her body with his other arm. “Or do I get to play here, next time we make love?”

She squeaked and wriggled even more. Though, damned be, if he’d ever held anything that wriggled so cutely before. His cock thickened, hardened. He pushed his finger in to the second knuckle, and she stopped moving.

“Is that...natural?” There was a breathless tone to her words.

“Maybe. Are you enjoying that?” Just to check, he slid the finger farther, made his other finger lie along her slit.

"I...I'm not sure," she said quietly, but the twitch of her labia said otherwise.

"Hmm." He nibbled her ear. "We'll definitely have to explore this another time. But it doesn't excuse you from answering."

She sighed. "Am I your...mistress?"

"I hope so. If not, I have no idea who I've been making love to." He maneuvered his lower hand and sneaked a finger into her cleft.

"Oh. Mmm. If this is your idea of torture." Her bottom writhed back. "No. I'm sorry. Theo..." She swallowed, and his heart skipped a beat. This was the second time she'd said his name without prompting. "Swimming reminds me of training. I learned how to use a knife and fight in water. Things like that." She shuddered. "I don't like remembering. I don't like killing."

"And have you killed?" He found he'd held his breath.

"Once. They made us kill a prisoner each. Said it would harden us, make us stronger in combat." Another shudder. "I threw up after. Do I have to talk about this?"

"No." She'd said enough to make him wonder at what, exactly, her employers were aiming at. The training was extreme for mere bodyguards.

She'd said *in combat*, which seemed a little askew from being a bodyguard. He filed it away. *Perhaps that avenue of investigation could stand further probing.* The thought brought him back to the present and where his fingers were embedded.

"Find something else to tell me. Something pleasant about your past." He couldn't resist moving his fingers again, down below. It mightn't have quite been appropriate considering what she'd just said, but it worked in distracting her. He figured she needed diverting as much as he did.

"You had a childhood, Claire? Surely they didn't deny you that."

CLAIRE STAYED QUIET a moment as she felt his fingers stroke inside her. This felt odd, even uncomfortable, yet combined with everything else he did, it triggered ripples of heat.

"My childhood. We're made to be about the same as an eight-year-old human," she said, opening her legs an inch and letting her eyes drift to half-closed. "Does that shock you?"

"No. I knew this. Our country has studied the making of, uh, the birth of, frankenstructs for some time."

"Birth?" She spat the word. She heard the hiss of exhalation from Theo. He withdrew his fingers. *Ah, now that was a pity.*

"You'd rather another word, Claire? Words are just words. How we use them makes them what they are. And I say, you were born. Your childhood?"

She shrugged, wondering what he hoped to gain from this. "Rarely, they let us run about the compound or play ball. The training runs outside were fun but not like the children's games in those books you gave me." She paused. "Is it really like that, all the time, for children?"

"Not all the time," he murmured. "But that someone is doing this deliberately to frankenstructs, simply to train you to do what they want..."

She turned her head and looked into those near transparent pupils, saw sadness there, and put up her hand to touch his cheek. "Thank you, Theo."

He raised those thick eyebrows, questioning her.

"For being so...nice."

"Nice?" His voice deepened to a sensuous baritone. "Nice is for men who wear frothy pink shirts and makeup." He smacked the side of her bottom, hard, and she jumped. "Come. Time to swim."

Naked, wading into the river, surrounded by reeds and water lilies, with the morning sun glinting off the ripples of water, and Theo by her side—it was beautiful enough to make Claire wonder, Why am I here?

Upon diving beneath the water, she saw the line between blue sky and the cold realm of rounded rock and drifting weed, submerged tree root and fish—it seemed to spell out the transformation of her life. *Why indeed. Why does Theo bother with me?*

The other side to it, she thought, as she parted the cool waters with her skin, was to speculate what would happen when Theo suddenly decided she was no longer interesting. She had nothing to offer, except her body. No matter how much she willed it otherwise. It couldn't last, could it?

Then why did it feel so genuine when he told her he wanted her as his mistress?

For a human, perhaps, it would mean little. A mistress wasn't forever. To her, it was a world of difference from "slave." The word made her someone of consequence, who mattered. Girlfriend, wife, fiancée, betrothed—any of them were wonderful because they all said she was a part of his world.

Yet humans are fickle. I know that too, and being a part of his world is no longer enough. I think...I know, I want forever.

More likely for the wind to always blow in one direction than for her to remain a part of Theo's heart.

She did a swirling kick to roll and swoop toward him.

Enjoy. Stop worrying. What else can I do?

She blew bubbles in the cold water, surfacing near him, gasping for air. Hugging her from behind, Theo's arms enfolded her below her breasts—hard, muscular arms. She felt across his biceps. Every muscle was delineated like a diagram from a book. No matter how much exercise she did, she never quite changed into this. His body pressed against her, and she laid her head back. Though their skin had grown cool, his breath warmed her cheek.

"What a lovely armful you are."

"I could say the same." She stretched back and ran her hand down his side. "I love the way you feel too." She heaved a sigh. "The way you hold me."

"Ahh. That's some confession—from you, Miss Blabbermouth. Maybe if I tickle you some more, I'll get even more out of you."

She giggled and slipped down through his arms. With a kick of her heels she dived away.

"Hey! Come back!"

For a while they chased each other through and under the water, until he cornered her in some reeds and forced a wet, slobbery kiss on her. It made her giggle even more. They ended up lying side by side in the shallows, just holding hands and looking at the clouds drifting past overhead.

Theo pulled himself upright and sloshed toward the embankment.

"Swim's over!"

"Oh."

Rising from the water, she found Theo staring at her. Feet sunk into the shallows, he stood straight and apparently unaware of how much he affected her. All that chiseled muscle, those broad thighs beckoning her to lay a hand on him, and, oh dear, the ridges of his stomach leading the eye down to look at his groin—

"A river goddess," he said, smiling. "Where have you come from? What have I done to deserve you?"

She blinked, then shook off some of the water dripping from her nose and eyelashes. A goddess? Embarrassed, she bowed her head.

"I'm the one who should be asking that." She gathered a rope of her hair and wrung it out.

"Never."

That struck like a spear into her middle.

Happiness wasn't normal for her. That one extra comment, it hit and tipped over the pile of compliments and joy that had been building up for hours. Too much, too soon. She felt sick. Deep inside a black mess of insecurities and anguish waited to boil over. Too damn much.

She wished she could go back to how she'd felt only moments before. Glumly, she turned from him.

"Claire?"

She picked her way back up the bank, the rounded rocks slipping underfoot. From the looks of the sun it must be midmorning. She barely hesitated before aiming for the pile of clothing.

"Claire, don't turn from me. Perhaps it's time to remind you of my rules of politeness." His words seethed with threat.

A distant crackle drew her attention. She slipped automatically into the alert state training had drummed into her—scanning the shadows under the trees a few yards away, listening. The revolver was holstered in Theo's belt at her feet. She bent, scooped up the belt, and nestled her hand on the butt. The gun slid out easily. A nice weight. It would kick up and back when fired.

"There's nothing here." Theo stalked up behind her. "My men have been through here hours ago. If you've seen a footprint, it'll be one of theirs."

"No," she murmured, still checking the perimeter. "Not a footprint." *Something is out there and running. Maybe coming this way.*

The loud crunching and rustling of something big moving fast came from the right, where the shrubs were barely four yards away.

She kicked into sharp time. The sound of Theo's next words slurred and stretched. A black bear burst from the tree line, heading straight for them. Droplets of sprayed blood glistened, falling slowly, like red diamonds frozen in the sun. The bear was wounded and angry.

A bullet might stop it quickly, or it might keep coming and shred them both before it died.

"Get back," she yelled to Theo. She aimed at the head—*Damn, I hate killing it*—then shifted and hit the foreleg. The impact spun the leg back and out before the bear compensated and came on, limping and even angrier. She side-stepped fast, then danced about wildly with her hands waving. "Hey! Here, stupid!"

Too heavy to shift direction quickly, it lumbered round, swung its head her way, and came for her, eyes gleaming. Yes, one very angry bear. Claire took off, sprinting, toes digging into dirt. *It's coming*! She could hear Theo bellowing. *Ignore him. Mustn't get too far ahead, or the bear'll turn back.*

A yard from plunging into the cool shadows of the forest, she heard a boom—echoing in sharp time like a cannon fired in small room. The high shriek of the bear followed, then two more shots, and silence except for the stamp of human footsteps from the forest and the burble of the dying exhalation of the bear.

One of Theo's house guards, rifle in hand, jogged from the trees near where the bear had burst forth. She strode to him, sharp time bleeding away—her steps slowing to normal. When she grabbed at a handful of lapel, his meaty hand intercepted hers and crushed her fingers, tried to twist her arm.

Another guard came up behind her. She ignored him. This one was the idiot.

"Why?" she asked him, attempting to shake him by the shirt despite the pain in her fingers. "You fool! I had it chasing me! Why'd you kill it?" She glanced away, saw Theo coming, and the bear's bloody corpse on the ground.

"Stop." The second guard reached under, taking advantage of her distraction to bend her wrist, aiming for an arm lock. "Let him go. Put down the gun."

"Frick!" *Dankyo.* She knew that controlled voice and the arm pressing on her. Theo was fit, but Dankyo felt like he'd been packed with muscle under high pressure. She growled and thought hard about *not* doing something seriously painful to him.

Succeeded, just. Instead she spoke through her teeth. "Release me."

He pushed and twisted; then her counter move was efficiently thwarted by his.

"Gah!" The pressure made her bend forward as her arm rode up her back. He levered the gun from her other hand. Absurdly, she felt pleased at the level of his training. Her own inattention had gotten her in this position—well, the bear had distracted her. A poor excuse, though.

Now, she suddenly became acutely aware, she was bent over naked in front of the guard and Dankyo. She shut her eyes, groaning in embarrassment when sounds from behind told her another two guards had arrived.

"Let her go, Dankyo!" Theo snapped. "Claire is not a threat!"

"She threatened Ericson, sir, and she had a gun in her other hand."

"Understood. Her own actions were wrong, and I will be explaining that to her. But she is not a danger. At all. I expect you to remember that."

"Yes, sir."

Her arm released, Claire brought it to her front, grunting at the discomfort.

"Here." Theo draped his coat around her, hugged her to his chest, soothing the ache in her shoulder with massaging fingers. "Now apologize to Ericson, please, Claire. And to Dankyo."

She fumed and said nothing. He waited a few seconds, then directed the guards. "Thank you for your help, all of you, but now return to your posts. Ericson, I apologize on behalf of Claire. She's a little ruffled right now."

With the stabs in her shoulder muscles subsiding to dull throbs, Claire relaxed into Theo's hold, snuggling up against him. She'd never tire of this, of his warmth and masculine aroma—even after the swim it remained to tantalize her. Her black mood was gone, burned away by the violence. She just wanted him. They stayed that way for a while, comforting each other.

His grip tightened. "Don't you *ever* do that again! I know what you did, trying to draw the bear away from me. Why?"

She shrugged. "I didn't want to kill it. I'm fast. I could have gotten it to chase me, then doubled back or climbed a tree."

"It was foolhardy. Next time, if there is one, let me have the gun. I won't hesitate. I doubt either of us wants to stay here with the bear. We'll return to the manor." He let her go.

She looked up at him. "You didn't tell me you had a cordon around us. All that time. They might have been watching!" She shook her head. "Dankyo even. I would never have—"

"What? Made love like you did? I told them to not watch the clearing, though considering the attraction..." He reached under the jacket, curved his hand under her breast. "Some of them may have watched, or heard your rather loud screaming. At least they'll know you're not a danger to me."

"Not Dankyo," she said tersely, remembering the way he'd twisted her arm. He'd still thought her a danger. *Screaming? Oh Lord, I did, didn't I?*

"Hmm, I don't know." Theo waggled his eyebrows. "You didn't see the look on his face when he had you bent over with your ass up."

"What! Oh!" She huffed. Dankyo had looked at her? At her bottom? She wished fervently she'd given the man a heart attack. "I'm getting my clothes on."

Having dried themselves with towels from the basket, they dressed quickly, packed the picnic gear, and hauled it back to the gyrocopter.

The bear lay where he'd fallen. A male. Unusually aggressive or maybe wounded after encountering one of the house guards? What did it matter now? He was dead, crumpled like a big furry toy. Flies had arrived, buzzing in a sociable crowd near the wound. Blood leaked onto the grass at his chest. *Hell and damnation. She'd never have made a good assassin anyway.*

After stuffing the last cushion in the gyrocopter, she turned to find Theo observing her with arms folded.

"Yes?"

"I haven't forgotten. There are two issues of disobedience to be dealt with when we get back. And this time, there's no excuse." That said, he climbed into the pilot's seat, leaving her puzzling over what, exactly, he'd meant.

Chapter Fourteen

The ride back seemed swifter, but she made sure to mark the distance and direction of the crash site when they passed to the south of it. Soon the manor lay beneath them. From above it was clearly U-shaped with two equal wings attached to the main section—the landing pad sticking out from the upper story like a gigantic tongue. The red armored balloon of the *Final Rebuttal* challenged the manor for size—equal in width if not in length.

Shadowing them from a half mile away was another gyrocopter. She eyed it sourly. Dankyo would be on that one. Maybe it could crash. She was going to have to have it out with him sometime. She'd get it through his head that she wasn't to be messed with.

On the flat rooftop of the manor, multibarrel cannon emplacements covered the approaches to the mansion. If war broke out, the property could be defended long enough to pose difficulties for the enemy. She noted where a small copse of trees would block off the overlapping arcs of fire. Perhaps Dankyo wasn't as infallible as he seemed to be.

Theo steered toward the landing pad. The *thwop-thwop* of the blades had barely dwindled to silence before Theo had hopped down and loped halfway to the doorway. A senior house guard stood there, and the two of them continued on together, discussing something. She thought better of intruding, instead pulling out the basket and carrying it inside. Theo waited in the bedroom.

"Theo?"

"I'll arrange for brunch in the inner study. Meet me in half an hour. There's an array of dresses ready for you in there." He indicated the long Gallic carved wardrobe on the far wall, then tipped her chin up with his fingers.

"Pick a nice short one. No leather this time."

Claire smiled nervously back. Something about his searching gaze bothered her. A little knot twisted in her stomach. Had he been serious about this punishment? She guessed she had agreed to follow his orders, but common sense should prevail. She'd been right. The other—Ericson—oh, heck, that was it, wasn't it? Frick.

One of the guards at Theo's door insisted on escorting her to the inner study. As she went through the outer study, that same jagged memory returned—tied hand and foot, scared and miserable. So different now, yet that could be her in a moment if she stepped wrong.

Ah, what am I to do? Every time Theo questioned her the urge to confess grew more terrible, as did the dread that he would discover her falsehood. Slowly, surely, he was picking apart her past. She should never have told him about Inkline.

She ran a hand through her hair. It had dried on the flight back. While she waited for the guard, who fumbled to unlock the inner study's door, she pulled her hair back into a rough chignon, sorted the hairpins she'd brought. On the dresser next to Theo's bed had been a bowl with four hairpins. One end was an enameled black and gold bee; the other end was pointed. Weapons, really. She weighed the last one in her hand before reaching back and thrusting it through her hair.

The door swung open, and she strolled through at the ushering of the guard. Left alone in the room, with the door shut softly behind her, Claire stood there amazed.

Books—more than she'd ever thought possible in one place. Timber shelves rose on the walls to her left, all the way to a high ceiling. On her right was a glassed wall that looked out onto a conservatorium awash with greenery and flowers. The sweet perfume of pollen invaded this inner study.

On the wall opposite the door, behind a long sofa, black-and-white lithographs hung in a row. More art? She walked across the white tiled floor, threading past a low table and two ochre sofas. The figures resolved into naked women. *My God.* She gaped. Even alone as she was, the sight drew warmth to her cheeks. She stared.

Drawn with an artist's hand, the pictures showed women intricately bound with ropes, in all manner of positions, some joined by men lording over them with whips and more ropes in their hands. In the last two lithographs, the man had the woman tied hand to ankle while he, as clear as day, made love to her. That someone would draw such a thing—

She leaned over to examine the detail and heard the sound of the doorknob turning.

By the time she'd spun on her heel, the door had closed. The skirt of her white *broderie anglaise* dress swirled and settled light as rain on her upper thighs.

In fresh brown linen shirt and black trousers, Theo walked over. His gaze went from her to the lithographs and back. "Which one is your favorite?"

As if I'd have a favorite! She couldn't meet the intensity in his eyes, shook her head the smallest amount. "I—" Frowning, she gestured at the artworks. "Why would anyone—I mean—" Unsure as to what she *did* mean, she fell silent.

He tossed something onto the sofa, then wrapped his arms around her as he leaned against the back of the sofa. His chin rested atop her head.

"Why would anyone do this? Because they enjoy it greatly. The women as well as the men."

"Hmph." She couldn't help seeing the details—the way the ropes emphasized anatomy, the rapt expression on the face of the woman being made love to—couldn't help imagining herself in that position with Theo. A tremor ran through her. She felt the warmth of his breath through her hair. Confused—she didn't want to do this sort of thing, surely? It was too close to real life, to what Inkline had done. He'd kept her bound in that chair for the whole day while he inflicted pain on her, and there'd been nothing she could do about it.

Getting her head around the fact that these women had wanted this... So strange.

"Not so different from what I did to you earlier," he murmured and kissed her hair.

The hardness of him against her buttocks and the sensual warmth creeping up on her confused her even more. Was she wanting this? To be tied up? She swallowed.

"No. It's different. I doubt I'd like it. These drawings are a fantasy. Looking at them—"

"They're all drawn from life. The artist is well-known to me." Theo's hand glided up her thigh and under the skirt of her dress, found the edge of her underwear, and a moment later, his blunt finger drew along her wet cleft. "Looking at them seems to make you wet. Perhaps you're lying, love?"

If she admitted anything, he'd want to do this. Quelling the need to take quicker breaths, she said, "No, I'm being truthful. It's just you, next to me."

"Really? I doubt that. I'm going to deal with the other matters I spoke of, and then, you are going to tell me the truth."

She made to rise from his lap but found he still held his arm tight beneath her breasts. "What other matters?"

"One. You walked away from me at the river. You attacked Ericson without cause. He was doing his job, and one or both of you could have been injured seriously. You refused to apologize to him or to Dankyo when I asked you. I will never allow that behavior again. Both are examples of rudeness and require punishment. Two. You denied a direct order from Dankyo, my second in command."

"Punishment?" This was sounding more and more like Inkline. "Let me go!"

Theo chuckled, snagged both her wrists, and drew them behind her. She froze in place, her chest heaving. Sharp time would get her free—let her read every single one of his reactions. If she wriggled her wrists the right way, microsecond by microsecond, she'd get free. But did she want to go that route? *No. An awful idea.* It would destroy everything. He'd never trust her again.

"Claire, do you agree you were rude, impulsive, endangered yourself and Ericson?"

The switch of tactic made her think. He wasn't going on about Dankyo. Thank God. He'd been plain nasty, and she'd not budge on that one. Her body betrayed her, as she recalled the way she'd been held while they made love at the river. That made it difficult to think. She licked her lips, tried not to be conscious of his erection.

"Was I rude? And, everything else?" Her words came out squeaky. She cleared her throat, hung her head. "Yes, I suppose I was. A bit. I'm sorry. There. Is that what you wanted? I'm sorry."

"It's a start," he said in a mellow baritone. "You have a choice." He released her, and she moved away, wide-eyed, her wrists stinging. "See this?" He reached over the back of the sofa and brought up what he'd dropped there—a round leather paddle with holes in it and the black corset.

"Uh-huh." She went round the other side of the sofa. One of the lithographs featured a woman being hit by one of those.

"Choose." Theo said grimly. "This, or you get to wear the corset all day under that dress." Now his eyes were twinkling.

"This amuses you?" She said it slowly.

"Oh yes." He came round the end of the sofa, paddle still in hand. Warily, she backed away. "Why not? Spanking your little bottom while I bend you over the sofa..." His mouth curved in a wicked half smile. She took another step back. "Stand still, Claire, while we talk. If you make me chase you, I will make this public, and *that*, I guarantee, will not please either of us."

She stopped, let him come up to her.

"So. Which is it to be? Ten strokes of this?" He jiggled the paddle. "Or wear the corset? You're accompanying me on a tour of the remaining outlying buildings after brunch." He cocked his head, raised an eyebrow.

How was the corset punishment? And then she recalled how it had affected her, wondered what she'd do in public, wearing it. She blushed. It was entirely possible, after ten or twenty minutes of that *friction* between her legs...that she'd come. A mortifying thought.

Theo stretched out, ran his finger lightly over her lips, brushed back some straying hair. "Having second thoughts? Perhaps, you'd like to see what one stroke feels like and then decide?"

Clearly, he wasn't going to budge on this. It couldn't be that bad. She'd had a knife slash in training, bruising from sparring. Though she had an inkling Theo would make the ten strokes take ages if she volunteered.

"No permanent injury?" she asked nervously.

"No. Of course not. Pain, yes. Well?"

"One then. Only, then I'll...see."

He nodded. "Pull down your underwear, bend over, and grab your ankles. Keep your knees a little bent to help you balance. Do not move, or I'll have to repeat the stroke."

"I thought—" She gestured at the sofa.

"No. I think this way is better. I get to see more of your pretty ass."

She looked at him, then down at her feet. Why was she obeying him in this? Couldn't she just walk away? She sighed. No. She couldn't, didn't want to really. Because he'd made it clear if she wanted to stay, she had to obey his rules. So, she'd bent a couple of them, and this was the result. Damnation, she wanted to stay.

Slowly she edged down her underwear, let them slip to the floor, then bent and grasped her ankles, staring at the brown pumps on her feet, waiting, biting her lip, wondering when he would—

The paddle slammed into her, hard enough to make her teeth slide and chatter. The vibration shot through her body as if she'd been shaken by a storm. A fraction of a second later, in its aftermath, her bottom stung like all hell, and heat flared, her lower body throbbing. She gasped and almost straightened. He'd said not to move. She glanced back at him, past her legs, her bottom up in the air.

Theo said nothing. Only watched and waited.

This, she suddenly realized, was as sexually arousing as anything could be without actually touching. The throb from her bottom heightened the pleasure. For a man to be watching while she did this... If she said nothing, would he paddle her again? Her mouth went dry. Fear awakened. No, she didn't want to go this route. Not pain. Besides, she felt sure Theo enjoyed wielding that paddle, and she wasn't going to give him the satisfaction.

"The corset," she muttered, her head feeling like an inflating balloon from all the blood pooling in it. "I'd rather that."

At least this way she'd be the only one feeling pleasure, and she could limit her reaction to a piece of clothing. With the paddle, Theo controlled her.

Theo nodded. He tossed the paddle onto the sofa.

NOT A SURPRISE she'd chosen the corset. He hadn't thought Claire ready to find enjoyment in pain. The potential was there, though. She'd liked it to a degree, despite her fear. The main aim of this was to impress on her his seriousness regarding her attitude to him and everyone around him, and one smack had achieved that aim—though the sight of her white posterior raised up high would never grow tiring. He stopped himself smiling.

He thought back to the reason for this. The sight of her attempting to shake Ericson, as if a man almost twice her weight were shakable, had been an eye-opener.

By only wounding that bear, she'd risked her life, and all because she didn't want to kill. They'd made her murder someone…and for what? Accustoming her to death? Mind-boggling. If he could have erased that awful memory, he would have.

Still, you were the sum of your past. Without that she'd be someone different. A someone who, perhaps, wouldn't have been appalled at the death of a bear. He'd wanted to grab her and cuddle her when he'd seen that. She was getting to be an addiction for him, far more than any other woman.

He folded his arms and tried to look stern.

The corset, despite what he'd told her, wasn't really a punishment. Not…exactly. The afternoon should prove interesting.

Efficiently, as if it were some boring task, Claire pulled her dress over her head, breasts bouncing enticingly as the bodice caught under them. Her nipples, pink-brown and soft, peaked as she caught him looking. "I think you need a hand," he rumbled, scooping up the corset.

"Um, I can do this."

Her upset tone made him hold the corset up high, so she'd have to stretch to reach it.

"Theo—"

"Yes?"

She sighed and shut her eyes a moment before looking at him. "Very well."

He tilted his head, wanting to see if she'd get the hint. "Hmm?"

Her brow wrinkled for a second. "Please, help me put it on."

He smiled. "Ahh. That's much better."

On bended knee, he helped her put each foot into the corset and draw it up over the long curves of calf and thigh, his hands drifting up her body, smoothing twisted pearls and cloth at bottom, waist, and breast, clipping the catch shut at her nape, and, naturally, nibbling his way up the slope of her neck. How he adored her neck. By that time, she was leaning back into him, her hand over his at her crotch, breathing fast... He could listen all day to her panting and moaning his name. But...no. He released her, stepping aside after making sure she was balanced.

"Put on your dress, Claire. Let's eat something." He smacked her on the red side of her bottom, grinned at the shock on her face.

Quickly, she slipped the dress over her head and adjusted the bodice. The pearls at her neckline were barely visible.

He'd not told her of the punishment for refusing Dankyo's order. If anything, that was the most important part. He couldn't afford this wedge she was driving between him and Dankyo. The business needed settling as soon as possible. But one thing at a time.

Chapter Fifteen

Theo swept his arm across, pointing out structures one by one. "Engineering and Vehicle Depot, the firing range, barracks. We'll go there first. Get your apology to Ericson and Blackman out of the way."

"Blackman?"

"The man you stabbed with a knitting needle." Theo started whistling, off-tune but cheerful.

"I see. I didn't know I owed him one. But yes, guess I do." The dress had a small bustle at the rear, with a broad bow tied over it. Apart from that and a little fussiness of satin ribbon about the bodice, the dress fabric barely registered on her skin—light and shifting easily as dandelions in a breeze. If it flipped up, *everything* would be on display—the rope of pearls running between her legs and worse things—for the farther they walked, the wetter she became. Impossible not to feel, yet she gritted her teeth and tried to ignore it.

"Uh." She nearly squeaked as a little jolt ran through her.

Beside her, Theo ambled, unconcerned and stopping to chat with staff.

She set her shoulders. Be damned if he'd get to her. She could do this, easily, to the end of the day; *then* she'd get this off and maybe ignore him for a little while...before she succumbed to his advances. If the last day was anything to judge by, he'd want to make love to her. *Mmm.*

He'd bent her over and put his fingers down there.

Her pussy ached like never before. Right, maybe *not* so easy. She sighed loudly.

"Something bothering you, dear?" Theo asked politely.

If she could have fried him on the spot with her eyes, she would have, but only for a moment; then the hard set to Theo's mouth reminded her of the alternative to wearing this thing—the paddle. "No," she said super sweetly. "Nothing."

"Hmm." He smiled back.

If I get aroused, so will he, surely. Maybe two can play this game? Maybe I can tease him?

Inside the barracks entrance, bunks lined the wall to the left. On the right, a man introduced as Dankyo's next in command waited before a squad of ten house guards.

First in line were Blackman and Ericson. Their faces like stone, they accepted her apologies, replying gruffly, "Thank you, Miss!"

In the midst of such a stronghold of masculinity, she felt exposed. *Silly.* As if the men could know what she had on under her dress. Yet, the scent of lust and sweat seemed to carry on the air.

Barely past lunchtime and just standing still, breathing in and out, made her focus on her clit. She could map the whereabouts of every pearl down there.

"Dear," Theo said quietly, taking her elbow, "you've been standing there staring at your feet for a long time. Let's move on."

Luckily the guards had been dismissed. She bit her lip, hoping they'd not seen her distraction.

Concentrating, she wrestled her feelings to the background. The Vehicle Depot was next.

The largest of all the outer buildings, the House Engineer's Vehicle Depot boasted double sliding doors of burnished steel. While waiting at Theo's side, she murmured hoarsely, "When I get this off, you're wearing it."

The doors parted by a few feet.

"Wouldn't fit me, Claire." Hand at her back, he urged her into the gap.

Landships. Two of them. Riveted steel and brass, wheels and track, stumpy funnels at the top and a large cannon swiveling in a turret at the front. *Wow.*

This place was almost on a war footing. The proximity to the border—that must be it. Theo's estate housed a quick reaction force.

A spare, tall man with gray cropped hair and a friendly face leaped down from a raised platform to the left. Past his shoulder, she saw a row of windows into a workshop. The smell of oil, boosted coal, and sulfur assailed her nose.

"Welcome, sir! And Miss!" The man advanced with his hand held out to be shaken.

“This is Henry Twine.” Theo shook Henry’s hand.

When Henry took both Claire’s hands between his, it was like being engulfed by a manic shaking machine. “Glad to meet you, Miss. What do ya think of my ladies? Delilah and Kate?”

“The landships?” She held out her hands, opening and closing them, trying to think of a compliment. “Big? Really big.” They were, at that. “Is that a Hotchkinn six-inch cannon?”

That froze him. “A six—you do know your guns, Miss. It is indeed!”

With little encouragement he showed off his ladies, pointing out features to Claire on the outside and climbing up the side of *Delilah* to lean in the square turret hole at the top. Keeping her legs together, she followed Theo up the rungs on the side.

“That down there’s the driver’s position,” Harry said. “Gunner. Navigator. Commander.”

“Let’s take her for a run,” Theo said.

“Of course, sir!”

Showed to the gunner’s seat in the bowels of the landship, Claire settled in while the engine fired up. Theo reclined in the driver’s seat. Henry raised the navigator’s periscope and shouted directions.

The rear depot doors had been fully cranked back, and the steam voltaic engine opened up to the maximum grinding speed of six knots. Sunlight flooded in through the overhead turret hatch as the vehicle growled out under the open sky.

Claire barely registered the meaning of Henry’s words or the changing of the light, for the rumbling vibrations of the landship motor had penetrated up through her metal seat and turned her lower body into orgasmic jelly.

Her nostrils widened, the metal walls dimmed to a blur, and the pearls jiggled like living creatures against her clit. Every sexual place in her body trembled with delight. She shut her eyes, clamped her mouth shut, and seconds later, came—nerves quivering, whimpering at the explosive release. All around her vanished in a seething wall of white.

Luckily, the cacophony of the engine disguised her noises. By the time *Delilah* cruised to a shuddering halt inside the depot, she was quivering yet again, despite sitting, most of the time, with her bottom an inch above the metal.

"You go first," Theo told Henry, and the man clambered up the ladder and could be heard jumping down outside. "Was that nice?" he whispered to Claire.

"Did you do that deliberately?" she whispered back, trying not to sound like a harpy.

No answer.

Fuming, she had a foot on the first rung of the ladder when Theo slid his hand under her dress and up the back of her thigh.

"Like a hand?" he said softly, as his fingers continued on, gliding along her wet folds, until two of them slipped up inside.

Impaled, she paused, her inner muscles tightening around his fingers. "Oh." She couldn't move. *Mmm.*

By moving his hand back, while still inside her, he reeled her to him. If she'd stayed still, his fingers would have come out. She didn't want that. She let herself step from the ladder and be shuffled back until her body met the hard muscles of his chest. Despite the residual of her anger, the way he surrounded her made her yearn to sink into his warmth and let the rich scent of cologne and man soak into every pore in her skin.

THEO PUT HIS arm across under her breasts and held her to him. "I love seeing you aroused, though no, it didn't occur to me that riding in Delilah would make you come. It wasn't supposed to." He brushed his lips along her neck, delighted when the little hairs stood up in goose bumps and pinkness suffused her skin. "I'll make sure to write it into my memory under things to be repeated."

He raised his voice. "Henry, go on back to your work. We'll be here awhile!"

"Yessir!"

"Won't he think—" she said weakly.

"Shh. Never mind Henry. I employ him, and I assure you he won't mind if we stay and examine Delilah a bit longer...or even if I sit you down on one of these seats and make you have a dozen orgasms."

"But, he'll know what we're doing," she said, mouselike, trembling.

He laughed and nuzzled into her hair, enjoying the simple perfume of soap and woman. Her subjugation...it stirred him far more than any of the bored aristocratic ladies who'd volunteered in the past. He could have taken her right then and there, bent her over the seat, but no, not yet. She didn't have everything sorted out in her head. He'd push her boundaries and truly see where she wanted to go.

"Perhaps, but he's not here. Why are you angry?"

When she didn't answer immediately, he removed his fingers, brought his hand around to the front of her thigh, then slid them back in, making her wriggle. This time his thumb could reach her clit, and he tapped it once.

"Ooh." Her breath caught. "You know," she said grumpily, "it's hard to think when you do that."

"Then I'll stop." And he did, only to have her press her mound up against his hand. "Uh-uh. You complained. Sit still." Pleasingly, she did, though her thighs trembled. "Now, what's bothering you?"

She swallowed. "This, it's not punishment exactly, is it? I mean, I feel like you're just showing me off as your newest toy. Your sexual plaything."

"You're not a toy, Claire. I don't want to demean you. But your sexuality, it's part of you. You're a woman with a body that makes me dream up new things to do to it every time I see you, whether naked"—he gently curled his fingers inside her—"or clothed."

"Everyone will think...bad things. This isn't what well-bred men and women do in public. It's because I'm a frankenstruct, isn't it?"

"Ahh, it's society's expectations that anger you then. You do realize you've lumped me in with the poorly bred?" He grunted. "Look. My sexual tastes are well known. I've had women in my bed before, some of them aristocrats. I treated them the same way. Will anyone here think the worst of you? No. I've always found it simpler to have staff about me who don't have any problems with such things.

"Besides, I'm taking great care not to let anyone really know what is happening here. Right now, it's me and you and whatever I decide to do to you."

The heartbeat under his forearm sped up.

"No ropes, remember?"

A challenge. Definitely time to see where the line was drawn. If she yielded, good. If not, he'd know where he stood. He closed his eyes to better appreciate the fresh scent of her hair. He'd be sorry when this ended. Sexual liaisons never lasted, not in his experience.

"It's time to take your education a little further, my dear."

He insinuated another finger around the string of pearls between her legs and felt her sharp intake of breath as he nudged her clit. The pearls slipped in her juices as his fingers thrust in and out.

"Theo. Not here!" She choked out the words. Her muscles twitched. He knew she strained not to curve her back and subtly increased the rhythm.

"Oh, yes. Here." At last, she arched into his palm. "Your lips need kissing." So swollen, so begging for a kiss, a pretty red. A bead of sweat trickled down her temple. He sucked her lower lip into his mouth between his teeth, caressing with his tongue. His cock twitched as a little groan escaped her, vibrating from her throat. "Now this," he murmured. His free hand dipped into a pocket, then sought out her wrist. Before she could resist, he put a loop of thin rope around it.

"No. I don't think so." She pulled her mouth away. Frowning, she shook her head. "No."

He released her except for the end of the rope, took his fingers from inside her, the liquid suction from her vaginal muscles dragging at them. A quiet "oh" escaped her.

Then, shivering, she got as far from him as she could inside the cabin of the landship, until only the short section of rope connected them—wrist to hand.

Her face was red-tinged, her eyes wild and widened. Blonde strands draped her face, like the bars of a cage with her an animal looking out.

"Give me your other wrist, Claire."

"No," she said through gritted teeth.

He stopped. The signals from her body said terror. He didn't want that. Yet she'd not said her safe word.

* * * *

Claire strained away. The loop tightened on her wrist, scraping her skin. She wasn't thinking straight and knew it. Rope, the idea of it wrapping her up tight, sent shrieks of panic along her nerves.

"Do you trust me?" Theo asked, those gray eyes weighing her up.

Did she? "Yes. But—"

He sighed. "But not with this. You're too frightened. Say your safe word. You need to remember that."

"Kokino," she muttered, knowing she was as angry at herself as at him. *Stupid, stupid word.* "I'm taking this off."

"No. Let me. Come here." He snapped his fingers.

The command went to her legs before her mind, and she took two steps.

"Good."

The praise calmed her and let her call up her mantras. Breathe slow, assess the situation, then act. Only she faltered at the first step. How could she slow her breaths when she stood next to him? His warm hands slipped the rope loose. His calluses brushed her skin—those of a man of force and action. She couldn't get enough of being handled by him, and shuddered at the rekindling of sensations. She hated denying him—yet rope…no, not that.

"You've liked everything else we've done together, yes?"

She nodded.

"Then, if you trust me, turn around, Claire." He kissed the top of her head.

She turned, felt him fuss with the bustle.

"An experiment. This isn't rope, so I expect you to be utterly still." He growled that and nipped her shoulder through the dress, making her gasp. Swiftly, he captured her wrists and pulled them behind her. She resisted the urge to rip them away. Not rope. Last time, at the river, the reward had been rapturous. Cloth wrapped around her wrists, tying them together. He must have untied the bow at the bustle and was using the ribbon. Not rope. *Not* rope.

"Now, that looks lovely. And you're not panicking." He came round to the front, clicked his tongue. "You have a rope phobia. Which means, presumably, I can tie you up with anything else. There's something about seeing a woman bound and helpless."

Claire found her chest heaving. Helpless. The word itself had a wicked ring to it. About the only thing that wrenched at her was not being able to touch Theo or make him touch her. Her nipples hardened and throbbed.

"Is this punishment?" She looked at him through her lashes.

"Ah, yes." He grinned, gripped her chin, kissed her once, hard. "Punishment. Almost forgot."

He popped the row of tiny cloth buttons on the bodice and opened it, exposing her breasts. Leaning down, he pushed aside the pearl strands and sucked on one nipple until the throbbing intensified, then the other, sending burning jolts to her groin. Something metal gripped one nipple and then the other, like tiny teeth closing about them. Wires trailed cold down between her breasts.

After her cowardice in the face of rope, a little bit of metal wasn't making her back away. She hissed through closed teeth. Pain spiked, then faded, and pleasure faded in, faded out.

"That's not so bad. Rather nice really." She managed a half grimace, half smile.

Theo knelt and lifted her dress. "I knew you were the woman for me. But…I haven't finished yet." He kissed her inner thigh.

He reached up under her dress and the corset and pulled the strand down over her stomach, fastened something over her clit, then some small device against her skin of her belly.

She watched him intently. Whatever was he up to? Each of her nipples poked out the center of an areola-sized cogwheel.

Frowning, she went to move...only her wrists were still bound behind her back. A wave shifted in her, connecting *everywhere* in the most pleasant way. Between her legs dampened.

"Let's test this. It should be fully charged." Theo looked up at her. "Ready?"

She eyed him back dubiously. Hands bound, her breasts bare, and some weird contraption wired to her. If she lit up like a chandelier, he'd find out what she could do with her hands and a skinning knife. Or maybe she'd just zap *him* with something.

"Sure."

He let her dress folds fall from where he'd bunched them to her waist and stood. With one hand at the small of her back, the other higher up, he kissed her, bent her backward in an arc.

Well, now, this she could do. She trusted him not to let her fall and let him have his naughty way with her. Surrendering seemed to be something that got easier with practice.

Then...the little cogwheels shifted and bit; the dress fabric and the pearls, caught between Theo's body and hers, rubbed against her clit and bare nipples. Something whirred at her waist...and lightning seized her, a buzzing in little bursts at her breasts and groin that zapped her straight into a mini-inferno of pain and pleasure.

"Mmmh!" she gasped, eyes wide open, and let out a small whine. The landship walls were spinning. "Ah." The inferno died away. Theo made sure she stood balanced and let her go. "What...was that?"

The aftermath left her body humming. If her clit could have talked, it would have begged for more. Excruciating and ecstatic all bundled into one. She couldn't walk around with *this* on.

"Voltaic energy. A small dose. Each time you move it will generate more energy. You'll get used to it. I tested it on myself, and I do believe Henry has outdone himself this time. It's a little random, so you can't quite tell when it'll happen." Smiling, he rubbed at his chin, then held up a finger and circled it. "Turn. I'll untie you."

"Henry? That Henry?" Crazy, maniac Henry? "Untie me then. I'll take this thing off." She turned to let him undo the knots.

"Take it off, Claire, and I'll make you walk about with your hands tied." He reached around and set his fingers to doing up the little buttons on her bodice.

"What?"

"You heard me."

Hungrily, she watched his mouth—those lips just inches away. Go up on her tiptoes, and she could... *No.* Her body wanted him, but after this, no, she'd not clutch at him. Maybe he expected her to. This silly contraption and the corset had her body so high with sensation, floating might be easier than walking.

His mouth was set in a hard line even if his eyes hinted at merriment. She bit her lip. *Right.* Every time she moved, it charged up? She could stand it. If having orgasms was punishment, she'd choose it any time over that paddle. Still—

"Better keep Henry away from me if you want him to live."

"Was that a joke?" Theo chuckled. "It was?"

She tried fixing him with a hard glare, but…it *was* a joke, and she didn't make jokes. Not out loud. A smile sneaked onto her lips. "I'll get my revenge on you both. You just wait."

He leaned in, murmured in her ear. "I like this new feistiness, but don't get your hopes up. You have no idea how inventive Henry and I can be."

She shivered, peeked sideways at him. *This could be bad, in a very exciting, sexy, sort of way.*

On the way to the firing range, the device discharged twice. Each time leaving her body a little more limp, her muscles and sexual parts tingling. Heck, as far as she could tell, the thing had even made her fingertips throb with pleasure. As long as she didn't come in front of anyone…

At the firing range, Dankyo was instructing four house guards in the art of long-range shooting.

Another jolt hit her. She bit her lip and screamed silently, holding herself stiff as that excruciating wave rolled through her. Pleasure. Pain. On the edge of orgasm, though not quite there. That little taste of pain kept it out of reach. She closed her eyes.

Opened them to find no one had noticed. Even Theo ignored her—occupied with talking to a guard about his weapon. Thank the Lord. Her pussy was so wet her pubic hair must be sodden. If she'd been alone, she would have put her hand down there. The ache subsided. She stood very still, careful not to set it off.

A breeze riffled her hair, drying the thin film of sweat on her cheek. She watched the men practicing in the prone position with the rifles spitting out shots at a slow pace. A puff of dust flew off the distant straw-backed targets whenever a projectile hit the mark.

She gnawed on her lip and resisted interfering.

At Theo's suggestion, Dankyo sent the guards off on a training run.

Theo turned to her, put a hand to her back. "Come. We're all going into the indoor range."

She didn't like the sound of this at all.

The indoor range was deserted. At ten, twenty, and fifty yards, there were circular targets. While Dankyo waited at the door—legs shoulder-width apart, hands by his sides, and a bland expression on his face, Theo led her along to the ten-yard line. She stepped slowly, trying not to set off the little engine.

Theo leaned back onto the wall and gathered her to him so she stood between his legs.

Something—the evenness of his brows, the line of his mouth, something told her bad news was coming. "Are you about to tell me something I don't want to hear?"

"Yes. This is the true punishment."

She narrowed her eyes.

He rearranged some hair above her eyes. "The paddle—that I meant. You do have to mend your ways."

"I will—I mean I have."

"Good, but there's one other problem—you and Dankyo. Shh. Wait." He put his finger across her lips. "He's my second in command. You don't respect or trust him, and he doesn't trust you, though I know he has a very healthy respect for your skills." He gripped her with his thighs.

"You are going to bend over and let him smack you once on your bottom."

She felt blood pour into her cheeks and down her neck. "No!" She shot a look at Dankyo. "No! Never. The man hates me."

"You are going to do it, because I know you, and I know him, and this will work."

She shook her head, looking down. "No. Don't ask this. Please."

"Claire. Do you know what would have happened to *any* of the guards if they had done what you did? Struck a fellow guard, endangered others, disobeyed a direct order? You'd be whipped in public. Discharged from the house guard."

"I'm not a house guard." She looked imploringly at Theo.

"No. You're not. You're my mistress, and you're a deadly weapon all rolled into one. And I love you for it. But I can't have you here if you disrespect Dankyo. What is your answer?"

"I don't know. This feels"—she swallowed—"sexual, not like discipline." *"I can't have you here?" No. Oh, hell, no.* This was an order, really. She couldn't stay with Theo if she didn't say yes.

"In a way. It's a dominance thing. A little like with you and me." He cupped her chin. "And I know Dankyo. This will settle you into the pecking order."

"You think? What if he says no?"

"I doubt it. Let's see." He set her on her feet then walked to Dankyo.

She chewed her lip. *Did I say, yes? Oh, hell and heavens and frick. Dankyo is going to smack my bottom. Only once, though. Once...isn't that bad. No underwear. Frick again.*

The two of them strolled back to her. She could see in the way Dankyo looked at her that he'd said yes. No smugness there; that was good. Curiosity? She pulled herself up straighter, taller, and returned Dankyo's appraisal.

Theo studied them both. "Let's get this done. After this, I expect both of you to be civil to each other. I expect you, Claire, to respect Dankyo as my leading officer and head of security. And, Dankyo, I expect you to trust that Claire is who she says she is and can be trusted. Yes?"

Dankyo inclined his head. Theo looked at her, raised his eyebrows.

"Yes," she said a tad hoarsely. Though, of course, a little voice spoke up. *You're not that, though—not who you say you are.*

"Turn around, dear. Put your hands on your knees."

She shut her eyes once, opened them, then turned and bent over with her hands braced on her knees. When Theo gently folded up her dress and bared her bottom, she flinched. She had her knees tight together. There was nothing to see, just bottom. Dankyo wouldn't get much joy from that, would he?

For the first time Dankyo said something. "One hit only, sir, with the flat of my hand?"

"Yes. Not too hard."

"Of course, sir. May I say something, sir?"

"Yes. What is it?"

"Thank you, sir."

Thank you? Oh that *was* smug!

He hit her, palm slamming down, and it hurt like blazes.

"Uh!" Eyes watering, she couldn't help saying, with a touch of annoyance, "Done?"

Silence. Then she recognized from the sound and a glimpse of clothing that Theo had stepped to the side.

She almost sprang upright only to find Dankyo had his hand on her back. To stand, or not? Wasn't this done with? The lack of reply to her question stirred thought. *No.* Disapproval radiated from Theo. *Damn.* She stayed in position. Dankyo's hand rested across the burning area on her bottom. So hard to not squirm away. Embarrassing. Intolerable. He'd be looking at her bottom like it was a target, and maybe at where the line of pearls disappeared between her cheeks.

And, oh… Realization dawned.

This was meant to impress on them both their respective places? She hadn't let it, though, had she? And they knew that. She gritted her teeth, clawed her fingers into her knees. "I'm sorry."

"Two more, Dankyo. Please. Ready, Claire?"

If Theo wanted her to do this...she had to give to Dankyo a little of what she allowed Theo every single day. She sighed, let her head and shoulders slump the slightest amount. "Yes."

The device gave a halfhearted buzz as if down there something nibbled on her clit. *Not now. Nooo.* If it triggered when he hit her, she'd die of humiliation.

The next two smacks were hard enough to sting, but she said nothing. Only waited. For an infinitesimal moment Dankyo left his hand there. The pressure of one finger trailed across her skin before he let her up.

When she straightened Theo was by her side and curled his arm about her waist. "There. Not so bad, was it?"

"No." She willed her heart to slow. Then she turned to Dankyo. Raising her eyes was difficult, and she had to brace herself inside, found herself bemused by her own reaction. *Where's my courage*? She looked up. "Theo said you respected my skills."

His eyes glittered a second. Not malevolence for once. Appraisal, like he saw her in a new light. *Damn him*. That *had* hurt. The man had a hard hand and could snap her in two if he so decided. She felt off-center and took some more slow breaths.

"Are you okay?"

She blinked, amazed.

"Uh, yes. Look. The weapon you've got your men using, the sights are inferior."

For a while, he said nothing. The man could have given a statue lessons in being inscrutable. Then he clicked his tongue twice.

“Very well. What do you recommend?”

“There’s a new parallax sight, experimental, but it’s for night use also.”

From an inner pocket, Dankyo whipped out a notebook and pencil, and gave it to her. Having scribbled down the manufacturer and model, she handed the notepad back. Still expressionless, he tucked it away.

She smiled nervously.

This time he raised his eyebrows a quarter inch.

“There’s something else,” she said, then rushed on before he could do his statue impersonation again. “I noticed from the gyrocopter that you have a problem with the firing arcs of the roof cannons. The trees to the north are in a bad spot.”

Dankyo’s left lower eyelid shimmied.

“Claire,” Theo muttered, “that one’s my fault. I’ve told him they have to stay. My great-grandmother’s buried there.”

“Oh. Really?” She nodded to Dankyo as Theo steered her away and back toward the house. “Uh, thanks for listening,” she called back.

“My pleasure, I assure you.” He flashed a mouth-stretching smile that for a millisecond touched his eyes.

Compared to Dankyo, she was an expert at small talk.

“How are you holding up?” Theo inquired, voice calm and unexcited.

"Perfectly. I think I see what you were getting at. He'd never have listened to me before. It's changed things."

He stared. "And how do you feel about him now?"

"I know he can hit hard." She thought for a few seconds, twisted her mouth. "Truthfully, I guess I do respect him a bit more."

"Good."

The device triggered. She hung in limbo for a full minute while Theo waited with hand on her elbow, steadying her. She'd managed a quiet gasp and shudder that time. Taken to the heights yet again by that *pulse pulse pulse.*

They seemed to take the long way back to the house, past the gardens and the laundry. She learned that just before it triggered, there'd be a little miniature sizzle of energy, and would brace herself, though never quite enough. The shock wore her down. Yet her body wanted more—each time requiring that little extra stimulation, and each time, instead, she teetered, agonized, on the brink of ecstasy. The effort in keeping still and not making a sound exhausted her and made her focus inward. Every part of her body sharpened and fizzed, her nipples swelled, it seemed, to twice their size, and down deep, she caged all the sounds she died to make. Only now and then, a tiny moan escaped her lips. Half the time, over the last hundred yards, she didn't see where they trod.

Chapter Sixteen

The sun had descended low on the horizon, changing the clouds to a vibrant purple and orange. The winds swung round to come from the east and then died to a sibilant breeze. Theo at last reentered the main back doors. At the sight of the massive curving staircase, Claire slowed, stopped, and found herself shivering. *No farther. Not a step.*

"Take this off, Theo," she whispered, her head bowed. She'd withstood forced marches, marathons, but never anything like this. Her feet seemed a long way down.

"Dankyo and all my staff call me sir. I think it's time I made that a rule for you also."

"Sir." It was too much effort to stop and think about that. She swallowed, only seeing his black shoes before her on the polished timber. "Please."

"Here? I think not." He swept her up into his arms with ease and began to climb the staircase. Beneath the tiredness, she marveled at his strength. It was a long staircase, and she wasn't light. But she clung to his neck and enjoyed the tranquility of resting in his arms.

The doors to his bedroom swung open. She heard the creak, saw nothing beyond the woven fabric of his shirt, embraced by his male scent. The doors shut with a slam. The floor lightly thumped under his boots. He lowered her to his bed, and she gazed up, unable to stir a finger, imagining all the things he might do to her, *wanting…*

"Ah. You need to drink." He rummaged under her clothes, unclipping and removing the voltaic device. She didn't stir, only glad that the tiny claws of that horrible yet irresistible thing were gone from her body. If she lay here for a little longer, perhaps her body would forget it completely. The hunger quieted.

"Mmm. Thank you," she muttered. Silence screamed at her. Peeking with one eye, she saw his stern expression. "Sir."

She felt herself raised by his hand at her back and drank as a cool glass pressed at her lips. He stripped the dress off her, then the corset, guiding her tired limbs. Another sip from the glass, and she lifted her head, feeling revived, and put her arms back to prop herself against the bed. Theo moved his thumb against her clit. She stiffened. At that single touch, every time she'd almost orgasmed surged to the fore, clamoring at her again. Her arms collapsed, and she slid to the bed in a boneless heap, whimpering.

Theo chuckled. "That's more like it." The glass chinked as he put it aside.

She shuddered and rolled onto her side, curling up around where his thumb resumed massaging, revolving round and round on her clit. Almost, but not quite, enough pressure.

"Maybe not ropes, but this—" He clipped a wide cuff around each wrist, buckled another pair around her ankles, leather on skin, and dragged her up the bed. Though she knew she had muscles, they weren't working right then, and she didn't want them to. Just let him maneuver her into position—kneeling, with head down against the pillow and turned a bit sideways so she could get air. She panted, mouth open, needing, wanting only one thing—him inside her, fucking her.

"I've wanted you like this since I first saw you. Bottom up, held down, with your legs apart." He rumbled the words against her ear, licking at the lobe, then fastened her wrists together and chained them to the headboard. Strapped her thighs against her calves so her heels pressed under her bottom. She let him. She was his.

"Nice." He slicked a finger along the line of her wet slit, and just when she thought he'd penetrate her...and put *something* inside her...

He carefully flipped her until she looked up at him, lost in the haze of lust and the pounding ache. He knelt between her legs, planted his arms either side of her chest, lowered his head, and applied tongue to her nipple.

She arched, her toes under her bottom, digging into the quilt. "Ah!"

The spark from his wet tongue spread, sending fire-laden streaks to her pussy. The stubble on his chin scraped. His hand was on her, down there. His fingers dancing, pressing everywhere...delicious and conjuring liquid heat. So stirred to the heights, she grunted each time he touched those vital places—clit, nipple, or his fingers in her pussy and ass. In and out, around, slicking, teasing her as her wetness spread. Flesh against tantalizing flesh. She groaned and tightened, felt everything roil together and explode in a blast of light.

A little choking noise came from her throat. Released at last. "Ohh, thank God," she said softly. As her memory replayed the sensations, new reverberations rocked her body.

"You're not getting off that easily, agapi mou." He lightly bit at her nipple.

She heard herself moan as if from a distance. Theo rose from the bed—then came the scrape of timber as he pulled out a drawer. Her bound legs slowly flopped out to each side. She left herself exposed but didn't care. Cool air caressed her pussy like the lightest of tongues.

She squinted and saw him holding something fat and long—shaped like a cannon shell with a blunt point. The rear half was gold-sheened metal and black seams, with the front half glass. Inside, clockwork cogs slowly ticked over. A miniature blue spark of voltaic energy fizzed across the internal workings like a tiny lightning storm. Theo dropped the thing onto the bed. She tugged; the chain clinked. Nothing gave.

Eek. Is that one of Henry's inventions?

"This first." He sat beside her and held a black blindfold out. Those gray eyes inches away gazed at her as he turned it in his hands, showing it to her. "I'm going to put this on you. It will make you concentrate on only the things you should be thinking about. As long as you trust me?" He canted his head, raised his eyebrows, waited.

This was the time to say no if she wished to. Here she was, still tied up, and he asked if she trusted him? After everything today? She licked her lips, nodded, despite the tightness in her throat.

Blackness descended as the blindfold was wrapped about her head and tied. Now there was only sound and sensation and the smell of sweat and arousal. The straps on her thighs were removed; then he pulled her ankles apart and attached them to something. She couldn't bring her legs together. *What had he done*? This seemed increasingly...odd and unnerving.

"That's a bar that holds your legs apart," Theo murmured in his smooth, deep voice. He slicked a finger along her slippery cleft. "It keeps you wide open so I can see everything. I could swim down here, Claire."

She opened her mouth, then tried to move her legs in. The ankle cuffs stretched taut. *Oh. Yes.* She imagined him looking at her and heated again, felt her lips down there swell a little more.

Something soft and warm covered her clit. His tongue. "Mmm." She wriggled as much as the restraints allowed. His tongue curled over her, flicking momentarily over the hood, then away again.

"Don't get all quiet on me will you, Claire? I think it's time to use one of Henry's devices."

Now that alarmed her. After his last device... Something buzzed—a mechanical sort of buzzing. She yanked on the wrist chain. No. Solid. She couldn't move her arms more than a few inches. The wondering, the anticipation of the unknown when she could do nothing to stop him, pumped her excitement higher.

Theo tweaked her nipple. A spike of pain jolted her. The buzzing approached, and...*magic*. The most incredible pleasure engulfed her clit. Unceasing, startling, microscopic tremors. She squealed, arched her neck, and thrust up her groin. “More! Please!” The buzzing stopped.

“You’re forgetting something, dear,” he said sternly. Which of these would you like?” He gripped her nipple, squeezed hard. “This?”

“No!” Forgetting something? What? Sir? Dammit, this wasn’t a parade ground! Yet... He pinched harder. “Oh! Sir! More of the other, sir! Not that. Please.”

Something hard nuzzled her vagina. The buzzing again, assaulting her with overwhelming pleasure, turning her mind to mush. It stopped.

“This then?”

“Yes! Sir!”

“Good.” It started again, and this time he also descended on one nipple with his mouth.

“Unh!” Nothing mattered except *that*. She strained, her mound pressing, grinding against *it*. In seconds, she came. Her body, shuddering as the device buzzed at her, consuming her, eating her up in a storm of racking spasms that kept on and on and on. And stopped. She twitched and tried to gather her sanity. *What...was...that?*

While she lay there breathing like a steam engine gone wild, Theo manipulated her body—sliding something beneath her, attaching straps about her stomach and chest, anchoring her ankles.

She cleared her throat. *Slow. Calm.* "What was that? Sir." Even behind the blindfold, her eyes were shut. Remembering. Would she ever be free of the pulsations of that thing? And what was he up to? Surely he'd let her go now.

He walked up until she heard him next to her head, and he stroked her cheek, kissed her lips. His larger mouth enclosed hers, and meekly, she let him open her with his hard tongue, then roughly toy with her lips and tongue. She wondered if he meant to suck the life from her. Any more of these devices, and she'd be unable to walk for days. Her core clamped down, tight. She wanted something inside her.

"That," he said, finally answering her question, "is what Henry calls a reciprocating sexual probe."

"What does it do?" she asked, her voice coming out low and ragged. Damn, she'd forgotten again. "Sir."

"It vibrates. You. And ever so nicely." Ample amusement colored his words.

"Then perhaps," she said sarcastically, "you should call it a vibrator."

"Hmm. I'll tell him that. But first, your cheekiness gets punished." He pinched both nipples, hard.

"Ow!" Warmth flared—the pain swiftly changed to something more as sensation homed in on her clit.

"I'm going to raise you up," he told her. "You'll be safe. Ready?"

Safe? She nodded, biting her lip, still uneasy.

He kissed her lips again, briefly. A chain mechanism ratcheted slowly, and her torso rose into the air. With her ankles spread and anchored and her wrists tied to the headboard, her spine arched. The straps about her torso tightened as they bore weight, and she felt the support of a padded board running under her back. Her neck and legs curved downward toward the bed.

She heard Theo climb up and stand on the bed.

“Is that hurting you anywhere? Your neck?”

Was it? She felt exposed. Her breasts, her pussy up in the air. She could move even less than before, but…no pain.

“No.” *Remember! Remember*! “Uh. Sir.” She shivered, imagining his eyes on her, as he stared at her naked, at her sex. *Oh, I like that idea, very much.*

“Good.” He rested his palm on her stomach. “And now, I’m going to do whatever I like to you.”

Said so calmly, so confidently, the words echoed inside her. She quivered, anticipating. Pulled at her bonds again, breathing hard and fast. He could do anything. And she couldn’t stop him. Every inch of her, from head to her curling-up toes, quaked.

The softest of touches, at her lips—his finger inserted slowly into her mouth. She heaved a shuddering breath, her pussy tingling, licked his finger, sucking him. He withdrew and, with that fingertip, trailed a cool shivery path across her lower lip and downward across her neck, then curving round the swell of her breast, into belly button, and slowly, at last, reaching her clit, though he skimmed past the side. One finger plunged into her moist slit. Another finger, thick with moisture, touched her other hole.

"Oh." She squeezed down there.

"You have to relax, Claire."

"I'm not—" She wriggled, but his fingertip stayed put. With all the stimulation, even that felt good. The fingertip inched in farther.

"Let's see if you like this."

The finger pushed, and as if it pumped blood into her clitoris, she felt the hood retract as her sensitive button engorged and tingled.

"Mmm. Oh." Different, awkward, but pleasurable.

His other hand curved around her breast and gripped it. He covered her nipple with his hot mouth. She made an odd sound—half squeak, half grunt. His tongue licked across and away, then to her other nipple, and back. His finger teased the nipple his mouth didn't attend to. She tried to pull her legs up and grind against his hand, and couldn't. Her back stayed arched and fixed there, available. Open. Her body wasn't hers anymore. It was his.

She needed, wanted, and all those things he did to her were driving her to trembling mindlessness. With her head upside down, blood rushed in, thumping.

"Let's try something else new." He left her unattended a moment, only to return and touch something slippery yet hard to her anus and slowly insert it.

"Ah!" She writhed and found nothing helped. The thing moved farther in, widening her, burning. Once past the entrance it plopped inside her. Seated there. The uncomfortable feeling churned and settled.

"That will stretch you."

The buzzing started. She tensed, feeling the new thing in her anus, then the vibrator slipping into her vagina. Hard and unyielding, her muscles clasped it, released. The vibrations traveled to her clit, and tension built. She inhaled, hard, her mouth staying open; the vessels at the sides of her neck felt enormous, pulsing with her heartbeats. Her head filled to bursting, every muscle strained, taking her up, up, and then his mouth covered her clit and sucked. She screamed and came in a wailing crescendo.

Coming down, subsiding from the crest, with her arms, her neck, her legs, relaxing...he sucked again and tongued the bulging nub between her legs. His fingers stroked her swollen nipples. Another wave of orgasm hit, flooding her, unrelenting. This time she could only let out a thin screech that went on and on until he released the wet grasp of his lips on her.

With the blackness over her eyes, she hung there, lost in an infinite throbbing space, punctuated only by the thud of heartbeats and the softness of gasping.

"My turn."

Dizzied, she could make no sense of the words at first.

The thing in her anus slipped free, the loss replaced a few moments later with a soft prodding as the head of his cock touched her there. She felt the rim of her anus expand and take him in, then the slow progression up inside. A dilating, an almost burning, that transformed into fullness. She groaned. The vibrator in her pussy had never stopped, and now every nerve ending wriggled in time with it.

* * * *

Theo stared down at Claire, transfixed by the beauty of her laid out with her arms outstretched and legs spread open, for him to take as he wished. She'd given in to him. Watching her be swamped by the joys he'd shown her was an incredible experience. Almost as good as burying his cock inside her. He pushed forward, watched his member slide into her anus, slow as treacle, slippery with the cream he'd applied. Her cleft glistened with moisture. The base of the vibrator jiggled in her vagina. As he built up a rhythm, he pressed on the vibrator. The tremors came through her flesh to his cock, and he butted into the thing at the deepest point of his thrusts.

Nice. So darn tight. Claire raised her head for a few seconds, neck straining, as if she could see him through the blindfold. Her mouth gaped open as she sucked in air; then her head sagged back down. Her inner muscles seized on him. Her breasts shifted as he reamed her. Not too hard—he didn't want to hurt her, and she might not register an injury until too late. He'd taken her to the very top.

Sweat beaded on her breasts. The veins in her neck stood out, and she sighed and groaned with every thrust, the muscles at the fronts of her thighs tensing and relaxing. Her nipples poked up like pink buttons. Next time, he'd put clamps on her. With that thought, his balls swelled and felt as heavy as lead.

Her breathing accelerated. Would she come again? Thumbing her clit, his other hand cupping her bottom, he grunted and slid back in.

"Ahh!" Her beautiful scream set him off.

The coiling tension took over; he shoved into her to the hilt, his legs pushing. Every muscle strained, shoved. His balls squeezed up so tight they might've been rocks. He grunted. His cock pulsed as he released into her, jetting, then twitching. *Yes*. He shut his eyes, then opened them to slits, devouring the sight of her body sagging with the aftermath of an orgasm. *Time to let her go*. He shifted a little, slipped the vibrator from her cleft, turned it off, and dropped it to the bed. He pulled back, his cock slipping out. She gasped. Gradually his ragged breathing came down to almost normal.

His hands smoothed along the contours of her belly; then he went to the crank and lowered her to the bed. The straps and ties came off. She barely moved.

"We're done, Claire."

Her eyes opened when he took off the blindfold, blinking at him through those long blonde lashes. He kissed her forehead, then collapsed beside her, snuggling her body up to his, her head in the corner of shoulder and arm.

"How was that? Happy?" he whispered.

She stirred a little, heaved a sigh. "Mmm. Tell you…later."

He propped himself up on his elbow and watched her eyes close, her breathing become shallow and regular. Ah. How could he even think of losing her?

Maybe...maybe this one was a keeper? He fingered a strand of her hair.

Chapter Seventeen

After having a quick bath himself, Theo had watched her from the door of the bathroom for a while, as if he thought she'd sink beneath the soapsuds and drown in the bath. Not a chance, Claire thought. Life was too good, too amazing right now, for her to go and drown. No matter how worn out she felt. And oh, Lord, everywhere ached or throbbed. She even had bruises on her wrists and ankles where the straps had been. Not from Theo putting them on too tight; no, she'd bruised from her own straining during orgasm. Several uncountable fricking orgasms.

Overcome for a moment by remembering, she slid underwater and let the muffling sounds of the water soothe her.

It was strange—to have done all those intimate and plain bizarre things with a man. Yet sex that way had been so much more wonderful than she'd thought it could be. An earthquake had shaken the foundations of her universe—an amazing, stupendous earthquake.

She rose from the scented water, let it stream off her body, and looked down at the pink-tipped mounds of her breasts, wondering at how Theo saw her.

Having dried herself and dressed in an apricot negligee and satin gown, she ventured into the hallway and down to the bedroom. Theo sat reading at one end of a sofa set at an angle near the huge bay window. Night had fallen. Insects tapped against the glass as they tried in vain to enter. On the table in front of him was a covered plate, a carafe of orange juice, glasses, and a bottle of red wine. A graceful flower-shaped voltaic lamp shone a blue circle of light upon the table. He lifted the cover off the plate, revealing a meal still steaming with heat.

"Please, sit and eat, Claire." He indicated the sofa next to him. "Charcoal-grilled pigeon, olives, and dolmades—stuffed vine leaves. I've already eaten."

"Oh. Thank you." The common courtesies seemed even more ridiculous than before. "Am I supposed to call you, uh, sir?"

"I like the sound of it, but...no. Only in public or"—he regarded her evenly—"when we make love. Sit." He patted the sofa next to him, then smiled.

She slid in next to him. As soon as her thigh touched his, she felt anchored. The world was in its rightful place. The food looked delicious, and her stomach grumbled.

Though he continued to read as she ate, he rested a hand near her shoulders and idly caressed her. When finished she pushed away the plate.

The bed had been tidied up—the quilt pulled straight and all that *equipment* put away somewhere out of sight. Not long ago she'd been stretched out there with Theo making love to her.

"What is it?" Theo massaged her back, leaned in and kissed her cheek, then settled back and waited, still massaging.

"Does"—she took a breath—"everyone have sex like that? Like we did?" She looked sidelong at him. The corners of his lips twitched upward. "Is it always that wonderful?"

"Hmm. No, perhaps to the second. Definitely a no to the first. So, you liked it?"

She shut her eyes a second. Sent back in time to how she'd felt, how she'd surrendered to him. "Yes. I did."

"No regrets?" He cocked an eyebrow.

"No. None. Though"—she held up her wrists, turning them to show the bruises—"this I could do without."

"Ah." He sat up and examined her, kissed her skin. "I'm sorry. Next time I'll use more padding."

Next time. Inexplicably, that saddened her. How many more next times would there be? The lie she'd told ground at her. He was such a good man, if she'd told him first off, she was an assassin…maybe? If only there was some way to be sure of what he'd do *before* she told him.

When would she ever feel totally comfortable and safe?

She sniffed.

"You look sad. Is it hurting that much?" Theo gently touched her wrist.

"No. It's not that. I'm just tired."

"Tired, we can fix. Here, lie back on me." He moved to put his leg along the sofa, with his back at the corner of the armrest, and let her snuggle into the space between his legs.

So warm and big. She felt safe, protected, and a tear rolled down her cheek. She let it, didn't touch her face or sniff, and held in all the other tears so he wouldn't know. Theo kept reading, the paper held up before him and to the right where she too could see it. After a while the sadness ebbed away. The words on the page coalesced.

"What is that?" she asked. Though really, she knew what it was, just not what he intended to do with it. *A study of the Frankenstruct.* Her heart beat faster. "You're reading about me."

He lowered the page. "Well, about frankenstructs in general."

"Why?" She prayed the answer wouldn't be a bad one. Was this that awful fate rolling in to get her? Her hands curled into fists.

"I'm putting forth a bill in parliament, proposing that frankenstructs be declared human and thus given all the rights of humans. We have to repeal another bill first, though. Hey, what's this?" He took her closed hand in his, raised it, and kissed her until she relaxed. "It's nothing for you to worry over. But it is important. Next week I fly down to speak on it before the members.

"You know, the report you wrote—it's been used in part to set out this."

"Could I help? Could I read this? Maybe I can tell you things that are missing or...wrong?"

He barely hesitated, and that was the best part. “Claire, that sounds like a good idea. Go ahead. If you want to write notes on it, there’s a pen on the table.” He laid the papers in her lap. “Even better, I’ll let you read the speech. This is important to me. I see it as a great injustice. You do understand that?”

“Yes.” She turned and smiled at him. “Thank you.” She kissed him on the mouth—a warm, soft kiss that he returned in the same way, their lips meeting as equals.

“Pour us both a glass of wine, love, before you start,” he said, tucking a loop of her hair behind her ear and kissing her there. “For once, I get to relax. You’re a godsend.”

THEO SAT WITH Claire in the fork of his legs and contemplated how she’d come to him. A sip of the red wine went down sultry and sweet. Pages turned slowly with a faint rustle and with the occasional scratch of pen on paper. He grinned. What a delightful warm, rounded bundle. Secretary, lover, and strangely talented bodyguard all rolled into one and smelling of his lavender soap.

A pink love bite at the nape of her neck reminded him of their lovemaking. Extraordinary how she’d taken to this. There was nothing about her that disappointed him. Nothing. For a barest flicker of time, unease stirred, as if they tempted fate. He gulped another swallow of wine. Foolish thought.

Chapter Eighteen

The days before Theo had to leave for parliament passed quickly. There seemed to be an endless number of variations of lovemaking that he wished to try out on her, though never rope, because she still refused to allow it. That he respected this boundary meant so much to her. Though otherwise, she trusted him absolutely and bowed to his will.

Two days before Theo was to leave, Dankyo found her at the garden nursery helping George prune the orange trees. She was at the top of a small ladder. As he crunched across the leaf-strewn root bed, she ignored him, hoping he wasn't aiming for her. He peered up. From above, his flat-shorn head of hair looked like it'd make a glorious broom.

"Might I have a word with you"—he studied her—"Miss Claire?"

She climbed down, put down the shears, then slowly wiped her hands on her apron. "Sure."

"Please." He indicated the path out down the aisle of trees.

This was the first he'd spoken to her since the day Theo had let him spank her. She eyed him warily. No hint of superiority or arrogance on his face. Well…no more than usual. Of course, the spanking had been Theo's doing—meant to impress on her the pecking order. Dankyo had participated reluctantly. It had worked. She couldn't imagine saying no to this straitlaced man anymore—though partly because, if Theo found out, the consequences might be painful.

After she took off her apron, he led her toward the vehicle depot. She thought of breaching the silence, asking him what was on his mind, but decided not to. She'd let him make the first move. Theo liked control, but Dankyo embodied it, *lived it*. A week ago she would have itched for a weapon in her hand when around Dankyo, but she'd learned. Not everything was solved by violence.

A muted roar came from within the depot. A shadow passed over. She looked up. The clouds had moved fast, and rain spattered cool dots on her bare arms.

Inside Henry was at work, lurking underneath the chugging steam limousine. Though Theo had called them both steam buggies, this was a sleek mean machine with an articulated chassis like a gold-adorned centipede given wheels instead of legs.

"Henry!" Dankyo shouted to be heard over the engine.

Henry slid out from under the steam limo, his mouse gray hair sticking up in disarray. "Yes?"

"I want to take out the buggy."

"Hex? Sure." He sat up and rubbed at his head, smearing a splotch of oil up into his hair.

He levered himself off the floor and stood, adjusted the crotch of his khaki overalls. "I'll have to fire Hex up with the voltaic generator an' keep the engine running, or she'll be impossible to restart. Needs a bit o' work."

Dankyo nodded. "I'll take care of it. I want something with speed."

Strange. He'd never struck her as the sort who liked adrenaline rushes.

Claire turned to the other vehicle Dankyo'd termed a buggy. It was plain ugly, with a myriad of spindly pipes cradling the engine and cabin. If the limo was a centipede, then the buggy was a spider with a huge ass on wheels.

"Get in." Dankyo pointed at the passenger side, then went to help Henry click some thick cables to points beneath Hex. She shrugged and climbed in, taking care to tuck the skirt under her and clip on the safety harness. Whatever Dankyo planned, he wasn't going to murder her or anything. The man unsettled her, but unease wasn't a death sentence.

The wide back doors were pushed back by Dankyo and Henry. Rain advanced across the expanse of grass, reaching the gravel road just outside, turning the stone dark in seconds.

Once started, Hex chuffed as fast as the gyrocopter, with an alarming tendency to lift up on the front wheels—and that was while stationary. Dankyo sat in the driver's seat and went through a fast but thorough checklist. He glanced at her, locked a sway bar into place between them and the dashboard, then accelerated away. She sank her fingernails into the bar. The seat shook with the vibrations of the engine as they drove into the gray drizzle.

The windscreen kinked back like an arrowhead to each side. She peered through the rain-spotted glass.

"Where are we going?"

"Nowhere in particular. Sometimes I just like to drive. It helps keep me sane."

She peered cautiously at him. "Sane?"

"Yes. I am human. I'll take the sealed road to start with, but this vehicle loves the dirt. She can take everything—shrubs, rocks..." The buggy took a tight curve in the road with a calculated slide and crunch of flying gravel. "I asked you to come because...I need to know what exactly your intentions are. Number one..." He wrenched the wheel and planted his foot. The road ahead ran straight for at least a mile.

He braked. Hex slid to a halt.

The patter of rain mixed with the throb and hiss of the motor.

"Are you loyal?" With a hand still on the wheel, he turned to face her.

"I am. Of course I am. I wouldn't do anything to hurt Theo or the others here...even you."

He smiled, his lips thin and even on that smooth face. He studied her. She knew he looked for the slightest clue that she lied.

"Would you lay down your life for him?"

"Would you?"

"Yes." His fingers went white on the wheel. "He saved my life, more than once, in the war. We had a traitor, and our fleet was betrayed. Lost a lot of ships and men, got badly damaged—only made it out because of the colonel. If there's one thing I hate—he hates—it is traitors."

Oh. Dear.

She summoned up courage, told the truth that rested in her bones. "I too would lay down my life for Theo." *Not for you, but yes, for Theo. He hates traitors.* She twisted her thoughts away from there. *No. I'm loyal.*

She must have passed inspection. He grunted. "Good. I believe you." He held out his hand, and she clasped it, her fingers dwarfed by his huge ones. With a small effort he could have mangled her hand.

Well now. It seemed they truly were at peace. Maybe Dankyo wasn't that bad after all. Something floated loose inside. Inkline was gone—it'd been weeks since she'd seen him, and it seemed as if he'd never return. Maybe her dream could come true. Maybe she could stay here.

Dankyo ratcheted the throttle forward. The buggy leaped into motion and surged over the road's edge, over the undergrowth, its legs telescoping out until they were a yard above ground level. "Now I get to show you what she really can do!" He grinned. They bounced over a small tree.

She clutched at her skirt as it billowed up, tucked it back under.

"Isn't that skirt a bit impractical for tree pruning?" he yelled.

Heat flushed across her face. It was true. She'd worn it because Theo liked to run his hands up underneath dresses and skirts to fondle her—not something she'd admit to Dankyo.

"I, uh, didn't know I'd be doing that when I dressed this morning."

He slightly raised his eyebrows, then gunned the engine again. The vehicle bucked like a horse while he negotiated a gully pocked with craters. Her teeth rattled. *Lord.* Dankyo truly had a thing for driving fast over impossible terrain.

He slewed the car to a stop. The rain had moved on east, and the sky showed patches of blue. She'd no doubt have smelled the fresh scent of the rain if it hadn't been for the nose-clogging odor of engine oil and singed rubber.

"One last question." From the way he gripped the wheel in both hands and stared forward, this question would be worse than the last.

What else could he need to know?

He cleared his throat. "You don't have to answer this, and…ah, do not repeat this to anyone. Why is it that a strong woman like you lets a man lord it over her?"

Perplexed, she stared. *Is he blushing*? She shifted in the seat, tapped her fingers on the sway bar. The question was exceptionally personal.

Ah. A ray of light dawned in her mind. She'd never seen him with a woman, though Kirsten sure wanted to latch on to this impenetrable man. If any man could be an island, that was Dankyo. But he'd laid himself open here, shown her the crack in his armor. Somehow, she doubted anyone else had seen this side of him. It pleased her no end.

Then she remembered the spanking. Had *that* brought this on? Heavens no, she was not *ever* going to follow up that train of thought.

She screwed up her mouth. “I don’t know. I don’t know myself the whole answer to that. But, believe it or not, I enjoy it. Maybe that makes you think I’m stupid.” She shook her head. “Or crazy.”

He raised his thick fingers on the wheel, one by one, like a pianist ready to play. “No. I don’t think that. But…thank you for answering. I’ll take us back now.” He revved the engine and drove off smoothly.

Puzzling. Maybe she should drop some hints to Kirsten. Would it scare her away?

“By the way, we’ve confirmation just today that the PME have admitted to planning mass assassinations. They’ve made assurances that all such plans are now defunct. Without your information, we’d never have known.”

“Oh. That’s fantastic news.”

“Yes.” He accelerated.

Thank the Lord. I’m free for sure. No Inkline to worry about ever again. Free.

Only, on the way back, in the far distance, she thought she glimpsed Francine de-camouflage from a tree trunk and then merge back in. It was for the barest second, so she couldn’t be certain. It bothered her all the way back.

If Inkline truly was gone, why would Francine be here? If that was her, was Francine spying on her, or had she too escaped the grasp of the PME?

Chapter Nineteen

The afternoon before Theo left, they visited Filip again at the kennels. He presented Claire with a wriggling puppy. All soft gray-brown fur and pink licking tongue, it squirmed until she had to put it down. Once there it went straight to Theo's shoe to gnaw on a shoelace.

"I'm sorry, but Angeliona's puppies are too little to leave her yet. This one is weaned and should make a lovely guard dog for the colonel's bedroom door."

"The bedroom?" Claire frowned and squatted to drag the puppy away. It refused and stayed, chewing. She rested her forearms on the top of her thighs, the sleek material of her leather tights under her skin. "Is it a boy or a girl?"

"A girl, of course." Filip's eyebrows waggled. "The colonel likes the girls."

Theo stooped and put a hand on Claire's shoulder. As always, that simple pressure, even through the cloth of her blouse, made her recall everything they did in the bedroom and sometimes out of it. She leaned her head into his arm.

"I'm not sure about this one." Theo grunted. "She bites. Is she house-trained yet, Filip?"

"Your lady?" Filip drew back in mock surprise. "You bite, Miss Claire? I would never have thought you'd let this one so out of control, mon Colonel." He chuckled.

"If you weren't old enough to be my grandfather, Filip." Theo sighed.

"He likes my jokes." Filip nudged Claire. "She will be house-trained soon. I will send her to you then."

"Good." Theo helped Claire to her feet.

When they walked outside and saw the rain-swept lawn, Theo held her arm, preventing her from stepping out from under the eaves. Frogs croaked their happiness from a nearby drainpipe. She shivered. The air had cooled by several degrees.

"It should stop soon." Theo turned those gray eyes on her. "I see that Filip likes you. That is your puppy, not mine"—he grinned—"and the first one to live in the mansion."

"It is? She is?" The facts astounded her. She put hand to her throat. No one had ever given her anything like that, ever. "Oh, that is so nice. I'm going back in to thank him properly."

"No." Though quiet, the firmness made her quiver to a stop. "No. You're staying here." He crowded her, hand slipping about her waist. "For this." He twisted her ponytail about his hand and dragged on it, bending back her head.

"Yes. Sir," she choked out. The tide of excitement rose in her. She'd come to know the ways of his voice, and right now, he would brook no disobedience.

His lips came down on hers, savage, as if he wished to provoke her. She wondered how far she might go and nipped back at his lip. It evoked a growl from Theo. “That, woman, you will pay for, tonight.”

She shivered, wondering what that meant. Tonight would be interesting.

“Perhaps,” he added, “we should try out a whip?”

She jerked away as far as she could, shaking her head.

“No? Ah, but I’ve seen how curious you are when I bring them out. Think on it, because, if I see the slightest hesitation on you, I will be using one.”

She said nothing, appalled, yet, truly, she was no longer certain what she desired. Things she’d thought abhorrent, she’d screamed in ecstasy at when used on her.

“Ah. Then that’s a definite yes.” He moved his hand under her blouse, long, heavy fingers outspread and warming her, then down into the crevice of her ass. He took her mouth again, even more violently, and as he did so, he gathered up the fabric of her leggings and drew them tightly into her cleft.

“Ah!” She gasped at the flood of sensation. They made love so often her body had no time to forget. Sometimes the merest brush of his body against hers would awaken her to desire.

She succumbed to the press of his tongue and lips, giving way to let him explore her mouth, opening wider and moaning. His finger wriggled between her buttocks, lower, into dampness.

His mouth left her lips, and he bit the juncture of jaw and neck.

Eyes half-closed, breathing faster, she tilted her head, allowing him better access. He took her throat again between his teeth and paid close attention to it for a while—sucking and biting. Her legs weakened.

"Hmm." He nuzzled her. "If I keep this up, perhaps you'll end up on the floor with your legs around me?"

No! How scandalous that would be here, in the open. *Surely not.*

The crunch and splash of nearing footsteps brought her up from the dazed world she'd been lowered into.

"Sir," said Dankyo, impervious to the droplets bouncing on the flat plain of his hair and dribbling down his face. "I beg your pardon, but I have urgent news."

With one hand still under her leggings, on her bare ass, Theo turned to Dankyo. "What is it?"

"The weather report has this rain turning into an electrical storm late tomorrow morning, sir. You might be wise to leave today if you wish to attend the opening of parliament."

"Ah. I see. Inform the captain to ready the airship for flight in two hours."

Dankyo nodded. "There is another matter, sir." His gaze slid to Claire and back. The slightest wrinkling of his brow betrayed his interest. She wondered what devious thing he'd been up to.

"What is it?"

Dankyo put his hands behind his back. "They're reopening the inquiry into the airship crash, sir. Apparently this employer of hers"—he nodded at Claire—"Mr. Inkline, is rumored to have been carrying some dangerous cargo, though as yet, no one knows what it was. That was the reason for the attack. The Brito-Gallic League have finally admitted to the attack and given us this information as a gesture of apology."

"Dangerous cargo?" Theo's fingers moved on her bottom. She had to restrain herself from wriggling.

Then a spike of fear drove into her. She was the dangerous cargo. Did it matter, though? That was the past, buried and gone.

She listened as they batted possibilities back and forth.

"Could this cargo have had something to do with the assassinations?" Theo asked.

"Perhaps, sir."

She'd decided that the assassinations would never happen. That they'd been aborted completely. But what if they hadn't been? Was it wise to completely dismiss the plan? Because someone called Theo had been on the list, and Theo, her Theo, was going off without her and Dankyo. Someone else might have been given her target. And that target might have been Theodore Kevonis. Anxiety knifed through her. *What if… What if he's killed because I've not told the truth?*

At last they gave up on the discussion, and Dankyo strode away.

"Claire?" Theo was staring down at her. "I'm sorry, but I'll be leaving sooner than I thought. I will send for you once I gain the agreement of parliament.

Once it's safe, Dankyo will bring you. There's a presidential ball being held in the capital. I would love to show you how we Hellenes celebrate." The smile he gave her was enigmatic, as if he had some surprise in mind.

She reined in her panic, thoughts churning. She had to either tell him everything or somehow get on that airship.

As they walked to the back entrance of the mansion, Theo casually asked her the question she'd been dreading. "Have you any idea what this dangerous cargo would have been?"

He barely looked at her, and she was grateful. He'd waited for Dankyo to go before asking her. To give her space to think and to answer without pressure. Ah, that almost undid her right then and there. He gave her kindness, and she gave back dishonesty.

She should tell him. Kneel down and beg his forgiveness and tell him. Only, she couldn't. Her bravery failed her. *Nothing* in this world was as important to her as Theo, and she couldn't bear to throw it all away by being truthful.

The hours before his departure tortured her. He'd learned her mannerisms so well, if she put a foot wrong, spoke with the wrong inflection, made the wrong gesture, he'd know she was concealing something important. Yet she didn't want him to leave.

As it was, they reached the front steps before she ended up crying. Beyond, the airship waited. Cold rain gusted across, swathing it in a curtain of gray. Theo's men waited patiently with umbrellas over their heads.

Theo hugged her to him. "Claire. What's wrong?"

She hugged him tighter, arms around him, her face buried against the crook of his neck, inhaling his scent. Her white dress had thick lacy petticoats and a cantilevered bodice. Though her breasts stood up nicely, there was way too much cloth between her and Theo. She wanted to feel his skin. A tear trickled along her nose. At least the rain would disguise the moisture left on his shirt.

"Claire?" He patted her back. "I have to go."

"I don't want you to go," she managed to whisper.

"I'll bring you to me soon. Dankyo will stay here with you. Parliament will revoke that bill; then you can come. I know we have the votes. This will happen. All right?"

He gently pulled her arms away, then held her chin up and looked at her. "Tears?"

"Stupid of me." She shook her head, trying to dislodge his fingers but not succeeding.

Damnation, she needed to give him a reason for her unhappiness. She clutched for another truth, not *that* one, and knew it had to be something that would distract him. Every second his gray eyes seemed to delve deeper into her thoughts, dissecting her, and eventually he'd hit bone. She let the sadness fill her.

Despite the others within earshot, she opened her heart to him, and she told him her fear, though not the reason why.

"I... You are everything to me, Theo. Without you, I feel I am nothing. I don't want to leave you, or you to leave me. I'm afraid of what might happen."

He frowned, then leaned in and said softly in her ear. "I'm not leaving you, Claire. I don't ever want to leave you. But this is not the place to discuss such things. When you come to the capital?"

Ever? He doesn't ever want to leave me? Oh, yes, oh yes. She nodded, sniffing. "Yes."

"Good, my love."

Ah, if there were two words she could listen to him say over and over, it was those—*my love*—even when he said them in Greek. She'd thought to distract him and ended up telling him she couldn't live without him. Then why couldn't she bring herself to say what she should have said long ago? That she was an assassin. Where was her courage?

She watched him stride away through the rain.

She could feel the words straining at the back of her throat to be said. *I'm an assassin, and I may have been meant to kill you. Please don't go without me.*

How did she say something that might end her world? This was like knifing herself. She could see herself cut down in an instant once Theo and Dankyo understood everything. She'd betrayed them both, but especially Theo. Her Theo. And she'd bleed for it. He'd throw her away like a dirty rag.

Yet if she stayed silent, he would go off without her and without Dankyo. And who else could protect him if he truly was the assassination target? If he died… Oh, that would be worse than ending this little paradise she'd found. She loved him. She thought he loved her back, but the person he loved wasn't real. He loved someone he trusted absolutely. Not her.

Theo was halfway to the airship. She quivered with indecision, felt the anguish and the words struggling inside her. She'd break in a moment. Shatter from the awful agony of wanting two impossible things at once. He took more steps, drew away. *Now! Say it now! There's time.*

He was almost to the stairs leading up. When he went up those, it would be too late.

She choked. Took one shaky step, then picked up her flounced skirt and *ran*. Mud splattered her ankles.

In a few minutes, the airship would lift off and sink into the fog of rain and wind, dwindling to a red smudge. Her mind seethed with grief and self-condemnation and more sadness, the emotions feeding on one another like circling sharks. *Run!*

For a few fleeting seconds, she even hit sharp time. People blurred. Raindrops fell, wobbling before her eyes, drifting like snowflakes.

Theo turned, slowly. He saw her and stopped; his broad shoulders seemed to jerk as if she'd shocked him. She wove through the two men in her way and fell to her knees at Theo's feet. The rain soaked her dress, stuck her hair to her neck and forehead, but she barely noticed.

"I'm sorry," she gasped out. "I..."

"Claire—" Theo put out his hand, cupped her chin. He sighed, a half smile on his face. "Very well. You may come. I never thought this would upset you so much." Someone else ran up. "You too, Dankyo. Arrange for some clothes for the both of you, please. Come with me." He dragged her up and to his side, then turned to the metal steps that descended from the belly of the airship.

Behind her, Claire heard Dankyo snapping out orders. He must have been right behind her, all the way, as she ran.

"You can remain in the airship while parliament goes through the stages of revoking the Frankenstruct Euthanasia bill."

Relief flooded her as they went up the steps together. She was safe again, and so was Theo. Everything was back under control. Perfectly safe. She didn't need to reveal any more of herself. She'd panicked for no solid reason. For an assassin to panic, well, they'd have failed her at classes, that was certain, and all because of one man. Strange, and it made her feel so queer. Going to her knees on the wet grass had been overly dramatic.

That her hands still trembled, she dismissed as a sign of the cold rain affecting her.

At the top of the stairs a uniformed woman cleaned her muddy feet with a cloth.

When they were behind a timber door, in some sort of lounging room, Theo sat on a tan leather sofa and pulled her onto his lap. She snuggled in. Her head found that ever so right space beneath his chin at his shoulder. Bliss. The engines of the airship had settled into a regular rhythm, and the rain seemed a distant event, lightly tapping on the porthole glass as if asking politely to be allowed in. Warm, comfy, and she had her man again.

"Happy?" Theo asked, his fingers playing in her hair.

"Mm-hmm."

"Thank the Lord for that," he muttered. But she could hear the amusement beneath the exasperation. She reached up and held on to the hand on her head. "Disobedient woman. I wonder what is the best way to punish you. I don't think I packed a whip."

She froze. *Oh, no.*

Theo chuckled and tugged her hair. "Don't worry, I'll think of something."

That almost sounded worse.

Chapter Twenty

Later that evening, a manservant knocked at the door and wheeled in a light evening repast of soup and crusty bread rolls, and cinnamon-topped apple strudel with little mounds of cream. After he quietly set the food onto the low table before the couch, Theo dismissed him. The door snicked shut.

She hadn't realized how hungry she'd become. She looked sideways at Theo. "Would you like me to serve?" It wasn't a role that came easily to her; at the barracks you were either a soldier or kitchen staff, with no in-betweens.

"No." He nudged her forward, and she climbed up from where she'd been nestled against him. "Turn." He indicated with his hand, and she moved until her back was to him.

"What is it?" Then she felt his hands at her back where the dress laced up from bottom to neck.

"No talking. Stay silent unless I ask a question." His voice had the steely backbone that made her shudder to a halt and her heartbeat thump louder. Her throat dried. She let herself be pulled until she stood between his legs and pressed her neck back as she felt his fingers working there.

He growled. “Still.” And she froze again.

The tie at the neck loosened, then the bodice as he undid the dress, opening it all the way down to her bottom. He kissed the center of her back and gently slid the fabric down her back and arms, baring her upper breasts, then her nipples to the cool air until at last she was nude to the waist. She strove to keep her mouth closed despite the quickening of her breaths.

“Close your eyes,” he said, and he kissed along her spine. A tingling blaze centered on where his soft lips pressed on her skin.

In the darkness of her mind, the light touch of cloth and fingers magnified. He drew the dress and then the lace and wire-stiffened petticoat to the floor. She stood there naked, wondering what he intended. From somewhere a wisp of breeze riffled her pubic hair. Was this to be his punishment?

He smoothed his hands from her upper arms to her shoulders and down her back, stopping a moment or two at her waist to rest his heavy palms on her hips. His thumbs revolved in feather-soft circles before he brought them round onto her buttocks, caressing the shape of her ass over and over, fingers flicking across the split. She heard the hiss of skin on skin, felt his calluses. His thumbs slid along the crease between each globe and on down to her outer thighs, then her inner, so very close to where her labia swelled.

She bit her lip, holding back a soft moan as her vagina twitched. A line of moisture leaked out, and she felt her labia part.

He kept on feeling her thighs and buttocks, shaping his hand against her rather than massaging.

Every so often his warm fingers wandered excruciatingly close to her mound.

"Are you wet, Claire?"

She sucked air through her nose. Just the question made her clench down there again.

"Answer me."

"Yes," she whispered.

"Turn," he said.

She faced him, eyes still shut, but her breathing came faster. Her nipples puckered. Though his hands hadn't done anything more intimate to her and only rested on her thighs, she was acutely aware of her nudity. A few inches away, he'd be looking at her with his mouth and tongue close to her breasts. He gripped tighter, kept her still. She imagined him probing through her slickness and quivered.

"Lovely." The word was said so quietly she almost missed it. She let her eyelids open the teeniest crack.

"Claire." She jammed her eyelids down, but he slid his hands up the front of her and tweaked each nipple, once.

"I'm going to shave you down there, dear."

She swallowed. Eyes still shut. *Mustn't speak. What did he mean? Oh. Surely not…*

"What do you think of that?" And yes, his fingers curled in her pubic hair and pulled.

"There, sir? That would be wicked! People could see my…"

"Who? Who could see? Unless you go about undressed, and that will only happen when I wish it to, in front of people of similar mind to myself." He tugged again at her hair. "Those who would appreciate this scrumptious body."

Her mouth was open. She shut it. "Sir, jokes." She scowled. "As for going about in front of others—"

"Silence. Open your eyes."

She did so. He regarded her steadily. "For that nasty expression"—his lips curved in a malicious smile—"I shall make certain to fulfill both of those options as soon as possible."

She spluttered and went to speak.

"Say another word and I'll gag you. Mmm, plus perhaps, you'd look good on a leash?"

Glaring...glaring would be bad. She blinked fast and held it in. How dare he threaten so? Yet, it made knees turn to water.

Oh, she adored him when he threatened and blackmailed.

Her pussy naked...and how did he mean the rest of her to be? Entirely naked before these others? Her imagination ran wild, and she saw herself paraded before a crowd, her lower body bared, a mask upon her face, and a leash around her neck. Heat swept through her.

Attentive, as always, he noticed, and little wrinkles framed the corners of his eyes. "Ahh. Perhaps you like my ideas after all?" She vigorously shook her head. "Don't believe you." He slapped her bottom. "Sit! Over there. Let's eat."

How was it that even when he suggested the most abominable things, she grew aroused? Her cunt dampened, even as she tried to think about something else—about *anything* else, except that embarrassing, exciting picture he'd conjured in her mind.

She knelt where he'd pointed, on the other side of the low timber table, and tried not to look cross or disgruntled. She was already in enough trouble.

With Theo sitting up on the sofa and her down on the floor, kneeling and naked, she felt exposed. Her breasts seemed swollen and heavy, and she was acutely aware of her sex between her legs. But apart from admiring her form at times, lingering on her breasts and making her blush with the attention, he stayed where he sat. Watching, smiling, like a big cat with something tasty trapped between its paws.

This was so...different. She'd slipped into this way of life so easily, and now she wondered how she'd ever lived before. True, he controlled her at times like this, but she thrived on it and adored him. She wanted so much to touch him, for him to touch her, and waiting like this under his scrutiny held her spellbound.

The soup and bread eaten, they started on the dessert. Theo placed a small mountain of cream in her bowl.

A dollop of cream fell from her spoon and, swiftly warmed by her body, trickled straight across her nipple.

When she went to grab a cloth napkin, stretching across the table, her breasts swaying, Theo said, deep and throaty, "Don't touch." His gaze seared her.

"Allow me." He reached over, plucked the napkin from her hand. Her chest constricted. She lowered her hands to her thighs, waiting, taut as a violin string.

Careful not to miss a single speck, he wiped her breast clean. His eyes were gray as storm clouds. Her nipple puckered. Would he lick her there, his tongue swirling, soft and hot?

She sat primly back on her heels and resisted squirming.

"You are so, *so* enticing. Time to get to work on you, dear."

She gulped. The room swayed, and it wasn't from turbulence.

Grinning, Theo put down the napkin, interlaced his hands, and stretched his arms, palms out, knuckles cracking. "I imagine Dankyo will have only packed essential clothing."

Relief settled. *Thank the Lord, he won't have brought the leather multibuckled coat.*

"However, I can improvise. Your breasts are underdecorated."

Her nipples stood out even more, and she had to resist the urge to cover them with her hands.

Her petticoat and dress lay over the sofa's armrest. He picked up the petticoat, took hold of the laced edge, then proceeded to rip the lace from it. *Such a waste of cloth.* The designer had spiraled the lace up the petticoat in one uninterrupted piece. Soon, Theo had the sofa covered in shreds of cloth and had gathered up several yards of tattered lace. He rose.

She shifted back a little, in apprehension, as he approached. The weight of his hand on her head halted her. "No," he said. "You'll like this. I promise."

She licked her lips as he stood over her, finding the middle of the lace, doubling it over, then finding the new halfway point. He trailed the lace across her, under her breasts, and quickly, efficiently, wove it around her back, to the front, crossing it between her breasts and returning. The lace tightened as he tied it. Being thin-edged, he tested how it pressed on her skin, slipping his fingers here, there, tracing a path under her breasts with those fingers and up to her nape.

She couldn't help half-closing her eyes at the pleasure, and sighed as he bent and licked where his fingers had been playing at the soft nape hairs.

He drew her earlobe between his lips, tongued her there before exploring inside her ear, while both hands cupped the mounds of her breasts. She had lace circling them and pulling them higher. The smell of him engulfed her—man and oiled steel and fine linen. If he wore cologne, it was the strangest scent, but it stirred her. Her nipples, her earlobe, and everywhere below her waist throbbed rhythmically.

She angled her neck, glancing down at his handiwork. "Mmm." Her breasts felt cared for, adulated, and indeed decorated. A lace halter neck that accentuated without concealing at all.

"Hands behind your back and wrists together," he whispered into her ear.

He sank his teeth in her earlobe. *Ah*! She jerked. Gently yet firmly he took both her wrists and drew them to the small of her back. She didn't resist. She'd done this before, let him bind her. Though the lace was so close to being rope.

Soft cuffs clicked onto each wrist—leather—and before she could speak again, he'd somehow linked them together with the spare lace. She couldn't separate her wrists, though she tried to. Theo's hands rested atop her shoulders.

"You won't get them loose. I can do what I like with you, dear heart. And I will."

Panting, she sat with her hands fastened at her back, head bowed, feeling what this truly meant. *Naked and tied again*. She shuddered. *Yes*.

"Okay? Claire?"

She nodded.

"If anywhere hurts or goes numb, tell me. Understand?"

"Yes, sir." The words came easier each time she said them. She looked up, found herself entranced by this large, forceful, yet tender man. Then he picked her up, put her over his shoulder, and took her into his bedroom through an adjoining door.

Chapter Twenty-One

For an old airship, the *Final Rebuttal* had some extraordinary design features. Draped over Theo's shoulder, naked, with her hands fastened behind her back and a bobbing upside down view of the room, Claire barely had time to look. Assassin training meant she could have still sketched the room in detail—though it might have come out upside down.

In the center of the bedroom, twin padded beams, joined in an X shape, with another strut sticking straight up from the middle, towered next to a pair of steel shutters in the floor. The shutters had been rolled back to reveal an oval bathtub-like window of armored glass. The green glass was cross-hatched with wire reinforcing. Clouds feathered past below, and condensed moisture dribbled across the large pane that formed the bottom. The air around this feature of the room was cooler. She shivered, though not entirely from the cold.

"A St. Andrew's cross," said Theo. "Or *crux decussate*. I haven't had occasion to use it for some time." He smacked her bottom as he swung around, and she jumped at the flare of sensation vibrating into her pussy. He deposited her standing up in front of the cross.

"There." He pushed until her back and tied wrists touched the cool padded leather. "Stay."

She looked at the strong features of his face, the heavy lips, iron-hard cheekbones and jaw, the stark black eyebrows above those compelling eyes, and sucked in a breath for strength before nodding.

He bent and kissed her, one hand at the side of her neck, thumbing her jugular furrow, toying with her skin. His mouth squashed down just enough to trap her against the leather. She melted into the cross, and only the knee he placed between her legs kept her upright. He took her mouth, as brutal and methodical as an army taking a fortress.

When he moved his hands behind her and released her wrists from the lace, she did nothing. Only waited to see what he was planning. When he pulled her cuffed wrists up to clip them to chains on the beams above, she let him, trembling as her arms were stretched up high. He slipped his hand between her legs, slid fingers along her cleft, then around her clit, leaving a cooling trail of her moisture.

"I think you like my cross."

With him inches away, doing *that*, no wonder she was aroused. She squeezed her thighs together.

He kissed her again, before buckling a leather strap across her hips and below her breasts and then kneeling to fasten her ankles to leather cuffs at the base to the cross. His light yellow shirt stretched tight across his back while he worked there. If her arms were free, she might have run her hands over him. The chains above gave very little when she tugged. He'd pulled everything snug, shortened the chains just right to make her feel totally restrained, unable to do what *she* wanted. Her clit felt swollen and hot, as if her body centered there. She shivered at the building tension.

Theo ran his hands up her thighs as he slowly stood. He kissed either side of her mound and belly button, then rose to his full height and went around behind, where she couldn't see. A double bed covered with a royal blue quilt was to her left against the outer bulkhead. The bathtub glass area dropped away a foot to her right.

The wind howled for a few seconds as it swept past the airship's hull, and the recessed glass hummed.

"Don't be scared. You'll be moving in a second."

She tensed as something clicked rapidly and the cross tilted back and swung out across the glass. When it stopped with a *clung*, she lay on her back, spread-eagled above the window, the padded limbs of the cross and the strut behind her head supporting her. It took her heart a while to slow.

Theo appeared at her side, gazed down at her while caressing her forehead. *He's standing on the glass. He trusts it not to break.* She tried to see past him. A long crank handle stuck out just beyond his shoulder.

"This used to be a gun platform. I had it adapted." Crow's feet crinkled at his eyes. He walked around her, out of the window tub, past her head, and as he went he slid fingers under the restraints, checking the cuffs and chains. "Wouldn't want you to fall off this," he muttered.

She closed her eyes a moment, striving for calm. This position on the cross rang alarms. She could barely move a muscle. When she opened her eyes, Theo was there, and he stroked his thumb across her lower lip.

"Are you okay, Claire? Take a breath. I won't do anything you don't want."

That somehow helped. She had a say.

"What are you going to do…to me?" And saying it that way, saying *to me* put the control back in his hands. She didn't mind. Her pussy clenched at the flare of lust in his eyes.

"I'm going to shave your little pussy until it's smooth as a gun barrel. And then I'm going to fuck you there. Does that suit you?"

Oh, yes.

She quivered and got her mouth working enough to say, in a voice that shook and dropped into a whisper at odd moments, "It suits me, though…we could've done this elsewhere."

His brow furrowed at that. "You think so?" Then he leaned over and fisted her hair, biting her neck in a most rapacious way, up into the hollow beneath her chin. His hand wandered between her strapped-open legs, and his fingers speared through her juices, into her entrance, and deep into her tunnel.

"*Unh.*" The suddenness shocked her. Today, slow and steady had gone out the window. Though hopefully not through the one at their feet.

He hooked those fingers upward, pumping, discovering some new delicious spot. She gasped and arched her back against the leather strap. Another pump lingered on that spot, and she writhed, wanting those fingers moving. *More.* When he stopped and pulled out his fingers, then stood, merely watching her, she blinked up at him, openmouthed.

He smiled. "I think this way is worth it, and so do you."

All that to prove his point? Oh. The spot inside her pulsed. *Maybe I should argue some more.*

Then he ducked away and came back with yet another device made by Henry—all metal and glass and cogs going *clickety click.* After an alarming glimpse of a row of little jaws at the front, she could only endure as Theo hooked up a long air pressure hose from the wall, and proceeded to shave her pussy.

The cold metal teeth made her jump as they cut her pubic hair. With her legs tied in a V, he could see everything down there.

He continually played with her clit and pussy and sometimes dipped a moistened finger into her nether hole while peering up to see how she was doing—still with a smug look on his face—and that only made her squirm and squeal. The man was insufferable, and now, she ached so much down there, she would explode if he didn't let her come soon.

"There," he declared. "Done. Now that looks so pretty and…hmm." He slid a moistened finger along and over the swollen bump of her clit. "Yes. Ready for me."

Panting, she craned her neck to see where he went and what he did.

The device set aside, Theo approached to stand beside her head and retrieve a leather strap from somewhere beneath. He laid it across her mouth, settled it between her lips, and buckled it down, pressing her head back into the padding and effectively gagging her.

She poked her tongue against the leather, swallowed. Why did he gag her?

But he said nothing and went over to the crank mechanism. She stared upward. The ceiling looked a long way away.

"Prepare for another move, dear. You can't fall off, so relax."

She squeezed her eyes shut. *What is this? Musical crosses?*

The beams under her tilted sideways until she looked at wall, not ceiling, and then kept on rotating until the cross stopped with her looking down at the glass, watching clouds curl past below. The leather gag took the weight of her head, pressing at the corners of her lips.

Freakin' hells and heavens above. She was upside down, and the only things holding her on were the chains and the straps on her body and spread limbs. She heard clothing being unbuttoned and tossed away, heard footsteps, and saw Theo's bare legs back there, between her legs, his hands under her thighs.

"I don't think you need arousing, do you?"

Those words sounded ominous. She tried to talk, but only a gargled sound emerged.

He thrust into her in one long move that threatened to split her in two. Joy, not pain, made her clamp down on him. The pleasure ratcheted up as he rocked out and in, slapping into her, in time with his roving fingers squeezing her clit and stimulating her nipples. And oh, her nipples stood out like bullets, stiff and throbbing. The clouds below, the ten thousand foot drop—all was forgotten.

"Ah!" Pleasure curled like a clock spring overwound a billion turns. Scrunching hard and tight, curling up her toes, making her body twist—she'd waited so long, and he'd teased her so much she couldn't have cared if she were upside down at the bottom of the sea. Her toes arched again. She cried out past the gag.

That was when he stopped, not the thrusting, just the movement of his fingers. He released her nipple and clit and clasped her hips for purchase, then slammed into her. Her heart drummed. Her inner thighs were slick with juices, and his legs rubbed on them as he slid down and back. She needed him.

Writhing was futile—the straps cinched her tight—but she tried, gasping moistly into the gag, slewing her hips that tiny bit, striving to push closer to him.

He put his hands back on her, in the right places, squeezing her clit and holding. He grunted, slammed in up to his balls. It was all she needed. She screamed into the gag until her throat was raw and aching. The room vanished. Fire tore through her in a thousand body-shaking bursts. Theo came, and the jets of his cum pulsing in her vagina triggered more spasms, while her wrists twisted, and her thighs pressed in vain against the cuffs and straps.

She had tears in her eyes when he let her down. He helped her to the bed; then, as she lay there trying to recall how to move, he went to the bathroom and returned with washcloth and a basin of water.

"Stay there," he told her, as if otherwise was possible.

Afterward, when they lay in each other's arms under the quilt, she dared to ask him, "Which part was the punishment?"

"Sir," he said, quietly, reminding her. A pause as he gathered his thoughts. "The shaving of your pussy."

"But I enjoyed that, sir."

"Tying you above my window then."

"I enjoyed that too." She couldn't help giggling. He'd forgotten.

He rose onto his elbows. "Insolent one." And that made her laugh even louder.

"Now you've done it." Chuckling, he wrestled with her until he turned her onto her stomach, then swatted halfheartedly at her bottom. "There and there! Punishment done."

She giggled again. Which meant another smack, but it was worth it.

In the night she awoke and found she'd curled up to his warm side, in the shadow of his muscled arm. His breathing came steady as a tide washing in and out. She lay there listening for a long time, being comforted, feeling secure, before drifting off to sleep again.

When she next awoke, it was to the jars and clangs of the airship docking. Still nighttime—the floor window was dark. With the room lit by a dimmed voltaic lamp near the recessed entrance, she studied

Theo. He snored quietly, lying sprawled on his back among the crisp white sheets. A tuft of dark hair at his armpit tempted her. Did she dare?

At the first foray of her fingers in his armpit, his opposite hand snaked across and snagged hers.

“What are you doing, insolent one?” Theo’s eyes glinted at her from slits. A hint of something dangerous lurked there.

She froze. Then temptation won out again. “We’ve arrived, and I needed to wake you. So...” She twisted her hand, aiming for the place to break his grip, between his finger and thumb. No luck. He was quick, too quick, without her resorting to sharp time. She grinned cheekily. This was fun, teasing him.

“By tickling me?”

He surged up with a roar, lunging for her other wrist and striving to flip her over. For once she resisted, testing him, using her knowledge to keep him off balance. They wrestled for a flurry of seconds, turning the sheets into a tangled morass. This close, without either wanting to hurt the other, Theo’s strength won out, and she ended up beneath him, her arms pinned at her back, knees crammed up under her stomach.

Her breasts heaved, rubbing her taut nipples on the sheet.

“And now,” Theo declared, breathing hard, “apologize. You do not tickle your master.”

My master? Oh, that sounds good. With her head jammed sideways and half under a pillow, it was difficult to talk. “Never,” she answered gleefully, wriggling a bit in a last-ditch attempt to get free. “Can’t make me.”

He growled. “You’ve sealed your fate.” He shook her.

The threat in his words sent her body quivering and robbed her of any will to resist.

Keeping his hold on her still, he wrapped and tied a twisted cloth, perhaps his trousers, about her wrists, then nudged her knees apart and took her from behind. This was no intricate seduction. Fast and brutal, yet she plunged into arousal. Wetness trickled into, then flooded her slit until she groaned at each thrust.

Theo laughed. “Don’t think you’re going to come. Not until I’ve had you at least twice.”

She groaned again in frustration.

“Will you tickle me again?” he demanded, slapping into her balls-deep, before twisting up her hair and lifting her head back.

She panted as she spoke. “No. Maybe. I don’t know. Oh. Please. Move. Sir.”

“Ah. I can see this will be fun.”

Though he made her wait for her own pleasure and did indeed take her using every orifice, before allowing her to come, by the end, she was left satiated and flopped across the bed. His love bites went from neck to buttocks, and she ached deliciously. The bed dipped, then sprang back as Theo left to ring for breakfast.

Heavens, she thought, dazed. If this was Theo at his worst, she never wanted to leave him. She wondered, with a little delightful trepidation, how else she might tease him and how far she could go.

Chapter Twenty-Two

"We're docked." Theo reached across the table and poured coffee into her cup. The steam rising hinted at some strange flavor, and she sniffed suspiciously. One side of his mouth curved up. "From Constantinople."

"Hmm." She wrapped the long sleeve of her borrowed black dressing gown out of the way, lifted the blue and white porcelain cup, and sipped. *Ew.* "Constantinople? How much camel dung goes in?"

He roared with laughter, and she couldn't help grinning at the sight of him rocking back in the cane chair. Life was good when she could laugh, or watch Theo do so.

He wiped his eyes before pushing the plate of fruit pastries and croissants over. Now *they* looked yummy.

"Maybe these instead then? I guarantee no camel dung."

After she'd moved two of them onto her plate, he caught her hand and raised it to his lips for a kiss. "Thank you for coming, Claire. You've made this a far more enjoyable journey. You'll have to stay on board and amuse yourself for a few days. There's a small library here."

He'd remembered. Pleasure spread through her in a warm glow. He still held her fingers, so she maneuvered them around. He let her pull his hand to her lips to return the kiss. His hand was heavy, his skin smelled awesome as always, and she couldn't resist giving a lick and then a nibble.

"Hey. I need my fingers."

"I know." She tilted her head to hold his palm against her cheek. "Thank you for this."

"For letting you come with me?"

"For everything. For just being you. I'm so lucky to have you."

His fingers curved and cupped her chin as he propped his elbow on the table. "And I you. I love how you obey me, Claire, and giving you pleasure."

She blinked, said quietly, "And I love obeying and...and wondering what you'll do to me next." Loved putting her hands in his and surrendering. She'd learned a little of why this appealed to her. The pleasure was only a part of it. The way he commanded her was his second gift, and one she treasured as much as the other. She put her hand to where he held her chin and slipped her smaller fingers underneath his.

"Somehow I knew this." He smiled. "Once this bill is repealed and you're officially human, I'm going to keep you, my little bodyguard, by my side wherever I go. Always."

Always? She felt a quiver of happiness inside. *Please, let this all come true. I want to be with this man so much it hurts to imagine anything else.*

He moved her head slowly, side to side. “Your answer?”

“Yes, sir.” *Always and forever.*

For three days, she lived in the *Final Rebuttal*, knowing if she set foot on the ground outside, she faced execution. Theo returned whenever he wasn’t obligated to attend parliament, sharing with her what was happening outside. She could feel their relationship cementing, enfolding, deepening. It was thrilling and satisfying all at once.

On the third day, Theo bounded up the airship’s corridor, his brown coat flaring behind him, and swept her into his arms.

“Done! Love! Done!” He kissed her, swung her about. “The bill is repealed. Tomorrow we’ll go explore the city. And tomorrow evening is the presidential ball.” His eyes changed, and he raised her chin, studying her intently. She wondered what he held back.

“After the ball is the president’s private function. There I shall introduce you to those friends I spoke of. We will have to visit Hinchcliff and Co. for something special.”

Ah. Those friends. Arousal dampened her panties; her stomach clenched. His friends—of similar persuasion.

Halfway down the steel outer steps, she stopped. She’d dressed sensibly in slim-leg red trousers, white shirt, and black jacket.

The airship field stretched away in the morning light. At one end were sprawling brick, steel, and glass offices, and at the other, backlit by an orange horizon, were low sheds and barbed wire fences. Smoke rose skyward in small tufts from a distant green and orange airship. Nothing remarkable, if it wasn't for the men running away from it at full tilt.

Just as one screamed a warning, a curl of flame licked from the rear of the airship. Theo and Dankyo had reached the ground below her and swung their heads at the sound. *Too slow.*

She clicked over into sharp time, leaped feetfirst off the steps, aiming to reach the bottom and land in front of Theo. *The faster, the better*. The ground drifted up to meet her. Wind fluttered her shirt.

Her boots thumped into the grass. Theo and Dankyo's mouths moved, but nothing had been said yet. At the airship the flame blossomed into a rolling fireball. Black specks whirled in her direction. Snatching up the round lid from a rubbish bin, she swept in front of the two men. A blurred ringing fed into her ears—sound lengthened by sharp time.

The specks preceded a wave of smoke. The running men were buffeted by the shock wave, some reeling, blood spraying, as metal debris clipped them. The specks shot closer, turned into shards. She flung up her bin-lid-shielded arm before Dankyo. One, two *clungs*. The pieces caromed and ricocheted off. The third she dived for, arcing into the air to catch it. The chunk zipped on a whistling path straight at Theo's head. Big as a crowbar, it struck, knocked her arm sideways.

She landed rolling, off-balance and skidding on her shoulder, scraping bits of jacket and some skin across the grass and gravel. She lapsed into real time. The explosion boom-shuddered past.

The crowbar debris chunked into the grass and stuck there, quivering. Theo and Dankyo whipped around and stared at her. Smoke whooshed past, carrying small pieces of acrid, oily ash. *Safe. They're safe.*

She bent her head and heaved a sigh of relief. Where had that come from?

Theo bent half-crouched over her, hand on her head. "Are you okay?"

God, even he shook.

She nodded. "You should check for sabotage. Airships don't explode that well." She should know. This had been one of their lecturer's favorite scenarios.

"True enough. Stay here. Get back up those steps, and don't move till I come for you." He turned his head. "Dankyo. A detail of ten men. Let's get over there fast."

When she made to follow him anyway as the men set off for the explosion site, Theo glared. "Stay. There." He gestured, and two house guards crowded her.

"Come on, Miss. Up the stairs." The guard took her arm.

Damnation. Still, Dankyo was with him.

Theo paused and fixed her with a look that said half *don't you dare disobey*. The other half, a mix of pride and exasperated wonder. "Thank you." He spun and stalked away.

It all could have been nothing more than an inconvenience and a jot of worry before the best part of the day arrived. None of the fallen men were killed or seriously wounded. Theo came back unharmed, and the explosion had, supposedly, been an accident.

Except when she'd reached the top step with the two guards behind her, a familiar yet subtle sign was affixed to the doorway. A tiny stain on the painted steel. A smell of lemon she'd forever associate with one person. With her stomach curling up like a dying animal, she felt at the hatchway frame as she stepped through. It was there. From the message bumps implanted and the distinctive odor, she could tell that Francine had been here. Her special ability would have let her breach the ship. That woman could get in anywhere given smoke or shadows.

Inkline wants to see you at the ball.

Inkline was not just alive. He was here. Her knees threatened to fail and deposit her onto the green carpet.

Panic didn't come close. Her insides had turned to ice. When she so desperately needed logic, it deserted her. *Frick, frick, frick. What am I going to do?*

Act normal. Act. Normal.

When she got to the study, she pushed the door shut in the face of the house guards, turned and leaned on it, then slid to the floor.

Fate had come back to bite her. She covered her face with her hands and bowed her head. What was she to do? She bit back a moan. She'd been backed into a corner.

After wiping her eyes, she pushed to her feet, then straightened her clothes. She'd find out what Inkline wanted. First...find out what. Then decide.

Maybe she could still wriggle out of this. As long as Theo was safe, she had room to move.

For the rest of the day, she struggled to appear normal. The visit to Hinchcliff and Co. was the only thing that distracted her from the growing sense of dread—the feeling she was walking into her own grave.

The clothing shop was located on one of the busiest and richest streets in the center of town. While Theo made purchases, she poked about the shop with wide eyes and a determination not to appear naive. Even the walls were decorated with accessories—whips, coils of rope and some rather suspicious pieces of machinery that reminded her of Henry's penchant for inventing sexual toys. There were skirt and bodice sets, where the breasts were bared. Long leather frock coats teamed up with crotchless leggings. The lingerie looked like it'd been shredded by shrapnel...and there were chainmail bras and panties.

On the way past a set of knightly armor, she found it too had been curiously altered. At the groin a segmented steel cock projected outward. After one long openmouthed stare, she tried not to look again.

When they left, Theo's house guards were burdened with several new packages.

"For you, dear," Theo murmured in her ear.

She blushed momentarily, until she remembered what awaited her at the ball. *Inkline.*

Chapter Twenty-Three

The steam limousine pulled up next to a bevy of blue-uniformed valets. Steam hissed, and their engine gyroscope whined to a stop. Their door was swiftly opened by one of the male valets. Theo disembarked, then reached in.

"Allow me, my dear."

She placed her white-gloved hand in his and let herself be helped from the carriage. Her white ball dress was demure with a neckline that went up to her throat, a cutaway section at her cleavage, and long star diamante gloves that matched the stars sparkling on the silk dress. The wide petticoat showed at the back in a bustle, and if any more material had been added to her apparel, she would surely have fallen over from the weight.

Being hampered by her clothes felt wrong, especially as the security here was so hefty. Some guards were in plain view, in black and gold dress uniform; others were less obvious. The bulge of hidden weapons, their stance, and the way they scrutinized the crowd were telltale markers. One guard noted her interest.

She was getting soft, losing her finely honed attitude of concealed wariness.

But was this normal for such celebrations, or did they suspect? Inkline had originally meant to send her to a state ball of some sort, and here she was, as a guest.

"You look beautiful, Claire." Theo swept her hand to his mouth, kissed the knuckles of her glove before adding, "Though I look forward to seeing you in your other garments." His gaze held an evil hint of laughter.

She ducked her head.

If he saw her expression, he'd know something was wrong. Luckily, the stream of people into the palace and then the formalities of their entry into the grand ballroom proved distracting.

She drew in a long breath. How strange she, of all people—and heavens, how she enjoyed slotting herself into "people"—how strange to be here, about to be presented to the president of the Hellene Nation.

Reality was only a misstep away. All those guards would have her on the floor in a flash with a pistol to her head if they knew what she was. She focused. *Stay calm. There's still hope. Got to be a way out. There has to be.*

The announcer, a slim bespectacled man in a black suit, standing by double doors of ebony and glass, bowed and took the card from Dankyo. The current assignment of four of Theo's house guards moved ahead to carry out their security check.

The announcer flicked on a voltaic-powered speakerphone. "Presenting Lord Theodore Kevonis and his consort, Claire." The lack of a surname had befuddled him initially. She gave him as confident a smile as she could muster, and he nodded, then swiveled on his high boots and waved them on.

"Come." Theo took her hand and drew her into the ballroom. Scent, sound, and sight overwhelmed her. Enough perfume and cologne seemed to have been used to poison an elephant. An orchestra playing a gentle waltz competed with a thousand voices and a thousand tapping heels. On all sides there were swirls of rich clothing, the flash of jewelry and laughter. Looking down on the ballroom from terraces were at least twenty guards. Likely, an equal number circulated with the guests.

Claire took a deep breath. *Concentrate. Somewhere here, Inkline is watching.* Each couple, after they'd entered and been announced, were greeted by another, elegantly dressed couple. "The president and his consort," Theo whispered.

Claire blinked. The president was as tall as Theo and just as imposing. He was older, perhaps fifty, with the red of his beard paling with gray flecks. Narrower at the shoulder yet muscular, from the way his coat draped him. It was curious to see such a long elegant nose allied with broad cheekbones.

Pale blue eyes... She stilled, seeing him studying her in return, only his gaze traveled blatantly down to her feet and back up, pausing momentarily at chest level. She tried to stay calm but felt the tension between her eyebrows and knew the frown showed. He smiled back.

"Good evening, Theo," the president drawled. "I see you have a lovely catch with you for tonight's festivities." He addressed Claire. "And if rumor is correct, my dear, you are the reason for Theo's"—he cocked an eyebrow, like a hawk poised before a dive—"avid pursuit of the Frankenstruct Bill?" He lifted her hand to his mouth and kissed it.

Theo chuckled. "Of course. I make no secret of this. Claire is worth anything to me." He looked sidelong at her, winked. "Anything."

She held her tongue, not wanting to make a fool of herself.

"Good evening, Theodore. I'm pleased to meet you, Claire. Theo has spoken well of you." The woman beside the president spoke quietly, but her voice was deep and assured. Her aubergine gown was so dark it seemed to consume light, except for at neckline and hem, where a wide row of brilliant white gems scintillated.

She added, "I do hope your passion is returned, Theo. If not, I'm sure others will be in pursuit of your lady tonight." She smiled at Claire, as if to say this was a joke between them. The lustrous black curls that framed her face and slender neck bobbed when she shifted, as though caressing her.

Claire squeezed Theo's hand, and he squeezed back. "His passion is returned, my lady."

The woman's smile deepened. "It's Antheia. Please, do call me that. I look forward to learning more about you tonight at our little party." She put her black-gloved hand on Claire's shoulder. "You'll find it far more exciting than this sterile affair."

And that settled it. Antheia was flirting. Claire blushed. A woman flirting with her? If she hadn't already grown used to Theo's strange ways... Then Theo said something that almost slipped past her.

"Excuse me?" she asked.

The president laughed. "Theo, you'll have to watch my Antheia. She has low intentions with regards to Claire. Your Theo was introducing us. The brash man stole my name. I too am a Theodore. Theodore Christakos at your service."

Laughter echoed around her. She managed to stumble through the rest of the conversation. Since others awaited their turn to meet the president, it was merely seconds before Theo continued on into the ballroom, and found their seats in the large alcove reserved for them. Arrowhead-shaped lamps illuminated the white linen of two oval tables and plush red chairs.

Theo directed her to throw her light fur wrap over a chair, then whisked her onto the dance floor. All the lessons in dancing over the past years allowed her to dance automatically without making a fool of herself. Her feet slid and spun across the shining timber floor while her mind skittered off into a maze of anxiety.

Above them hung crystal chandeliers, dangling from the ceiling three stories up. She knew who Inkline wanted assassinated.

The name had penetrated like a spear—Theodore Christakos. He'd been her target all along. Inkline would have already instructed her to eliminate her Theo if he'd been the target. Why wait for a highly guarded ball?

She twirled and flounced about the dance floor while her thoughts swirled far faster, and she sank deep into a mire of grief. Her lies had returned to torture her.

And still, she could not bring herself to do what she knew must be done. Not yet. One last time to be held in his arms...then, maybe. Her eyes brimmed with unshed tears. The dance music died away.

Their table was covered in delicate gold-embroidered linen. She stared at the fine needlework as waiters came and went, bringing food, before they withdrew and pulled the curtains across for privacy. The goblets, cutlery, and plates were beautifully designed. She ran a finger along the moisture on her goblet. Bubbles raced to the surface of the pink champagne.

What to do? Inkline wouldn't just go away.

A scent of lemon came to her. The room jarred, shifting as if an earthquake had struck.

She found the next instruction under the table's edge. Francine again—some imbalance of her body's chemistry, something to do with the camouflage mechanism perhaps—meant the fragrance of lemon always accompanied the woman.

Inkline had the gall to request a meeting before she terminated the target. It was the first part of the message that had made the room spin.

Your mission reaffirmed. Kill Theodore Christakos. She was right. Shocking despite everything.

She stared at Theo.

"Claire? Claire?" He took up her hand, unclenched her fingers from the table's edge. "What is it? You're cold." A deep crease furrowed between his eyes. Stricken, she bit her lip. Tears rolled from her eyes and down her cheeks, across her mouth. Here it was, the end of her world. She would not betray him this way. If someone was to be hurt, it must be her.

She slid off the chair and stayed there on one knee, feeling as if her throat had seized up. Not properly kneeling. True submissive posture seemed wrong. This was business, not sex, and begging off and pretending she was some little brainless type who hadn't understood what she was concealing... So very wrong. If she'd hurt him, she'd take whatever was coming.

She bent her head, tugged her hand from Theo's. He let her go, his fingers sliding across hers...and gone. Would he ever hold her hand again? The depth of her sorrow had stung him. He must guess she had something awful to tell him.

Dismayed, terrified, she looked at the tip of his shiny shoe and whispered. "I'm sorry. So very sorry. I've lied to you." Her mouth and voice shook. She paused a few seconds to collect herself, then looked up at him. "I'm not a bodyguard. I'm an assassin and"—she swallowed—"I have just learned that my target was the president." Behind and to her right, where Dankyo stood, she heard a sharp hiss of shock, then the *thring* of a sword blade being drawn.

"If you would let me make amends, if you trust me enough, I will help you to...to find Inkline. He's alive, and here, somewhere."

Theo said nothing. The silence deepened.

Did he not hear her? "The palace security is breached," she added. The tension ate at the insides of her stomach. Impassive, he gave only more silence, deliberately maybe, to see how big a hole she'd dig for herself. "I… We need to do something. There's a message in braille, under the table's edge. I can tell you what it says. Please, please, let me help."

Enough! I've said enough. Stop.

She clasped her hands together, tried to control herself, but the shaking in her hands spread until her entire body trembled. Where had all that training gone? She'd happily, almost, take a knife to the gut rather than wait like this, knowing she was losing him. Her teeth chattered. Bereft, she shut her eyes. His gaze fell on her still, flattening her, making her into a nothing thing, filled up with leaden pain and sorrow.

Slowly, unable to stop, she lay out straight upon the timber, prostrate at his feet, the white gown and petticoat frothing about like a wave crashing over her.

The opposite of heaven is hell, her inner voice whispered, and I've gone straight from one to the other. A high keen sounded in her head. That's me, she thought. That's me, screaming. But there was no doubt she deserved it, deserved whatever happened next. *I've betrayed him all along.*

Chapter Twenty-Four

With her head to the floor, she couldn't see what expression Theo wore, but she could hear the grinding of his teeth—this from a man she'd never seen truly angry. He was always in control. Eventually Dankyo broke the silence.

"Sir, we must act on this."

Theo let out a hiss.

"Very well. Send for the officer in charge of security. Do it quietly. We need to find this Inkline and whoever is with him. Locate, isolate, capture, or kill if necessary." She heard a sound that made her think he was scrubbing his hands through his hair. There had been no inflection in his voice. Dead and cold and angry.

"I'll do that, sir."

They left her there, on the floor until the officer returned; by then the tears had dried on her face. She heard the click of his boots, then the murmur of discussion as they talked near the curtained entrance.

"Claire," said Dankyo. "Sit up. Get yourself on a chair. We need to ask you questions."

She got up off the floor, rearranging her skirts, trying to catch a glimpse of Theo's face without looking full-on at him. It was as expressionless as his voice.

So she sat on the chair as they bid her, then repeated the braille message. They found the message themselves, and Dankyo shot her a hard look. Surprised perhaps? She didn't think he'd seen the technique before.

Finally the officer grasped the back of the chair he'd sat in the wrong way round, pushed himself upright, and twisted the chair back into a spot at the table.

"If the lass is sure this Inkline will be there, we'll set up an ambush. But the lady has to walk in without alerting him. It'll be dangerous."

"I'll do it," she spat out before anyone could say otherwise.

Dankyo nodded grimly.

"So be it." Theo shut, then opened his eyes. He rose, pulled his morning coat on, and carefully buttoned up. "Weapons? Dankyo?"

"Sir." A curt nod, and Dankyo left.

What was this? What weapons did they speak of? Had they arranged something unusual? Knowing Dankyo he might have an electrorocket launch platform tucked away somewhere. With her eyes only, she pleaded with Theo. A simple acknowledgment of her presence would do, but he swiveled on his heel and strode away through the curtain.

So be it. She'd known this would happen. She'd known.

* * * *

If palace security shadowed her to the rendezvous point, she couldn't spot them. Just as well, for Francine de-camouflaged from a wall of tropical plants halfway up the grand stairs that spiraled to the roof. On her slim, muscular body, the greens and creams of the wall and the plants slowly moved across her skin. She was naked, as she had to be, when going *quiet*.

The patches of chameleon color merged, then faded to the dark chocolate Francine favored. For the thousandth time, Claire thanked her stars that she didn't have Francine's ability. Going naked in enemy territory wasn't tempting. If things went wrong, Francine had minimal time to grab a weapon or even clothes. There'd be a stash somewhere, though.

Francine nodded. Though silent, her eyes spoke of the same ache to tell all that Claire felt. Best friends in the past, but what were they now? Could she trust Francine?

She wrenched her thoughts back on track. How would the Guard watch her when this was going to be out in the open on the roof? If Inkline had some auxiliary plan and security turned up, the wrong people might die.

The last flight of stairs took her out through a door with a newly disabled lock. Confirmation that they'd infiltrated the palace. Someone was out here. Francine followed her through. She stepped out under the stars, felt the cool breeze, smelled the tang of the sea off to the southwest. Her bustle ruffled and fluttered in the force of the wind.

Assassin's garb, this was not. She hungered for a black slink-cloth coat and tights, with a side order of gauss pistol and knife.

The palace wasn't made to be overlooked and the only structures, on the same level or above, were watchtowers a quarter mile away.

Hopeless. Where was security? They'd not given her the plan apart from engage him in conversation and keep him here.

Slowly her eyes adjusted to the low light.

Off to the right she saw the glint of moonlight on a swimming pool. In front of her, rendered in gray and black courtesy of the night, was a lounging area flanked by potted palms and sculpted plants in tubs. Ivy on lattice walled two sides of the garden. Inkline sat forward on a white sunning chair. The others, she detected and marked their position.

She went to him, stood there at parade rest. It was automatic even now. And, she wanted him to think her harmless.

"Good evening, Claire," he said crisply. "How have you been?"

An inane question. She licked her lips. Nerves. Damn, she couldn't afford nerves. She needed precision, unmistakable purpose. Instead she got nerves.

His bald pate glimmered with moonlight. Black shirt and leggings—*he* got to dress properly for the occasion—and a belt weighed down by a pistol on one hip, and sheathed bayonet on the other.

He unfolded, standing over her. Slick and malevolent, he drew the bayonet and crowded her eye with the tip. She strived not to lean away, succeeded.

“I’m well actually. I could take that off you in a millisecond.”

“Of course, but...I have four of my best watching us.”

She didn’t look. Let them think they were concealed. Francine would be the fourth. God knew where she’d found to hide.

“You are the fifth, darling.”

“Fifth?” The knife tip wavered at her lower eyelid.

“Yes, fifth best. And my, how well you’ve done since we parted ways. Found yourself a Theo and hung on to him. Waiting, were we? For instructions?”

“Mm-hm.” *Fifth best*? With sharp time she could run rings around the others. Not the strongest or smartest, but she was fast, and tonight, she prayed that was all she needed.

“What a pity he’s the wrong Theo.” He laughed. “Of course, I’m not stupid. You’ve been rutting your little brains out, haven’t you?”

Oh, hell. She swallowed. The knife tip slid down, pressed on her cheekbone.

“Haven’t you?” The knife went down her face and then throat, never quite cutting, then across to her left nipple. “Haven’t you?” He dug it in a little, and she felt a spike of pain and the wetness of blood on her breast.

“Yes,” she whispered.

“And here I was holding myself back because I thought I’d hinder your performance. Why did I bother? Tut-tut." Even in moonlight she saw the narrowing of his eyes. "Well. It's good though. After this I'll know where to come for my relief. Won't I?" He grabbed her breast, squeezed hard.

She winced. The churning mess in her stomach threatened to spew from her mouth. "So," he said cheerily, with eyes as dead as stones. He stepped away, sheathed the bayonet. "Now we've settled that, I need you to kill the president. Don't fail… Fail, and your lover dies. Understand?"

Oh God. My worst fear. She wanted to shut her eyes and scream. A droplet of sweat ran between her shoulder blades. *Inkline doesn't trust me at all. No one does.*

She couldn't walk away and let the palace security deal with this, wherever the hell they were hiding. Inkline alive meant Theo would die. He'd not renege on his promise.

"I understand."

Inkline liked to pull all the strings. No second in command. The PME had stopped the assassination order. He was out on his own with no support. If she eliminated him, it would be over. Theo would live. The president would live.

"I'd like a kiss before we get down to business," Inkline said.

She snapped her gaze back on him. The grin on his face made her ill. His lips were parted. His skin glistened.

Ugh. Her stomach flip-flopped at the thought of him pressing his mouth on hers. She backed away, circled. It didn't matter if she lived or died, only that

Inkline died. The others were fast, if not as fast as her. If she stabbed Inkline, they might still get her, and a knife might not kill. She needed something surer, something that couldn't fail.

He turned on his heel, following her. "Where are you going? Stop...right...there."

She froze. A habitual reaction. He snared her cold hand and brought it soft and trembling to his mouth. Ice ran down her arms, her spine. She needed to let him get close anyway. Needed him stirred up so he thought she was easy prey.

Five yards back was the edge, with a railing to stop anyone accidentally toppling over. She didn't aim for this to be accidental.

"There." His lips pressed against her knuckles like an amorous snail, wet and squishy. He cupped her breast, wriggled his hand into her cleavage. She could feel his fingers scrabbling about until he grabbed her nipple and clamped down hard enough to make her wince.

She had to be certain Inkline died. The man always had liked kissing her, groping her. She knocked away his hand, though it made his fingers jerk painfully on her nipple, and fled a few more steps.

"No. No more." She put a tremor in her voice, kept on backing away, then let him catch her again.

"What? Shy?" He chuckled.

A few more unsteady steps with him pushing...and her bottom hit the railing. Inkline put a hand either side to trap her against the rail. *Predictable, arrogant man.*

Up close, silvered by the moon high to her right, his lips shone wet and dark; his eyes were wide, devouring her.

"Better, pet. Stay." He leaned in, angling his mouth.

Sharp time.

She took his forearm, slithered down, and ducked beneath his arm, whipped around behind, and pushed. He went over the rail like a fish sliding over a dam, with a death grip on her wrist that twisted painfully. A jerk, as his weight yanked on her arm. He tumbled sideways slowly, legs, arm flailing.

She overbalanced, bent at the waist across the railing. Another second, they'd both be falling.

The scuffle of shoes from behind warned of others. If they shot her, Inkline would fall.

She twisted to free her arm, but the swinging weight and his strength defeated her. Inkline's mouth was wide, lips stretched, teeth bared. If she fell, death would take her. Irrevocable. Sharp time couldn't stop death.

The parapet dragged on her dress, ripped fabric—another inch, and she'd be too far over to pull back.

The lights below called to her. Inkline screamed, but the sound hadn't hit. She leaned into the pull, let herself slide, headfirst, toward the ground. Trails of superheated air sped past her ear, shedding red sparks, heading inward to the roof—bullets from somewhere out there. The watchtowers, of course. Inkline's head exploded in a puff of slow-moving blood.

Snipers. What the—

A sword flashed, carved straight through Inkline at the elbow. She threw her left hand up, clawed fingernails into stone, swung from head down to right way up to hang from her hands. Her back felt like a target. She hauled herself onto the palace roof.

Sharp time...ended.

Where are those snipers?

She staggered and sprawled onto the tiles, on top of a soft body. She'd survived. Her nails were torn to the bleeding edge, her thighs and waist had been scraped raw...but she lived.

"Francine?"

Her friend grinned back from underneath her, clapped her on the arm. "Whew. Thought I was too late there. Let's go." She wriggled out from under Claire, went to rise.

"No!" Claire slapped her back down. "Stay. There's snipers." She glanced about. Three bodies dead or at least unmoving. No more bullets incoming yet. They'd have to crawl. No telling who those snipers would shoot.

Inkline is dead.

She looked at Francine. At least the woman had managed to pull on a pair of loose pants and a black top along with snagging her favorite Hai-na-go sword. Curved and super sharp, the blade had severed Inkline's arm like it was made of cheese.

In the moonlight, Francine's face was a study in *chiaroscuro*—classic lines of black and gray and silver—serenity, beauty, and a no-nonsense attitude to life. She laid her hand across the back of Francine's shoulder. Death had been so damn close. Elbow propped, she sucked in a lungful of air. *Calm.*

Francine just waited. Like always, she was the tougher one. Nothing knocked her off center.

"Thank you. Thank you for helping me."

Francine grinned and patted the hand on her shoulder. "Hey, it's what I was here for. Not Inkline—that bastard can rot, and those others, pah, no better."

"Inkline's dead," she whispered.

"Yeah. Unless he's very good at bouncing and can regrow his head. And we might be dead too unless you got friends here."

Claire sighed, her throat full of putty. "I've got you. That's about it." She should have jumped with Inkline. Then she wouldn't have to remember Theo.

"That'll have to do. We can get out of here. You know, those snipers didn't shoot at you. Maybe we're okay?"

"I don't think they were aiming at me. You, though, be careful." She figured they were Dankyo's snipers.

Security erupted onto the rooftop—boiling out the door like ants on a picnic mission and climbing up from below the edge of the building. *Clever.* A bit late, though, to catch her or Inkline going over. She hoped none of them had been brushed off the side of the building by Inkline's body.

Yes, she was okay. They'd only let her rot in prison for a few thousand years.

She stood up, put her shoulders straight, and tried to look strong. But Theo and Dankyo were nowhere to be seen. They'd not even bothered to see if she survived.

"I'll try to get you out of this, Francine. Francine?" Her friend was gone. She smiled. At least one of them had a chance at life.

When they came for her, she said nothing, only holding out her hands to be shackled along with her ankles. And they led her away, hooded, in blackness, with no idea of where she was going—and she didn't want to find out, for her heart was wrung empty of hope. No one cared, and no one would ever love her again.

Chapter Twenty-Five

Theo put down the binoculars. The flare was fading, but he'd seen enough.

"Claire's safe. You can pack up now."

"Good." Dankyo watched him a moment before issuing quiet orders to the snipers.

The long rifles sheened with blue all down their barrels. Evil-looking things, but they did their job well. Nothing else would have hit with such accuracy at this distance.

He caught Dankyo eyeing him. "What?"

"Claire recommended these."

"Yes, I know. Your point, man?" If there was one thing he hated, it was people trying to nudge him toward the pathway they wanted him on. He'd make his own roads, thank you very much.

"They'll be taking her to a cell for interrogation…unless sir intervenes." Dankyo helped a house guard manhandle a rifle into its case and snap the clasps.

Theo narrowed his eyes. "Are you presuming to tell me my duty, Dankyo?"

"No. Sir. I would never presume to do that. Only to inform sir of facts of which you might be ignorant." On the word *ignorant*, Dankyo had jerked the bottom of his suit coat, as if adjusting it.

"Hmph. Good." Why had he ever hired the man? Dankyo could be an irritating bastard. Besides, exactly why was he taking the woman's side in this? Maybe he thought it was protocol to give an employee a fair hearing before taking them out and shooting them.

He sighed. Only she wasn't an employee. Dammit, this was an insufferable problem. It felt like someone had stuck their hands inside him and ripped out his guts.

He strode to the head of the spiraling stairs that led out of the watchtower, then paused. "Let's get everything back to the airship. And, Dankyo, just to give you the facts...I've given instructions to palace security that she's not to be hurt. Satisfied?"

He cocked an eyebrow. If Dankyo showed the merest hint of a smile, he'd demote him to cleaning pistons. To his disgust the man was straight-faced as a statue. *Damn.* He needed to get angry at somebody, and Claire wasn't here. Whatever would they do with her? She'd laid herself open for the worst. An assassin who was in on a plot to kill the president.

He laid a clenched fist on the wall, felt the grit of brick grate on his skin. He couldn't trust her. How could he let someone like that close to him? He wanted to never see her again...yet he also wanted to see her little white backside in the air so he could turn it so goddamned bright red she'd not sit down for a week. *Damn!*

He lifted his fist from the brick and looked at the spots of blood, felt the pain and the cold blackness inside him spread.

Chapter Twenty-Six

The cell they held her in was stark yet comfortable—cream walls, a bed that folded down from the wall, a sink, a toilet, and a few books. The barred door was set into a wall of steel bars. Still, she'd have thought it luxury a month ago. Though the first guard was a hulking brute who refused to leave even when she used the toilet, he was soon replaced by another more accommodating one—one with a friendly if rugged face, and he didn't stare at her like she was some exhibit. Thank the Lord. Having a man watch her pee was going too far.

Though they'd tried to deceive her, she was sure this cell was somewhere in the palace. The fake carriage trip and the frequent direction changes hadn't fooled her direction sense one bit.

Not that it mattered—she wasn't trying to escape. And she doubted she was going to manufacture some weapon while on the toilet. Maybe they thought she could squeeze through the plumbing. The odd vision made her smile. Where had that come from? She hadn't thought she'd ever smile again.

She thought awhile. Things had a way of coming out even when you didn't think about them. The changing of the guard…it meant something. It meant that maybe someone was looking out for her. And that *maybe* was like a light at the end of a very, very dark tunnel. There was only one person she wanted that someone to be. If there was the slightest hope—her eyes watered, her heart picked up the pace—if there was any at all, she'd try her very hardest to make things right again.

Only a few hours after her arrival, at maybe four or five in the morning, an officer and a squad of six soldiers in black and gold marched up to the cell, stomping to a halt before her guard.

"I have orders to escort the prisoner for questioning!" the blond officer barked, his words as exact and energetic as his marching. In his hand was a sheet of paper.

Her guard had been sitting on his chair. He glanced at the paper and stood to snag the key from his belt. "The document's good. Do you need her in handcuffs?"

The officer looked at her appraisingly. "Just the cuffs. No hood. Can't believe she's an assassin. Got the captain in an ass-tearing mood." He stepped up to the bars. "Put your hands through the little door and wait until the cuffs are on."

A small section of the cell door hinged out, leaving just enough room to put her arms through. Questioning? To be expected. Being difficult would only get her roughed up.

When she stepped up the officer shook his head. "Nope. Turn around. I'm cuffing them behind you. No sense being too lax. 'Specially considering I've heard you can tie a man in knots faster than a blink."

She sighed, then did as he asked, turning to put her hands behind her and out the hole. Metal cuffs snicked around her wrists.

They marched her out of the cell and down a long corridor flanked by cells. Only one other cell was occupied. They went up a flight of stairs and to the third door.

Inside was a long room lit at one end by a dangling blue light; the other end was in shadow and divided off with a mesh screen. At a plain table were three chairs. The officer sat her down in one chair, chaining her at the waist facing away from the darkest part of the room, before exiting.

Silence. She made herself listen, slowed her breathing.

She could hear someone breathing back there. The outer door clicked and creaked open. A woman in an ultracrisp uniform stepped through—a lieutenant. She was accompanied by a skinny pimple-faced young man bearing a sheaf of paper and a typing machine. He adjusted the machine until it was square to the table and sat, his hands poised, ready to type.

The officer nodded, her sleek red bob swaying, her gaze already keenly advancing over every inch of Claire like a scalpel looking for a place to cut. She pulled out a chair opposite and eased into it.

Claire sat up straighter.

"Good morning, Miss... Claire."

"Morning."

"No *good* in there?"

"I'll wait and see."

The officer flash-smiled, showing teeth. "I'm Lieutenant Griffin. I've been assigned to question you regarding the attempted assassination that was averted last night. Have you anything to say before we begin?"

What a cold fish. Claire wriggled a bit; the chair was hard as steel. "One, I helped to stop that assassination. Two, I will cooperate fully. Three—" She stopped. What was three? No longer *please execute me,* that was for sure. She'd had enough of being sorry for herself. She firmed her mouth.

"Three, I never intended any harm, though I know that by not speaking up…I may have done the worst harm ever to the only person who really mattered to me." She blinked and braced herself. The lieutenant seemed mildly stunned, so while she had her attention, she launched into her story.

Maybe that wasn't Theo back there, but she thought it was. This wasn't for the lieutenant or for any record; it was for Theo. If he was back there listening, this was her confession to him.

She went through everything that had happened from the start. The early history of her with Inkline, the recruitment of those suited to assassination duty, the training, and her trip in that airship with Inkline…and more.

Her reasons for what she'd done spilled out across the story. Her regrets had been many, and she detailed them. How she'd not told Theo about her mission and why. That, she needed to say. How she'd known of his hate for betrayal and his deep feeling of responsibility for those he employed, and his hatred of assassination—that needed to be told, and she did so. By the end her face was wet with tears, but she kept her voice steady.

The final moment, when she'd discovered she could no longer conceal her lies and then the elimination of Inkline, spilled from her mouth like the last spatter of rain hitting the earth after a thunderstorm. Then she was done and exhausted.

The lieutenant said nothing, only staring as if she'd witnessed something extraordinary.

"Well." She tapped her fingernails on the table, kinked an eyebrow. "They said you'd likely be forthcoming, but that was different. Looks like I don't get to use any auxiliary means of persuasion, hey?" She chuckled grimly. "Joking. They said I wasn't allowed. Pity. One of the perks of the job."

She scraped back the chair and stood in one motion. "Farewell and good luck. I'll send in the guards. There's been...pressure to set you free. My assessment will be that you're not to be prosecuted." She saluted, signaled to the hastily packing stenographer, and headed for the door. It swung open smoothly, let them both through, clicked shut.

For a lieutenant, the woman seemed to have her fingers on the pulse of power.

Even so, Claire was alone with whoever was back there, and still chained to the chair.

Chapter Twenty-Seven

Dankyo leaned close and whispered in Theo's ear, "She knows you're here, sir. Or suspects."

"Yes." A monotone answer. He wouldn't give Dankyo the satisfaction. He was, had been, so angry, and even now with it ebbing, he knew this couldn't work. Sadness was taking its place. They could have had so much.

He'd thought he'd loved her, but this would break any relationship. He couldn't deny that he wanted her safe. Seeing her there chained to the chair and sad, it wrecked him. She was crying too. Not something he could see, but he knew. Wanted to go and wipe away, kiss away those tears. Not to be. He'd make sure she was sent somewhere she could start a life anew, and be done with her.

He rose. "Let's go."

"Sir?"

"I'll see those blasted tortoise-like guards get in here and release her. Come." The less said the better. God knew how acute her hearing was, and he didn't want to raise false hopes.

* * * *

It had been him. The whispers had carried. Yet he didn't come to her.

So be it. She'd wait. If he bothered to be here now, there might be another time. She wouldn't stop trying. Couldn't.

She slowly caved in until her forehead rested on the table, needing the support. *God. Please, let this be over.*

* * * *

Later that day, Dankyo visited her. She'd never seen him so haggard. His uniform bore creases, and his eyes were red. The guard clanged shut the cell door, locking him in with her.

She hauled herself into a sitting position on the bed.

Dankyo looked about and seemed to realize the bed was the only structure made for sitting. He sat gingerly next to her, bowing the bed enough to make the springs groan.

This was the man closest to Theo. If anyone could help her, it was him. Yet, if she were drowning, Dankyo was the last person she'd want throwing her a rope, for it seemed likely that attached to the very end would be a crocodile.

"Why are you here, Dankyo?"

"I'm here...because it's clear that you are the one thing Theodore Kevonis thinks he needs that he cannot have. Not having you is destroying him, and I aim to help you two get together again. Clear?"

"Ah. Whoa. Yes. You really don't mince words, do you?" And—*oh my God*—her little spark of hope kindled and rose to a blazing fire.

"No. I cannot see the point. But, also, let me state that this is more a catharsis. I want you out of his system, and the only way to do that is to let him see you're not who he thought you were. You've hurt him deeply. I believe he will then realize you must leave, permanently. And once that's done, we're done. Clear? You get a last good-bye from this."

She sat back, feeling like he'd grabbed her by the throat. *Huh. This is the crocodile at the end.* Did Dankyo think so little of her? Her resolve solidified into a metal-girded juggernaut. Be damned if she'd let Dankyo tell her what to do.

She'd never been a doormat—well, unless it was Theo, but then he stepped on her so...pleasingly

She'd run over Dankyo in an instant to get to Theo. Be a darn big bump in the road, but she'd do it. Disappointing in a way, though. After the talk in the buggy, she'd begun to think Dankyo an almost ally, even a potential friend, and she didn't have enough of those to go losing them.

Hmph. We'll see who gets to say good-bye.

"I get a last good-bye?" She eyed him narrowly. "What must I do? And, let me be clear here. I will do anything."

"Well. That is the problem. I don't really know." He ran his hand over his short hair.

"Not much help then, are you?" But still, she grinned weakly at him. *Dankyo, sitting with me, wanting to help. No matter his strange back-to-front logic, this is my best hope. Lord.*

He glared. “I’ll send you word once I get something sorted out. Don’t disappoint me.”

Her grin shrank to a flat smile. “I won’t.”

For the rest of that day, and most of the next, she was left alone. At five o’clock in the afternoon, a summons was delivered. The president, the man she was to have killed, had asked to see her. She’d been part of an assassination plot. Was this to be the passing of judgment or something more terrible?

The guards marched her in, without handcuffs, free to move, and left her in the ballroom, though now it was filled with emptiness and silence instead of people and laughter. Three men stood fifty yards away, waiting. Theodore Christakos, her Theo, and then Dankyo, looking self-satisfied and a few steps back from the others.

“Claire.” The president beckoned.

She started.

“Yes?” She walked over. Her shoes tapped, echoing, sounding so small and lonely in this monstrous room. She halted before them

“You’ve been brought to hear my decision. I’ve assessed all the evidence, from your testimony through to what we know of the PME’s plans. Lieutenant Inkline seems to have been working independently with this plot to eliminate me. I’ve heard what Theo Kevonis has had to say, as well as my own security about your actions.”

Every muscle hummed with tension. She curled her toes in her shoes, made herself look straight at the president. Not at *him.*

"My decision is that you shall be exonerated of any ill will toward this current administration. That you have a separate case to answer to for misleading Theodore Kevonis. I give you a choice." He paused, his chin lowering, mouth a straight line.

"Either you can be extradited to a place chosen by the state. This place to be outside the influence of the PME as much as we can possibly ensure. In gratitude..."

What? Gratitude? He plans to reward me?

"For your courage in the face of enemy forces, we will award you an annual salary of forty thousand drachma in perpetuity.

"Or, you may instead surrender to Theodore Kevonis and accept his decision regarding your future." At that, the president clasped his hands before him and waited.

Theo? How could this be? But, she had her chance, small though it might be. Afraid of what she might see, she glanced at Theo.

The president leaned forward and whispered, "Go to him."

She blinked, raised her chin, nodded.

From the red suffusing Theo's face, he'd not known of this alternative. Was this Dankyo's doing? "I will accept the decision of Theodore Kevonis." Thank God, she'd said that without quaking.

Heart thudding, she walked to Theo, every step under his furious gaze feeling like it might crumble her legs to dust, and stood before him.

She moved her mouth, trying to say something, *anything* that would make the determination leave his eyes.

"Please."

He shook his head. "How can I accept this? No. I cannot trust you, Claire. I have people who need me as much you. People who do trust me to keep them safe."

"I never meant to hurt anyone. I know what I did was wrong. I've said as much. You were there, weren't you?" She searched his face for clues. "At the interrogation? I know you were there. I could feel you." She clenched a hand over her heart, gritted her teeth until her jaw ached. "I can feel you. That's how close we are. If you make me go away, I will never be whole again. Without you, I am *nothing*."

"No. You're stronger than you think, Claire." Yet his eyes softened, and for the first time, something stirred between them.

She shut her eyes, shook her head. "Am I? You convinced me I wasn't just a weapon, a thing. You're the only person I've ever been this close to, and...I had thought you loved me. I don't know what else I can say. How can I show you that you can trust me again?"

Pain coiled tight in her chest—she wanted to fix what she'd broken *so* much. But wishing wouldn't work.

He sighed. "How? That's just it, Claire. It's not just that I don't trust you. Or even that I don't—" He swallowed. “You did not trust *me* enough to tell me what you were. I could have helped you.”

Her heart faltered. “Is that it? But…” Confused, aghast at this apparently impossible problem, she thought back and knew what she must say, then hesitated. If she was wrong, this would destroy her chance of ever putting things right.

“Would you have, Theo? Would you have helped me? Because, back then, when you knew me so little, I believe you would have sent me away.” She stopped. There it was—she’d thrown her last hope at his feet. *Please. Please, let me be right.*

He seemed to loom taller. His forehead wrinkled. “I would never…”

She sank to the floor; the timber jolted hard on her knees. “No?”

The hurt in his eyes and the deep breath he took told her she’d hit the mark.

“Perhaps,” he whispered. The frown melted into a new curiosity, and then he shook himself. “It matters not at all. Not now. I can’t trust you now. I can’t.”

Hands on her thighs, she bent her head. “Why not? Why not? I’d put my life in your hands. Here I am, at your feet. Please, I do trust you. Do what you will with me.” She scrambled for something that would be solid proof.

“Do what I will? You know, Claire, that I would never hurt you. This proves nothing. I can’t know what is in your mind or what other secrets you might hold from me.”

His legs moved. He was leaving. She gasped and looked up. “Use ropes on me! Tie me up if you wish! Let Dankyo do it. I don’t care! I...I trust you.”

“You think that offering to let me hurt you is some sort of proof? And since I *will not* do anything to hurt you, this still proves nothing.”

“Please.” He slowed. “Please, Theo.” She put her head in her hands. “I’m sorry but please, tell me, what I can do to make this *right* again.”

She heard his footsteps grow louder. He returned to her. They slowed and he stopped beside her. She held her breath, hoping.

“What can you do, Claire? Nothing. There is nothing more you can do.” Gentleness suffused his words, yet there was that same fearsome resolve in every syllable. “I’ve listened to your arguments and your logic. I’ve listened, earlier, to Dankyo’s arguments also, though in some amazement. I never thought I’d hear him defend you.”

His hand touched her head, and without thinking, eyes shut, she raised her head, wanting to feel more of his presence, to feel his warmth, to put her nose to his broad palm and smell his heavy masculine scent.

“Listen, Claire.” He pressed his hand down, so she stopped and waited. At least he was near. “There is nothing you can say that will change my mind. Nothing.”

“Oh.” Claire’s heart tore in two, and a twisted ache burrowed through her middle. “Oh.”

“Yes.” He patted her head once, then exhaled slow and hard. “Trust is something that should be earned. Yet if there’s one thing I have learned over the years, logic doesn't always work where trust is concerned. You can't change my mind, because only I can do that."

Hope fluttered to life.

"And I have changed my mind."

She wrenched her head up to meet his gray eyes, didn't dare to speak.

"I let my anger fool me. I will trust you again, my dear, because despite everything, you've not wavered in trying to fix what wrongs you've done, because Dankyo trusts you, but most of all, against all logic, because it's what, deep down where it counts, I want to do."

"Thank you," she whispered, putting her hand on his as he traced the curve of her face.

Theo smiled a little grimly. "And because, strangely, I do love you, my little assassin." He drew her to her feet and kissed her hands, then her mouth while she hugged him tightly, arms molded to his chest, her thoughts awhirl.

Ohmigod. He's forgiven me. Yes. Yes!

After resting awhile with his chin beside her ear, breathing slow, Theo leaned away, studied her. "Did you hear me?"

"Yes." She groped for something to say. "I-I'm sorry for lying." *He loves me? Can I say those words*? She glanced over. Dankyo was watching.

"Do you have something else to add?" Theo raised one eyebrow.

She mouthed those words. *I love you too.*

"Hmm." His smile stretched and amusement reached his eyes. "A little louder would be nice, especially after I've forgiven your...errors. I believe I may have a way to make you say it properly and louder. You did volunteer to be tied up."

She nibbled her lip. Elation was fast being tainted by a shivery kind of fear, and her knees were suddenly jelly. *Ropes. I've done it, though, haven't I? I've won him back.*

"Only there will be more than just tying up. You've earned the flogger. How many strokes, I've not yet decided."

Wide-eyed, she blinked up at him. Yet this was the Theo she wanted. Curiously, the fear stayed away. Somehow, in all this, her worries had been bent out of shape. Her fear now linked to her victory, to the rising sense of pure joy. He was hers, and she was his again.

Ha. Maybe this wouldn't be quite so bad. Theo had restrained her before, and she'd loved it. She squeezed her thighs together, feeling excitement rise.

"Well." The gravelly voice came from over her shoulder. "What an interesting outcome. And what a pity I have no time to witness the result."

She blushed. She'd forgotten the president.

He strolled into view. "May you all enjoy yourselves immensely. Perhaps another time, my dear, we might become better acquainted?"

She stiffened, alarmed, remembering the clothes Theo had bought for the party after the President's Ball. She'd never quite seen what went on...afterward.

"Sir. Thank you for your forbearance," Theo said. The president nodded and walked away. He left through a side door.

"Come, Claire." Theo took her by the shoulders. "Let me show you the facilities in the Machine Room. Both Dankyo and I are eager to demonstrate."

Machine Room? And... She swiveled under Theo's hands and looked over at Dankyo. She *had* offered to let him tie her up. He was back to being impassive. Theo hooked his fingers beneath the little straps of her dress, wiggled them. "Before we leave here, though. Remove the dress and your underwear."

She gaped at him. "Here?"

"Yes," he said, straight-faced except for the tiniest wrinkles at the corners of his eyes. "Here. I promise, there is no one else to see, except Dankyo. Trust me?"

She swallowed. "Yes. Oh, definitely yes."

"Then don't look around." He raised both eyebrows.

Without the slightest look, though with trembling hands, she crossed her arms, took hold of her dress, and skimmed it off over her head, let it fall, then took off her underwear—both bra and panties.

Naked, standing naked, in the middle of the ballroom. Her nipples beaded; her cleft and clit swelled in arousal. But she had Theo again. She did.

Chapter Twenty-Eight

Theo led her by the hand into a large room with walls painted a feral combination of black, red, and gold and a ceiling festooned with dangling chains. Padded machinery, crosses, tables, and other devices she couldn't decipher the function of, were set up here and there on the floor and walls, like metallic creatures ready to pounce on straying humans. White rope hung, coiled, from pegs and struts. She shuddered, her mouth dried.

"Don't worry, Claire." Theo stood behind her, combed his hands through her hair then twisted it into a rope, and carefully tied it together at her nape. "I'll take care of you."

"That's what I'm afraid of," she murmured.

He kissed her neck, then turned her to face one of the devices. All black, the device was some form of sawhorse, like one used in timber work, only padded on top, with rings attached here and there. Her mind raced ahead—rings for tying ropes to.

"That?" she whispered and swallowed past the lump in her throat.

"Yes. Give me your wrist."

Sometime while she'd been distracted—which meant as soon as she'd entered this room—he'd picked up a coil of rope.

The thumping against her ribs would be her heart. She licked her lips and raised her right wrist. The loop of rope Theo placed around it was white as an angel's wing. Pure and so not innocent. This whole place, every movement, every instruction Theo gave her, made her feel like she'd plugged into his galvanic machine. *Thud, thud,* went her heart.

With a few deft finger movements, he wound it about her wrist, snugged it down firmly, and waited.

She stared at the rope. Hung upon a revelation, an epiphany moment. This wasn't just possible, just bearable—it excited her. Letting Theo take charge of her had always been the utmost thrill. This too. Rope no longer sank talons into her gut. Whatever he wanted, she could do.

Oh, yes.

"Good, sweetheart. Lie down."

She blinked at him, nodded.

He guided her until she lay on her stomach across the length of the padding with her bottom in the air, sticking out past the end. Slowly, precisely, he wound rope about her limbs and body. She wriggled at times into the padding, until he pressed his hand to her back and made her stop.

Her bent knees and her ankles and wrists were tied with enough rope to set a ship's rigging. Her breasts were bound so firmly they felt round and filled with blood. Each heartbeat made them throb and made her so aware of them resting against either side of the padding.

She couldn't move a single inch, and it made her so hot, she bit back a groan when the ends of the flogger grazed her pussy.

"I must admit," Dankyo said, "you look far more interesting like this than when you're glowering at me."

Dankyo? She'd been unaware who was back there. Did he have the flogger?

"Why are you—" Then she noticed Theo lounging against the wall, watching, still in his coat and trousers. "Huh. Aren't you stretching the limits of your duties a bit?"

"Not really."

The fire-laden smack of the flogger's tendrils on her bottom startled her. "Ah!"

She strained at the ropes fastening her arms to the sawhorse, closed her eyes as they pulled taut…and held. *Dankyo, of all people.* She bit back a swear word she might have called him.

Mortifying, yet, strangely, knowing Theo watched Dankyo smack her… She arched the tiniest bit, wriggling the inch or two her ass could move…and heat blossomed.

No. She went still, made her breathing slow. This was awful. Dankyo would see, know she got off on this. Say something. Distraction needed here.

"You've played us both, haven't you? Arranged this. You *wanted* us together."

"Possibly."

"Why?"

He bent down, squatting next to her head, then putting a hand up to hold her chin. "Maybe because I can see that in your own way, you're good for him. That he does need you as much as you do him. Maybe because you've made me realize something about myself I'd never have known otherwise."

Unable to look away, she looked, really looked at him. A hint of a smile curved his lips. *Oh. Frick.*

He stood and removed his coat, folded it, and put it on the floor. Next, while she watched, tongue-tied, he stripped off his shirt and placed it on top of the coat. His hairless torso gleamed. He flexed his shoulders, making slabs of muscle slide like earthquaked rock. The man could lift a landship.

Claire swallowed, throat almost too dry to move. Her muscles were tiring with the effort of keeping her neck up so she could look Dankyo in the eye. But she didn't want him to see her lower her head. That would be like giving in. And...she was lying here with her bottom out. She let out a long breath, cursing softly. Her head sagged an inch.

He'd said he realized...something. "What have you realized?" But, in the blink of saying it, she knew. *Lord, am I in trouble. Tied down, can't move, and this rock of a man has a flogger.*

His eyes glinted. "That I like this." He picked up the flogger from where he'd left it on the floor, gave it a twitch. "That I like *this*. Beating the backside of a stubborn, annoying, cantankerous woman. You have no idea how angry I've been with you."

"Angry?" Her voice squeaked.

"Not now. Now I'm happy because I've been given permission to deliver your punishment."

All of it? She pulled on the ropes again. *What was Theo thinking*? "Maybe, uh, this is a bad idea?" She craned her neck to plead with Theo, but he shook his head, folded his arms.

Dankyo came close, caressed her hair. "After this, perhaps I'll see if Kirsten shares a common interest."

"I know she does," she managed to croak out. "Why not practice on her first?"

"Oh no. You're first. Don't worry. I've used a whip before and know what I'm doing. I won't break your pretty skin, and I'm only going as far as the colonel's approved."

He pushed her head down and stepped back where she couldn't see. She shut her eyes. The blow fell. She jerked and clenched her teeth.

"Count."

"One." *Or was it two? Oh frick.* The pain flared and spread. She glared coldly at Theo. *How could he give me to Dankyo?*

"Wait, Dankyo." Theo walked over and put a hand to her shoulder. "Add one more for insolence."

"Yes, sir. With pleasure, sir." He striped her across the right thigh, so close to her wet pussy.

She hissed, tried hard not to spit out some nasty word. "Two!"

"You can do this, Claire." He looked her right in the eyes, massaged her shoulder, trailed his fingers across to and down her backbone. "Soon, it'll be over."

She heaved in a breath and really looked at her man. Her Theo. Took a mental step back from the pain and thought for a moment.

I do deserve this. “I know, sir. Without this, I’ll never feel right again...about us, about lying to you.” Another swat fired streamers of pain across her thigh. “Three.” She panted. “What happens, after?”

He bent down and kissed her full on the lips, murmured sweetly into her mouth. “Then we do more pleasurable things. Does that appeal?” He kissed her again, lips moving slow and sure over hers. The pain in her butt swirled, mingled, and she parted her lips under Theo’s.

His fingers found her nipple and circled it. Despite the pain throbbing through her bottom, her nipple spiked to a peak. Her slit moistened. Warmth traveled *everywhere*. She writhed, trembled, feeling every rope tying her down, the crisscrossing rigidity about ankle and wrist and breast.

He was helping her through this, mitigating the pain with some pleasure.

“Oh, yes. I’d like that, sir.” Her eyes half-closed at another light brush of his hand. This seemed wrong, yet so arousing, with Dankyo watching everything Theo did to her.

“Yes?” Those evil fingers of his reached the crease between her buttocks. His fingers—how many she couldn’t tell, didn’t care—slid into both her holes. She jerked and gulped in air, clenching around his fingers, reveling in the sensation. “Yes, dear?”

“Umm. This isn’t just...temporary, is it, sir? Before a good-bye?”

He laughed. “No, it’s not temporary, though now I’ve decided to keep you…” His fingers slipped in farther and stopped. She squirmed. “I plan on doing some most devious things to this lovely body.”

“Uhh. Good.”

“Sir.”

“Mmm, yes. Sir.” She swiveled her head, trying to look back at Dankyo, but only spotted his feet.

Theo’s fingers moved again, sliding thick and slow. He swirled his other hand over her breast. The invasion of her pussy and anus, the tight swelling of her breasts made each touch and thrust echo the other until her back muscles strained to arch more, higher. That Dankyo saw this, she no longer cared. *Yesss. What was I saying?*

Something puzzled her. Her words came out low and husky, though loud enough to carry. “Dankyo, if you wanted us together, why did you tell me you meant this to be a last good-bye?”

The flogger licked gently across her thigh. “Because you didn’t deserve to have it too easy. But also because I knew it would make you fight all the more for it.”

Uh. Well, she guessed the first part was fair. “But…what if I’d given up instead?”

Theo leaned in, put his forehead to hers, and murmured, “He knows you, dear, as I do. I don’t think he ever thought you’d give up. You can’t imagine the smile on his face.”

"What a bastard!" she whispered. *Boy, am I going to find something bad to do to Dankyo. Maybe tie his shoelaces together before parade? Yes. For sure.*

"Yes, he is, isn't he? But he's mine, just like you are." He kissed her again, gently. "If you call him that again, I will tell."

She wriggled back into his fingers to feel how they penetrated her. Deep. She sighed. "Sorry. And thank you, sir, for forgiving me." Then she kissed him back, so thoroughly that nothing back there hurt at all.

Theo removed his fingers and drew a squiggly line of wetness over her buttock and up her spine.

Smack!

"Ouch! Four!" *Maybe I can put chili powder in Dankyo's uniforms.*

Five more smacks of the flogger—enough to make her legs quiver and sweat pool in the small of her back—then Dankyo was done. Panting, she heard him walk away. Loop after loop Theo unraveled, releasing her from all the ropes except the ones around her chest.

"Finished, dearest. Come here." He helped her upright, steadying her when her legs shook. With her breasts still bound, the press of her rigid nipples onto his shirt made her squeak. He squeezed her bottom.

"Ouch." But it wasn't all ouch. The way his hands massaged her ass was sending out all sorts of interesting signals. She squirmed against his coat and subtly shifted until her legs were either side of his trouser-clad thigh, so it pressed onto her mound just *right.*

Theo chuckled and reached up to pull on her ponytail, so she couldn't help but tilt her head back and meet his eyes. He wiggled her head a little side to side. "I see what you're doing, Claire. My trousers are going to need cleaning."

Despite the chastisement in his words, embarrassment refused to surface. He didn't mind at all. Neither did she. She'd do it again just so she could stare up into his gray eyes and hear the mellow timbre of his voice. The way he said Claire sank right into her and traveled to her heart. He hadn't gotten her to say those three words, but she did love him.

"Thank you, Theo."

"No more thanking. We're done. Even."

Relief flooded her. For days she'd been existing with the weight of all her lies on her shoulders. *Done.* When he let go of her hair, she snuggled in right up next to his solid chest, pressed her nose into his shirt, and breathed, just breathed.

"Thank you." *Oops.* The words had come out so naturally, she'd not had time to stop them.

"Claire." Exasperation showed in his voice.

Uh-oh. "Sorry." She sucked her lower lip onto her teeth, didn't dare blink. Maybe she could hide in his coat.

"You know, I have an idea. Your little derriere looks so delightful all red like this." He patted her ass lightly. "There's a paddle on the wall over there that has a cogwheel shape cut into the middle. Since your bottom needs to be white to show it up, I'll have to wait for the redness to go; then we'll try it out."

Strangely, the idea excited her.

* * * *

Six months later

Claire wandered through the shop. Hinchcliff and Co. never failed to surprise her with the variety of goods on display. Something new turned up every visit. This time, she kinked her neck back to see properly—it was an inflatable dirigible in the shape of a penis hanging from the ceiling. She shook her head and prayed Theo wasn't planning on buying that.

For months she'd been doing her job, off and on, as his bodyguard. Without a weapon belt, her waist felt wrong. No weight—it damn well imbalanced her. At least the pastel green dress had a quick-tearaway skirt, so if someone bad turned up, she could get her legs free for action real fast. Theo hadn't said no to that. The lack of underwear he'd insisted on, though. She frowned, wondering what he planned, as she squeezed past the phallus of the knight on the way up the three steps to the next level. Someone had hung a key chain on the steel dick. She grinned. At least the knight was still here. Some things never changed.

"Found you." Theo gently settled his hand on the back of her neck. "Hands on the sofa, please, bottom up."

She almost turned to protest but didn't. By now obedience to Theo's orders was close to ingrained. Even if some of them were embarrassing, surprising...

Like a match under a bonfire, excitement flickered. Gray-haired, distinguished, Mr. Hinchcliff, the proprietor of the shop, watched with arms folded, face impassive, as she leaned over the armrest of the maroon sofa and put her hands flat on the seat.

Bottom up, he'd said. Striving to stop the blush rushing to her face, Claire tilted up her bottom. He was going to spank her; she just knew it. Why here? Why now? The back of her dress was flipped up, and air cooled her skin, slid like mist between her legs, where wetness already gathered.

She shivered. Whatever his reason, she couldn't help her reaction. Did he know how someone watching made everything so much more enthralling?

"I have a paddle or two to test, Claire. Hold still."

Two jolting blows hit her ass—one each cheek, and she yelped at the second. *Ow*. The familiar heat suffused her lower body. She breathed fast for a while into the fabric under her mouth. It didn't take long anymore for the pain to transform. Not when she recalled all those other times when he'd pushed his fingers into her, played with her...

Six months—and every day of it, when they weren't making love, they were still together. As his unofficial bodyguard and his consort, she was always by his side. Sometimes it seemed as if Theo had memorized every part of her, mind, body and soul, he knew her so well.

"Turn your head and look, dear."

Through the tendrils of her hair that tumbled across her face, she looked back.

The smug grin on Theo's face was the first she saw, then the mirror he held, and what it reflected. Her bottom showed bright red around two backward words. On one cheek was *Just* on the other was *Married*.

She gasped. “Theo!”

“Well?” He lowered one hand, smoothed it forward over her bottom to the inward slope of her lower back. “What do you think?”

“Um.” Confusion scattered her thoughts. He couldn’t mean...did he? “Of course it’s nice...Sir.”

He smiled and knelt by her side, kissed her once, softly. “So, you like the idea of a wedding?”

Oh, dear. Oh yes! A wedding! But... She screwed up her mouth, shifted her head closer to his, then tangled her fingers into his shirt cuff while he played with a lock of her hair. “Do I want to know when you plan to use those?”

This time he licked the top of her nose. “Afterward, at the party when there’s only a few close friends left. I plan to bend you over a table.”

The wet spot on her nose cooled. She smiled at his silliness.

Uh. Not so bad...except for the public smacking part—one was okay, but a whole crowd? Then she noticed the delighted look on Mr. Hinchcliff’s face. Was it the smacking and her naked bottom he liked, or the prospect of a wedding? Maybe both?

“Congratulations to Sir and Miss.” He dipped his head slightly.

Ah. Well, he certainly didn’t mind the wedding. She swallowed past the big lump in the middle of her throat. “Thank you, Mr. Hinchcliff.” Tears overflowed and trickled from the corner of her eye. Theo, his face only inches away, raised his eyebrow. "It's just the smack, really. It's not… I'm okay. Thank you, sir." If someone had checked her insides right then and there, she was sure they'd find her full of fluttering butterflies.

Everywhere within her felt on edge and jittery and…just so fricking wonderful.

"I know how to stop you crying." He moved in and kissed her again, gentle at first, as if her lips were some fragile wondrous creation, then harder and more determined. Soon all she could hear was the gasp of their breathing and the rasp of his stubble on her skin and the sofa. All she could feel was his lips and tongue. All she could smell and taste was Theo. She screwed her fingers tighter into his sleeve. She was never *ever* letting him go.

THE END

Cari Silverwood

Though I'd much rather stay invisible and spin you all tales with my words, here's a little snippet of my world.

I have a lovely family here in Australia, with the prerequisite teenager who dwells in the dark bedroom catacombs, a husband who raises eyebrows when he catches glimpses of what I write, and a furry menagerie of animals barking, meowing, and swimming about the place.

Before writing *Three Days of Dominance* I had never dipped my little toes in the hot and lust-swirled sea of erotica. Now every time I turn around, there's some new character making me write down their story in the most lurid way. My people are quite adamant about explaining creative new ways of making love, so I doubt I'll run out of ideas anytime soon, though I may go cross-eyed.

And, dammit, I can't seem to stop reading other erotica authors either. I have come over to the dark side. Someone please find me a candle...and some rope. 'Cause if Darth Vader's here, I'm going to see if he's up for some bondage and wax play.

Main Web site: http://www.carisilverwood.net

Blog: http://somewriteithot2.blogspot.com

Loose Id® Titles by Cari Silverwood

Available in digital format at http://www.loose-id.com
or your favorite online retailer

Three Days of Dominance

* * * *

The STEAMWORK CHRONICLES Series

Iron Dominance

Lust Plague

* * * *

31 Flavors of Kink

Co-written with Leia Shaw

In addition to digital format, the following titles
are also available in print at your favorite bookseller:

Three Days of Dominance

* * * *

The STEAMWORK CHRONICLES Series

Iron Dominance

CPSIA information can be obtained at www.ICGtesting.com
Printed in the USA
BVOW02s1136071013

333096BV00001B/8/P

9 781623 000318